G000021782

# SILENT DEATH

# SILENT DEATH

## CRYPTID ASSASSIN™ BOOK TWO

## MICHAEL ANDERLE

DISRUPTIVE IMAGINATION®

This Book is a work of fiction. All of the characters, organizations, and events portrayed in this novel are either products of the author's imagination or are used fictitiously. Sometimes both.

Copyright © 2020 Michael Anderle
Cover Art by Jake @ J Caleb Design
http://jcalebdesign.com / jcalebdesign@gmail.com
Cover copyright © LMBPN Publishing
A Michael Anderle Production

LMBPN Publishing supports the right to free expression and the value of copyright. The purpose of copyright is to encourage writers and artists to produce the creative works that enrich our culture.

The distribution of this book without permission is a theft of the author's intellectual property. If you would like permission to use material from the book (other than for review purposes), please contact support@lmbpn.com. Thank you for your support of the author's rights.

LMBPN Publishing
PMB 196, 2540 South Maryland Pkwy
Las Vegas, NV 89109

First US edition, January, 2020
eBook ISBN: 978-1-64202-703-7
Print ISBN: 978-1-64202-704-4

The Zoo Universe (and what happens within / characters / situations / worlds) are Copyright (c) 2018-20 by Michael Anderle and LMBPN Publishing.

## Thanks to our Beta Readers

Jeff Eaton, John Ashmore, and Kelly O'Donnell

## Thanks to the JIT Readers

Dave Hicks
Dorothy Lloyd
Peter Manis
Diane L. Smith
Micky Cocker
Jeff Goode
Jeff Eaton

*If we've missed anyone, please let us know!*

## Editor
Skyhunter Editing Team

# CHAPTER ONE

The establishment was definitely more upmarket than what he was used to. It wasn't that class was a foreign concept to him, of course, but this definitely wasn't anywhere he felt at home or even remotely comfortable. The fact that the elevator itself looked like it was made from burnished gold—although it was more likely some kind of polished bronze—was all he really needed for him to know that it hadn't been designed or decorated with someone as ordinary-citizen as him in mind.

The touchscreen showed the numbers climbing slowly as he was taken up to the top floor of the building. The burnished gleam that surrounded him was enough to blind most folks to the fact that three cameras covered every possible inch of the elevator.

But not him. Not Jon Harper. He had learned to notice things like that and knew exactly what they were there for. Nor did he have a problem with it in principle. While some might say casinos were paranoid about security, they needed to be overly vigilant or they wouldn't make much money come the end of the year.

Or semester or quarter or whatever it was that casinos worked to—he didn't know, and frankly, didn't care. He wasn't there to gamble and there was no chance that he would be involved in the business at all.

Well, technically, he would be involved in the business but only—and always—as an outsider. He wouldn't take freelancer jobs if he had casino money, after all. That said, he could wholeheartedly approve of caution, excessive or otherwise, that would ensure a healthy remuneration for him at the end of whatever operation they had in mind.

The elevator dinged softly to confirm that he had arrived at the top floor. A young, attractive secretary waited for him with a tablet in her hand.

"Mr. Harper?" she asked crisply and flicked a few errant strands of brunette hair back behind her ear.

"That's me." He proffered a hand but she had already turned away and motioned him down the lavish hallway. They entered an office that looked like it was meant to be showy but still somehow elegant and professional. He could tell that the owner had aimed for shock and awe, especially with the fantastic view of the Strip below.

While he could acknowledge that it was as impressive as shit, his honest opinion was that someone was putting on a show. They clearly wanted to impress people and worked hard to achieve that.

It reminded him of the opportunity this meeting presented. While he thought he could see beyond the façade, he was also sufficiently impressed by the tactics to have a healthy respect for the man he had come to meet.

His instincts said to tread warily and he sure as fuck intended to listen.

"Mr. Marino will be with you in a moment," the woman said before she exited quietly.

It took him a moment to realize that he wasn't the only one in the room. The second man stood from the sofa at the back and pulled at his jacket to straighten it.

His suit was obviously of a decent make but not expensive enough to belong to the guy who owned this office.

"Hi, Jon Harper," he introduced himself.

The shorter, black-haired man smiled and shook his hand firmly. "Mike Terrance. It's nice to meet you."

"Were you called in for this job too?" he asked as they both settled on the couch.

"Yep. People I take seriously told me to take this Marino guy seriously, so here I am."

"Same deal with me. Wait, are you working with Bryans?"

"Yeah," Mike said and narrowed his eyes. "How long have you been with him?"

"Ever since Coral Springs."

"Yeah, I was there for that." The man grinned. "Oh, my God, the Benihana there was to die for."

"I know," Jon said and laughed. "I've been back to Coral Springs maybe three times to get another taste of that stuff."

"I won't say I've done the same, but I've been to the other restaurants in the chain around the country and none have been like that one."

"Agreed."

Their conversation ceased immediately and both men

stood from their seats when the sound of voices outside intruded. It wasn't long before the secretary returned, closely followed by the man they assumed was the one who had called this meeting.

He certainly didn't look the type to rub shoulders with freelancers, which obviously came as no surprise. His suit was understated but clearly cost more than what both men made in a year—maybe even twice over given that they were both fairly new in the business. The watch was of similar quality and so were his shoes. He wore a pair of glasses that were probably meant to show that he wasn't all business and had a fun side too.

Hell, even his haircut was expensive.

Two burly men stepped in on his heels. Their matching suits, the telltale bulge under their jackets, and the unmistakable combination of muscle and alertness were almost a bodyguard cliché. A single glance at them was enough to confirm that they looked formidable. One remained near the door and the other took a position to the left of the massive desk. Their appearance didn't surprise him in the least and especially not given that armed security downstairs had searched him for weapons, wires, and other devices before he'd been allowed into the elevator. He assumed the other operative had endured the same treatment.

"Gentlemen, sorry for the delay," the casino boss said. "I have been dealing with family issues, which include endless interruptions because casinos always need attention, you know what I'm saying?"

Neither of them did, and it didn't look like Marino even noticed their silence as he made his way to the truly impressive desk and dropped onto the chair behind it. He motioned for the two visitors to sit across from him.

"Julia, would you mind getting me an espresso and... something for my guests?" Marino asked and looked from one man to the other. "Coffee? Water? Maybe a beer?"

"Water's fine," Jon said quickly. A sudden attack of nerves clamored for something a little stronger, but he needed to present a professional front. Bryans had stressed that in the short briefing. He'd pointed out that this was his passport to the next level and hopefully, a better future. That meant losing the rough thug in favor of the tough professional, especially since Bryans had stuck his neck out with the referral. He wondered what his finder's fee was.

"For me too," Mike agreed. He'd probably had the talk as well.

"Two waters and an espresso, please." The secretary nodded at her boss and left quickly. "You know what they say—always hire a secretary who's easy on the eyes and you'll never work a day in your life, am I right?"

"Sure?" Jon glanced at his fellow freelancer and bit back a somewhat crude response.

"She still thinks I hired her for her qualifications," the man said with a laugh. "I mean, she has a ton and she's only working here to put herself through law school, but still. Now, enough of the pleasantries. We can focus on the business I called the two of you in for."

"That's why we're here," Mike said and stated the obvious in a hopeful tone. "How can we help you, Mr. Marino?"

"Look, you guys know that my father is the late and

great Marco Marino." He leaned forward and took a sip from his coffee while he watched them speculatively.

"I'm sure we don't know anything about your dearly departed father and certainly not about any connections he might or might not have with La Cosa Nostra," Jon said and wondered if he'd phrased that a little too obviously. He wasn't used to dancing with the mob but the man seemed to take it in stride.

"Yeah," Mike replied casually. He picked his water up and toyed with the lime on the rim. "All we know is that your father was a very successful businessman in the city who opened a number of businesses and gave thousands of people jobs."

"A real titan of industry, your father," Jon confirmed. They weren't trying to be disrespectful to the man but everyone in the city knew that Marco Marino was the head of Sicilian Mafia in the city. Everyone but the local law enforcement, apparently.

That said, everyone also knew you didn't fuck with the Sicilians, and that included being very careful how you talked about them.

"Good." Marino nodded as if they'd passed some kind of test. His face was affable enough but there was a hard light in his eyes that belied the pleasant demeanor he presented.

"So," he continued. "The reason I need the two of you is with regard to my father's less than legal dealings. That's why I made sure to recruit operatives from Bryans whom he knew would have no issue working with organized crime. The list was long, obviously, but you two were the ones he personally recommended for the job. He said something about…Coral Springs?"

Both men looked at him in implacable silence and appeared to have not noticed the deliberate question. It seemed the Mafia boss wanted more details, but while they might not be top-level professionals, they knew enough to not shoot their mouths off.

The fact was, Jon reminded himself, that he'd simply been in the right place at the right time. Bryans had a situation that escalated and needed extra people in a hurry, and he'd repaid the favor by pushing work his way since then. He'd be a fucking idiot to blab about the man's business—a dead idiot, probably.

While Marino perhaps wanted to assure himself that they were the right people for the job and had what it took to get it done, they didn't kill and tell. It wasn't worth the risk to their own skin.

Or maybe, he thought, it was a test to see where they stood on confidentiality. That seemed more likely. Either way, he'd not get a peep from either of them about that particular adventure.

"So Bryans told you we were dependable and known for our discretion when dealing with illegal matters," Mike stated calmly but he shifted a little uncomfortably in his seat.

"Of course, that's why you're here." The man smiled a thin smile and shook his head. "Like I was saying, I need the two of you to deal with a sensitive matter regarding my father's less than legal enterprises in the city. As you are aware, he died earlier this month—"

"I'm so very sorry for your loss," Jon said.

"Very sorry," Mike added quickly.

"Thank you, I appreciate that." His expression seemed

untouched by sentiment, but perhaps that was merely a public mask. "The situation is complicated. When he died, I inherited his ties and business relationships, although I was not the obvious choice as a younger son. However, the rest of my siblings are either out of the country and...uh, unable to return for...let us say legal reasons and the heir apparent is languishing in prison. Suffice it to say there is very little likelihood that he will ever have the liberty— quite literally—to assume my father's mantle as was origi- nally intended."

He paused and his face assumed an even harder expres- sion. "I now control his business as a whole whereas before, I had merely managed the casinos. As a result, I was never too familiar with the criminal element with which he was involved. In all honesty, I didn't think I ever would and so never concerned myself with it. However, his connec- tions in Sicily came for the funeral and a somewhat compelling discussion. The outcome is that I'll control everything from here on out."

"It sounds like you have your work cut out for you," Mike said.

"Agreed." Marino leaned forward on the desk again. "There is a small problem, unfortunately. While I'm well- versed in how businesses are run—even when they're run illegally—I'm not yet fully confident to run a criminal enterprise. Getting millions of dollars in tax write-offs that would make the folks at the IRS shriek if it ever hit their radar? No problem. They teach that shit at Harvard Busi- ness School. How to keep the criminal element in line and working for me and no one else? That's something I'd rather leave to the...uh, professionals at this particular point in time."

"I assume your father had a number of these professionals in his employ," Jon said cautiously. "Why not bring them in?"

"If there's one thing I do know about the game is that it's about respect," he explained. "These guys were loyal to my father, there is no question there. But their loyalty to me only goes as far as they trust me to keep their wallets full while they're with me and make them regret it if they're not. If they realize I don't know enough about the business to run it effectively yet, their loyalty will decrease.

"On the other hand, if I bring outsiders in to take care of issues, they fear for their jobs and they don't know how much I still have to learn. Let me be very clear here, gentlemen. This operation has a dual purpose. The first is to send a very clear message to my existing workforce that ineptness and mediocre loyalty will not be tolerated. In my father's time, failure was not considered an option and I see no reason to change that. This is my opportunity to reinforce it and to compel anyone who might be on the fence to adjust their thinking very quickly."

Jon nodded. "So you want them to see that they need you more than you need them?"

Marino nodded, his expression implacable. "To accomplish this, I require you to give me a demonstration of your abilities." He held a hand up as both men opened their mouths to protest. "Hear me out, please. The operation for which you will be paid is the actual demonstration. This will deliver the message as we've discussed, but it will also open the door to the possibility that I might use your services in the future. To be honest, I rather like the idea of having a select handful of mercenaries on hand should the need for them arise in the future. But whether that works out or not, I will still pay you above the going rate for your assistance in this problem. To me, it's win-win, but how do you feel?"

"Well...there is the small matter that the pros your dad hired will lose," Mike pointed out. His mind had obviously gone in the same direction Jon's had—to seriously pissed-off mob-owned thugs in need of retribution against those who'd done them out of a good payday.

"Those guys need a lesson in the chain of command, so they win too—once they have learned it, of course." The Mafia boss shook his head firmly. His eyes, now, were glacial. It was as if the real man behind the mask slid out for a moment, and it was chilling. The glimpse vanished in an instant, however, to be replaced by a winning smile. "So, what do you guys say? Are you in?"

Jon shrugged. It honestly didn't sound too difficult, although they hadn't heard everything yet. "Sure. I'm willing to listen further. What kind of demonstration do you have in mind?"

"There's a problem out on the East Side." Marino picked up some papers and slid them across the desk. "My father ran a couple of insurance businesses there that mostly operated on the racketeering model in the area. One of the recently opened businesses resisted the marketing attempts of our local salesmen. When more persuasive measures were taken, the man resisted aggressively and involved local law enforcement."

The translation for that was obvious. The local racketeers failed to intimidate the business owner sufficiently, and when others arrived to inflict more painful persuasion, they had their asses beaten and handed to the cops.

"This situation is unacceptable. It must be known that trouble on the East Side will not be tolerated." The mob boss tapped the file with a well-manicured finger. "I need a message sent and an example made so the rest of the local businesses don't decide that our insurance is not for them and move on to other providers."

Mike took one of the files off the table and inspected the contents. "Do you have any preferences for the kind of example you need us to make?"

"Nothing excessive," he said decisively. "We need to encourage repeat customers, not scare them off. Perhaps something along the lines of a ruptured-patella-based encouragement package. You merely need to make sure they realize we're the only business for them."

Which translated loosely to blowing this guy's kneecaps out to make sure he and everyone else knew there wouldn't be another warning.

Jon nodded. "And what kind of commission do you think we would receive for peddling this...package?"

"I thought forty thousand each would be fair for your services. Twenty thousand now and the rest upon completion of your work. What do you say?"

Neither man wanted to show any kind of surprise and both nodded.

"Well, we would normally wrangle a better price out of you," Jon said in what he hoped was a suitably casual tone but strong enough to get a point across. "Negotiating is the silent skill of the best freelancers, after all. But, out of respect for you and your late father, we'll agree to that rate."

"Excellent!" The Mafia boss stood quickly and the operatives followed suit. "I'm really glad we could come to an agreement. Julia is waiting outside with your checks, to be deposited in a bank of your choice."

"We will focus on familiarizing ourselves with the files and the job immediately, Mr. Marino." Mike took the man's proffered hand.

"It's a pleasure doing business, Mr. Marino," Jon said with a smile and motioned with his head for his new partner to join him.

Both men collected the checks the secretary had waiting for them. Once the doors closed behind them, they exchanged a knowing glance. They obviously knew better than to say anything in the building and didn't even try until they were off the casino floor.

"What did you plan to charge him?" Jon asked while they waited for the valet to bring their cars around.

"I was going to say ten grand, plus expenses. Although I would have seriously fucked him with the expenses, of course."

"Yeah, me too." He chuckled. "I guess this guy is desperate."

"Or he has no idea how much the going rate really is. Either way, it's a good payday for an easy job."

# CHAPTER TWO

The drive from Vegas to Los Angeles would never inspire real complaints from very many people. The roads were smooth, easy to move on, and already accommodated the AI-powered vehicles. If Taylor wanted to simply lean back and take a nap for the duration of the trip, he could.

Maybe the easy journey was why the rich and the drunk or high of Hollywood headed to Vegas for an instant marriage that would immediately be dissolved once they sobered up. He still wasn't sure how an entire state had somehow legalized and profited off the business of rapid-fire marriages followed by rapid-fire divorces. He simply chose to assume that the people who cooked the crazy scheme up were both geniuses and unbelievably evil.

Still, that was thankfully not something he would ever have to worry about. He honestly couldn't ever see himself being so slammed that he actually married anyone. His personal philosophy definitely precluded Elvis impersonators and cheap rings.

For this trip, he chose not to use the AI-driver function. He liked driving Liz and he would be able to cut the four-and-a-half-hour drive down by an hour or so as long as he kept the gas pedal down and he was careful about traffic cops and cameras.

He could always call Desk if he got any tickets for speeding, of course, but he would rather not. It was an annoyance for her, he could tell, and that was enough for him to try to avoid them, at least. Despite the fact that his feelings still rankled somewhat over what he considered her hacking of his suits, she had put effort into making his work with the FBI a little smoother. If only for that reason, it was the least he could do to return the damn favor.

The only downside of doing the driving, of course, was the fact that the AI knew how to make Liz an efficient gas guzzler, whereas he did not. He wasn't terrible, but he needed to pull into gas stops along the way to fill up perhaps a little more often than he might if he relinquished control.

Still, it was for the best since Liz wasn't the only one who needed to power up. It wasn't strictly legal but he liked to snack while driving. His first choice was always something salty with a preference for beef jerky, but there was time and space for sweets in there too, especially if they were the sour kind.

But first things first. Taylor stepped out of the truck, closed the door, and took a moment to stretch his sore muscles. It was technically a short drive, but he still needed to stop and get the blood flowing around his body.

He couldn't wait too long, though. Banks still needed him and from the sound of it, they wouldn't wait for long. The chances were that they already had a couple of other cryptid hunters on the list waiting for him to fuck up.

Once he'd set the pump to fill the tank, he waited rather than head inside. Liz was a thirsty gal and she had a tank to match. When she was full, he replaced the nozzle, locked the vehicle, and entered the building to purchase snacks, drinks, and other items he needed for the rest of his trip to LA. It took only a few minutes before he paid for them and the gas at the register.

Someone had told him once that to save time, he should simply leave the pump to work while he did his shopping. It sounded logical, but in situations where a car had issues or the pump did, the tank could end up only partially filled or even too much.

Liz would obviously not present those problems. He had worked on her himself and was confident of that, but he couldn't say the same for the pumps. It really was better to be safe than sorry, especially when he was in a hurry to face monsters that might be the precursor to the Zoo apocalypse.

"Is that your truck outside?" the cashier asked.

"She's mine, yeah," he replied with a small, polite smile.

"She looks like a beast." The young man cast a quick look out the window.

"Thanks, I guess."

"That wasn't a compliment. Trucks like that are bad for the environment."

"Says the kid who makes a living working in a gas station," he retorted and snatched his receipt up as well as his purchases. "Besides, the environment's spent way too much time trying to kill me so returning the favor seems like the smart thing to do."

"What?"

"Never mind." He shook his head. "You have a nice day."

Maybe he'd been a little too sarcastic to the kid. He worked in a gas station, true, but with the economy the way it was, people needed to take whatever jobs they could get their hands on. And as social causes went, the environment wasn't a terrible idea—even if a little slow on the draw what with all the shit happening in the Zoo.

Then again, no one trashed Liz with impunity, regardless of their good intentions. She was his baby and he would defend her to his last breath, either physically or verbally.

As he returned to the vehicle, a powerful engine revved and drew his attention toward the other side of the gas station. A convertible Mustang pulled up and "Girls Just Want to Have Fun" blared from the juiced-up speakers.

The song made him cringe every time he heard it, but the young women who spilled out of the car to fill their tank definitely held his attention. They had the look of a sorority on a road trip somewhere, for which one of them had "borrowed" their dad's car.

The only reason for that perhaps incorrect assumption was that the Mustang didn't seem like a sorority-girl car. Then again, he didn't know what would be, so any assumptions he made would inevitably be from a position of ignorance.

"Hey there, honey," one of them called and waved to him. She looked a little beyond merely tipsy as she leaned back on the car to display the skimpy tank top and extra short jean shorts she wore.

And what was underneath, of course, which he could more than appreciate.

Admittedly, they were a little young for his tastes. He preferred women who knew what they were doing but in the end, when all you intended to do was look, there was nothing wrong with enjoying the view.

He didn't wave in response and simply smirked as he opened the door and tossed his purchases in.

"That's a nice ride you have there," the same girl called when she realized she hadn't received the kind of attention she had so obviously fished for. "Where are you headed, matchstick? To Vegas?"

"Out of Vegas, as a matter of fact," Taylor replied.

"Do you think I could do anything to change your mind? We're headed to Vegas for a bachelorette party and we decided to start the party early."

The other three girls responded with a resounding and drawn-out "Woo" that was only drowned out by the sound of another distinctive rumble of motors. Three heavy motorcycles roared into the gas station. They were built to look like choppers but the shiny quality gave them away as straight out of a Harley dealership, as did the clean and shiny appearance of the cyclists' leather jackets. These guys had just bought their bikes and wanted to ride them on the open roads.

He could easily identify with that. There were few better feelings in the world than taking a new vehicle out for a spin.

All three seemed like they rode a little high on the

testosterone their powerful machines had filled them with. The moment they saw the younger girls flirting with him, he could see it riled them a little. It had happened before. Hell, he'd felt the same way himself at times so he knew what the warning signs were.

Those particular signs were currently up like red fucking flags and he knew what was coming.

"You girls are wasting your time with fire-crotch over here," one of the bikers said and laughed. "If you ever need a real man, don't look for one hiding in a truck like a bitch. Find a guy who knows how to ride you like Lionel fucking Richie, baby—all night long."

Taylor narrowed his eyes as the four girls around the Mustang backed away quickly. They were used to being the ones to make the bold advances, and when the bikers looked like they needed to get some of their thirst out, they were suddenly no longer interested.

"I wouldn't worry about that if I were you," Taylor said and drew their focus away from being annoyed by the girls' reluctance. "They say spending too much time on a bike does funny stuff to a man's bait and tackle. The chances are you'd need an extra short night if you want to follow in the steps of Mr. Richie."

If things were going to escalate, he preferred that they escalate in his direction.

His instincts once again proved to be correct. The bikers strutted over to where he stood, which gave the girls an opening to escape into the convenience store.

They were safe. Him? Not so much.

"Do you think you want to say that again?" one of the men asked and tilted his head in an unmistakable challenge.

"What? Oh, you mean pointing out the well-known statistics regarding men who spend too much time with something vibrating between their legs?" he asked cheerfully but kept his voice down. There were a couple of security cameras in place around the building that would help him if the three decided to sue for damages.

Cameras would show him standing calmly while the other three began to lose their shit and became more and more aggressive before he acted in self-defense.

It was annoying that he needed to think that way, but he was technically a government employee and as much as he liked to piss Banks off, he didn't want to lose that particular job.

The three moved in around him to cut off any avenues of escape, which left him with his back to Liz.

"Do you have something to say now, bitch?" the man in the middle asked. He stepped aggressively into what he thought was his adversary's personal space and tried to seem intimidating despite the fact that Taylor had about five inches and twenty pounds of muscle on him.

"Not really." He kept his hands down as he watched the other man's fist cock in readiness. "I merely wondered what three guys have to prove to a stranger at a gas station. Although it's probably the same thing you had to prove to the cute saleswoman at that dealership you bought those bikes from, right? Do you need a little help to get your collective gear sticks up?"

As anticipated, that was all he needed to say. The first fist hammered forward with as much power as the man could muster thrust into the haymaker. Taylor could see it coming a mile away, but he didn't move.

The fist connected with his jaw and although it was a little low to be effective, he felt knuckles connecting with the bone. It was a little jarring and slightly painful, but not as painful as the man's hand would be.

"Fuck!" his assailant shouted as pain exploded across his hand and wrist. Still, it was nothing compared to what he had in store for him.

"You know, they say never to hit a man with a closed fist, but it is, on occasion, hilarious." He rubbed the place where he'd been hit. "Observe."

He ducked low and drove his fist into an enthusiastic uppercut between the biker's legs. The man was unable to manage a scream of pain and barely even grunted in agony. Taylor straightened, grasped his opponent by the collar of his leather jacket, and hauled him forward to pound his lowered forehead into the man's nose and mouth.

The biker was already on his way down, and the head-butt merely sealed it. He sprawled into a groaning pile with one hand on his privates and other over his face.

"A crotch shot?" one of the other bikers asked and backed away a step or two. "Classy."

"Yeah, because three guys attacking one totally screams fair play, right?" he retorted and glimpsed the third man's approach out of the corner of his eye.

He turned to face the second as if he hadn't noticed the sly advance. Calmly, he mentally counted every step until his would-be attacker was close enough. At the perfect moment, he leaned back on his hip, snapped his right elbow back, and caught his target in the temple. The blow hurled the man into Liz and he slid soundlessly to the concrete.

The second tried to take advantage of what he obviously thought was a moment of distraction. He threw a wild jab that Taylor blocked with his left arm. He shoved it aside, which left the man wide open, and swung his right from above. The blow hammered into the side of the man's head and dropped him to his knees.

While he probably didn't need to, he brought his knee up under the last man's jaw to disable him completely.

"Like I said." He looked smugly at the three men, who were still conscious but wouldn't get up anytime soon. "Hilarious."

They made no effort to respond and he rolled his neck, took a deep breath, and looked around the gas station. He didn't expect that anyone would run to help—not for him and not for the three who actually needed it. The kid behind the counter talked rapidly into his cellphone, though, likely calling the local cops.

The girls stepped out when they saw that the fight was over and it was safe to emerge. Most of them appeared to want to get out of the area as quickly as possible, but the one who had addressed him before was either a little bolder or a little drunker than her friends. She sauntered over to where he cleaned some of the blood biker number three had left on Liz's coat of paint.

"Thanks for the help, giant stranger," she said softly. She seemed shyer than her previous overtures had suggested.

"I'm not sure how I helped you, but...you're welcome?"

"Well, I guess I should have opened with the fact that these bikers have given us trouble all the way from LA," she said and glared at the injured men. "So thanks for that. I honestly think they planned to follow us all the way to Vegas."

"Oh, well, it's definitely no problem," Taylor said. "It looks like your bachelorette party will be safe. Wait, is that why you were trying to get me to join you?"

"Partially," she admitted. "There was also some intention to find out if the carpet matched the drapes if you know what I mean."

"I do, and believe me, I am tempted." He winked. "But have urgent business to take care of in LA that can't be pushed back. But they do match if you were curious."

"I won't simply take your word for it," she said and glared at her friends who honked the Mustang's horn to tell her to join them.

"You'll have to." He pulled the door of his truck open and stepped inside. "Have a great party. Maybe raise a drink for...what was that charming little nickname you gave me?"

"Matchstick," she said. "Sorry about that."

"No worries." He started the vehicle and eased onto the road. He could see the girl watching him drive away in the rearview mirror.

# CHAPTER THREE

Desk took her time getting back to him, although Taylor wasn't really surprised. She couldn't have been happy that he'd simply walked away and left a mess like that for her to clean up.

The woman was sulking, that was all. It was annoying but he had come to expect it from her at this point and he decided not to bitch about it. She'd earned a little silence from him.

He was about an hour away from the coordinates Banks had sent him when his phone rang. All he needed was a press of a button to answer as he had connected the device to the Bluetooth in Liz when he'd left her the other three voicemails.

"Desk, it's nice to hear your voice again." He deliberately laid it on thick. "How have you been doing?"

"Don't you try to sweet-talk me," she grumbled. "Did you think I wouldn't find out about you getting into that fight at the gas station? Or that you walked away when you damn well knew the cops were on their way to deal with you? Are you fucking serious right now?"

She sounded pissed. Not that he really expected anything different.

"Now I know I might not have done that by the book—" Taylor said, instantly defensive.

"I wasn't finished," she snapped. "And then, you have the nerve to call me not once, not twice, but three times to help you deal with a little 'situation' you left behind?"

He paused, reluctant to interrupt the tirade she obviously needed to release. Sometimes, it was best to simply let the person vent.

The silence lasted a few seconds longer than was comfortable and he began to wonder if that had been a wise choice.

"Well, don't you have anything to say?" she demanded.

"I…uh, do you not have anything else to say?" he asked. "I don't want to interrupt."

"Are you fucking serious right now? Situation you left behind, full goddamn stop!" It emerged as a roar through the speaker.

"Oh, right, cool. First of all, I saw a situation developing in the gas station and decided to diffuse it as quietly and efficiently as possible while staying on time with the schedule to reach Banks."

"Is that what you call a situation developing? Three bikers flirting with a few sorority sisters?"

"Well—not that I knew this from the beginning—but as it turned out, those bikers had followed the girls all the way from LA," he explained. "They had the look of guys who would cause more trouble down the road and they were getting pushy. I decided to leave them in a condition where they wouldn't be able to do so—or follow the girls, as I later discovered—while I also tried to move quickly enough to stay on schedule."

"Wait, what?" Desk asked. "Okay, yes, I can understand being the reluctant knight in shining armor, but how could you think it was quickly enough to stay on schedule? You dealt with the bikers efficiently enough, but you had to know the cops would be involved and that means a whole ton of trouble for me to deal with. I assume you don't want to be taken to their police station and interrogated for half a day while Banks is dealing with a real situation."

"Well, I made sure all the evidence the cops would recover would be the report from possible witnesses about how the bikers harassed the girls, from the girls them-selves, and from the kid cashier." He paused for a moment and frowned. "Then again, maybe the kid wouldn't be too much help since he didn't like me too much. Oh, and there is the camera footage in the station that should show how they approached me first, became all aggressive, and threw the first punch before I introduced them to an intimate relationship with the concrete."

"Oh…hold on. Let me look into that." It sounded like she put him on hold while she looked for the footage he had mentioned. There was nothing they could talk about until she'd seen it.

All she really had to go on at this point was the police reports, apparently, and those wouldn't have his side of the story. That would be quickly updated once they knew what actually happened. Taylor had made sure his voice was low enough that it would not be picked up by the average security system microphones, so all the cops would know was that he tried to talk the bikers down and they attacked him.

They would still want to have a word with him and take a statement and whatnot, but with a little insistence from the FBI, they could probably be dissuaded.

There were benefits to working with or for the government.

"Okay." Desk returned to the line. "It looks like you're supported by the data available, although the cops are interviewing the cashier in the convenience store so we'll know more about what I'm dealing with in that scenario once that's done. It was still an incredible risk to deal with those three."

"For them, maybe," he replied. "Those guys acted all tough, but my money's on them being finance guys who wanted to try out their new toys, were a little too hopped up on it all, and decided to take up the biker lifestyle for a while."

"You're not that far off, actually. All three are members of the same law firm in LA and all had just received a bonus for their work in a recent case."

"Now how the hell would you know that?"

"Because I'm good at my job?"

"That still seems like you might have overstepped the jurisdiction of the FBI," Taylor said. "I don't say that in a bad way, of course," he added hastily.

"Local news covered the case and mentioned the names of all three of those gents," Desk replied with total unconcern. "I won't bother you with the issues and details, but the short of it is that they came into a large amount of money and bought themselves motorcycles to celebrate."

"So, if they're lawyers, will they be a problem? I've heard the assholes can find all kinds of ways to twist the law to make themselves look like the victims."

"I'm already about three or four steps ahead of you," she assured him smugly. "I sent their firm's partners a message saying that if they try to press any charges or make a fuss about excessive force in your little altercation, the FBI would charge all three with the attempted assault of a federal officer. That, of course, would damage the company's reputation in the state and tie them into a quagmire of legal issues before it even reaches court."

"In short, you made sure their bosses know that the best thing for everyone involved is to let this be a brawl that goes by the wayside, yeah?" He raised an eyebrow, secretly impressed by both her logic and her efficiency. "Wait, how am I a federal officer?"

"You are designated as being employed by the US government and were currently in the performance of your official duties when they threw the first punch. That opens them to felony charges on a federal level, and no law firm wants *Three Llawyers Facing Federal Charges* on the front page of every newspaper. It should resolve itself in no time, but I'll keep an eye on the situation as it develops. In the interim, I suggest you high-tail your ass over to Banks because you have considerable problems on your plate in that regard."

"Wait, what is that supposed to mean?" Taylor asked.

"Well, let's say that on top of issues with bikers in gas stations, you will also face less than great changes to the original contract you were called in on," Desk said. She sounded less than happy about it, which didn't offer much in the way of reassurance.

He'd had a feeling this would happen. Having a job come up only four hours' drive away did seem a little too easy for him. He'd somehow known it was unlikely that he could simply saunter in, eliminate the damn monster, and head home with another fat stack courtesy of the FBI.

With a heavy sigh, he prepared himself for what was to come. "Go on, tell me what kind of shit I'll walk into. Assuming you are allowed to brief me on that, I guess."

"I am, don't worry. But unfortunately, that is the end of the good news. The long and the short of it is that they have established that there are Zoo monsters in the area, and they are incredibly aggressive. Witnesses have reported them attacking people they encounter."

"Who are these witnesses?"

"Firefighters, for the most part," Desk said. "They have agreed not to spread the word on social media and the like so the situation has been contained but we can't trust them on that. Banks wants this job over and done with as quickly as possible before hunters decide to get in on the action."

"Right," Taylor said. "Quick question, why are there firefighters in the area?"

"Haven't you watched the news?" she asked.

"Well, obviously not."

"Well, anyone with any kind of connection to the outside world knows that much of the area is engulfed by serious wildfires that have necessitated the involvement of considerably more people than we'd prefer. They're evacuating the area, but if the news gets out that there are Zoo creatures there, you know there will be dumbasses who want to catch a glimpse or maybe more. Getting the job done quicker would be better."

"Fun times." He shook his head against the rising frustration.

"There is something of a silver lining in this for you, of course," Desk continued.

"Oh yeah?" He already had a bad feeling about this assignment and it hadn't even started. When people mentioned silver linings, it usually meant the storm clouds had begun to obfuscate anything else from view.

"Well, more of a silver lining for you than for anyone else. They did some calculations on the assignment and will probably raise the ceiling for an acceptable asking price. They wouldn't tell you any of this, of course, but let's say I have your back more than those of the penny-pinchers. The way I see it, you're clear to give them an invoice to the tune of the lower six figures for this job."

"How lower?" Either it was a really bright silver lining, or it was a fucking dark cloud.

"Well, Banks will only make a fuss about it if you ask her for anything higher than a hundred and fifty thousand dollars," she told him. "That's not to say she won't go a little higher, but if she does, I doubt it will be by much."

"Noted," he said. "And thanks."

As silver linings went, he had to admit it was a good one. That amount of money was not something to turn his nose up at. All things considered, he could do with a little extra seed money as orders for their work at the shop had begun to pour in. The influx of work meant more parts and more working hours, and the extra money would go a long way to meet those needs.

It wasn't something he looked at with a great deal of anticipation, of course. Dealing with Zoo monsters was normal for him—or as close as it could be given that they were inherently abnormal by definition—but fire had never been an issue in the Zoo. Still, it was nice that this job provided a couple of different challenges. It was good for his mental health to be pushed out of his comfort zone from time to time. He would become soft otherwise.

"Well, not that you needed to know, but color me interested," he said finally to end the silence. "It sounds like it has variety—like a video game, where I have a number of targets and a ticking clock to get it finished by. I can't ask for a better challenge."

"Look at you, being all positive," Desk said and laughed. "I like that look on you. It gives us all extra hope for the future."

"Don't be ridiculous," Taylor grumbled. "I'm a positive person—always have been and always will be. I'm one of those guys who has a glass half-full and don't ever let Banks make you think otherwise."

"Well, I'll take your word on that. Oh, right—in other news, it looks like you'll meet other members of CREG for this mission."

"CREG?"

"Cryptid Research and Elimination Group. Banks has put a high enough priority on the job that she thought it would be worth it to bring a couple of other freelancers in as well."

"Oh…" He immediately felt a little offended—did the

woman still not fucking trust him or something? After a moment, though, he accepted that she wouldn't have pulled in extra guns if she didn't feel it was necessary. "Well, as long as I won't have a pay cut—"

"You won't."

"Then it's all gravy, I guess."

Not too long after, massive black clouds billowed in the distance, visible for miles. They seemed to grow blacker and far more ominous as he pulled off of the main road, headed up into the hills, and followed the map Desk had sent for him. Each moment brought him steadily closer and all too soon, he drove past vehicles that had been loaded with essentials by people evacuating the area. Fire trucks could be seen ahead, moving into the same area.

Finally, he pulled Liz to a stop at what looked like a field HQ the firefighters had set up to coordinate their efforts.

"So, will I work with the firefighters?" Taylor asked and kept Liz's doors and windows closed for as long as he could. He knew that the moment he stepped out, she would begin to smell of the smoke that suffused the whole area.

"Well…technically, yes, because you will work with the intel they have collected from the area," Desk said. "But also no. Again, the priority of this whole operation is to keep the word from spreading, so having the FBI set up an HQ would attract too much attention. Since there is already an HQ on-site, Banks thought it was a good idea to set up here with them. There are fewer prying eyes that way."

"I can't disagree with that," he admitted. "Although I

have to say I don't really want to get in the way of the people who are actually fighting the fire, so to have two teams out there could be problematic for both of us. Not only that, they might well encounter the monsters and none of them are equipped to deal with them, so I'd then also have to worry about keeping them safe."

"Are you equipped to deal with the fire, though?" she asked as he disconnected his phone from the car and pressed the device to his ear.

"Partially. The suit I have can handle some fire for a little while, but it was never a priority in the Zoo. Things simply don't burn well out there and if they do catch alight, it's not for long."

"That's interesting but irrelevant," she said crisply. "Do you know how effective the suit is?"

"Nope," he replied. "But I guess I'll soon find out."

# CHAPTER FOUR

Taylor took a moment to lock Liz before he moved toward the tents that had been erected on the side of the road. Most of the area had been cleared of any brush, trees, and other organic material to keep it from being overrun by the fires that blazed ferociously across the nearby hillsides.

Thankfully, Banks stood outside of one of the tents and watched him intently as he approached. It wasn't until he got closer that he noticed the yellow stump of a cigarette that protruded partially from under her boot.

"Who the fuck smokes anymore these days?" he asked as he stopped beside her.

She shook her head and exhaled one last lungful of smoke. "I the fuck smokes these days, that's who. What the hell took you so long?"

"Well I was—wait, didn't Desk fill you in on the details?"

"If I wanted her version of events, I would ask her. Which I did, obviously, but I now want to hear your explanation for what happened at that gas station."

"Three wannabe bad boys thought they were tough," he replied. "I taught them otherwise. Aside from the inconvenience of having to deal with their company health insurance, they'll be fine. And, hopefully, think twice about picking a fight with a dude twice their size. How's that for explanations?"

The agent scowled. "That's actually not the worst explanation for tardiness I've heard all day. You're lucky the other two only arrived a couple of minutes before you did or we would have moved on with the job without you."

"No, you wouldn't have."

"Try me, bitch." The tone was sufficiently acerbic but her grin gave her away at the last word. "Hell, I would suit up and head out there with them if they needed a third wheel."

"Yeah, right, and that would be such a smart idea. Should we get inside?"

Banks smirked and gestured for him to precede her through the tent flap. As headquarters went, he had seen better over the years. A solitary bulb hung over a single metal table that was placed in what appeared to be the dead center of the tent, where a variety of pictures and papers rested. That was the sum total of what it contained.

Then again, he had seen many that were far worse. This looked like the average field HQ, the kind they needed to set up close to the front lines of a fight while still being far enough away from the action that the brass didn't need to worry about bullets.

Fortunately, bullets wouldn't be a problem in this situation.

He noted the two others who stood inside the tent,

clearly waiting for them. Neither were firefighters or any kind of law enforcement, that much was clear. The woman was tall and lean with short brown hair and was dressed in jeans, a tank top, and a pair of combat boots. The man had long, black hair and wore a black Slayer shirt, cargo pants, and boots. They looked tough, but that alone wouldn't be enough in this business.

"Taylor, meet Tanya Novak and Hector Ribera," Banks said and strode toward the table at the center of the tent. "They've worked with CREG for a while now and have been two of our most valuable assets since our inception. Tanya, Hector, this is Taylor McFadden, our newest recruit."

"It's nice to meet you," Taylor said, and they nodded in response. "How long have you guys worked here? Hell, I still don't know how long CREG has been around."

"About two and a half years," the agent replied. "Hector joined us in the beginning and Tanya about three months after that. They might not be what you consider qualified for the job, but they have survived and done so for a while, and that should be enough for you."

He nodded.

"Wait, in what way aren't we qualified?" Tanya asked.

"That's not important," Banks said.

"It seems kind of important to me," Hector pointed out.

"Moving on," the agent said a little more forcefully. "We have monsters to hunt and you guys have money to make. Or is that not important enough for you?"

Both shrugged, and Taylor couldn't help but do the same. They were there to do a job. For the moment, finding out more about what that entailed had a higher priority than who he would do it with.

"These are pictures taken by some of the firefighters and reporters in the area," Banks said and pushed some of the images across the table to him. "We've managed to convince them to keep a lid on it for the moment by talking about how people might go in to try to hunt it and be killed either by the fire or by the animals themselves. So far, it's worked—mostly because we appealed to their better natures—but we all know it won't last. We need to get rid of those creatures as quickly as possible before the fucking ZooTube enthusiasts head in there."

"Hurrah for a ticking clock," Hector said and scowled. "How long do we have?"

"Until the end of the day. They'll want it up on the evening news by then."

"Nothing like a little pressure." Taylor picked one of the clearer pictures up. The monsters were a little difficult to make out in the photographs taken by the firefighters since it appeared that most of their pictures were more about the fire and the creatures were an afterthought.

The reporter pictures were much clearer, however, and far more alarming. From their images, it was easy to tell that there were multiple mutants—at least seven of them by his count. They resembled bobcats and were up in the trees as well as on the ground and bared their teeth at the man who held the camera. Their black fur did indicate that they weren't regular bobcats, though, as well as their long tails that ended with what looked like a scorpion's stinger.

"That was one brave reporter," he noted, impressed despite the fact that he thought the man—or woman—was a total idiot. "And this is definitely our kind of case. It doesn't look like these little beauties have dropped too many bodies so the fire and the timeline aside, what's with the rush? Are the rich and famous of Hollywood Hills not fans of having Zoo monsters in their back yard?"

"What tells you they haven't dropped bodies?" Hector asked, his tone marginally scornful.

"For one thing, we'd see fewer firefighters in the area," he explained calmly. "When Zoo critters are in a murdering mood, they don't tend to be picky about who they kill or why, which would include the guys who got close enough for a picture. These don't look aggressive enough to be killers."

The other two hunters narrowed their eyes at him but Banks merely shrugged.

"The worry is that the fire will drive them out of the woods and into populated areas," she said. "You know how that song and dance goes. Some people die, people panic, and my bosses have a shit-ton of alien egg on their collective faces since it was their job to prevent precisely that. So…yeah, you guys are on a clock here."

"Point taken," Taylor said and looked at the others. "Assuming we have a location to work with…" He waited for the agent to nod in the affirmative. "What say you guys that we get this show on the road?"

"You seem really eager to head into a location where we not only have monsters to deal with but a blazing fire as well," Tanya pointed out.

"I'm eager to get out there and earn a hefty paycheck is what," he replied. "Which…yeah, is the kind of check I'll be looking for in this job. So, why are we wasting time here?"

"A hundred and fifty grand each is the bounty set on this job for all three of you," Banks said.

"Wait, why the hell does this guy get to call the shots?" Hector demanded. "Not to start measuring dicks, but I thought we would have some seniority over the newbie."

"Because I've seen the real thing." Taylor fixed the man with a hard look. "I've been out in the real Zoo and dealt with every kind of fun trick that jungle of nightmares has to offer. This is… Well, I don't want to say child's play by comparison, but it sure as fuck ain't the big leagues either."

"Bullshit." The other man laughed. "The chances are this guy lied on his resume to get the job and now wants to look all tough before he goes in there and hides behind the real pros."

Taylor looked at Banks, who raised an eyebrow.

"Do you want to say anything about that?" he asked. "You are the one who read through my allegedly fake resume, so this might be damaging to your reputation."

"I look forward to you being able to prove your worth to this team on your own," she replied with a cheeky grin. "Don't come to me and expect me to fight your battles for you."

"Fair enough."

"Come on, back me up here, Tanya," Hector said.

The woman shook her head. "You're crazy if you think I'll get anywhere near the splash zone in this particular pissing contest. You two are on your own."

"I can live with that," Taylor said. "Now, unless you want to throw out any other doubts regarding my credentials, why don't we go and earn ourselves a crap-ton of money?"

"That works for me." Tanya pushed out of the tent,

quickly followed by the other three and they moved to where their equipment waited for them. Taylor had been directed to park where he had and as it turned out, all three of them had been made to stop in the same area. It gave them some time to get better acquainted as they prepared for the job they would have to accomplish.

The firefighters looked on curiously and tried to determine exactly what the hell the three newcomers were doing there. The FBI had commandeered one of their tents and they were supposed to cooperate with the feds, at least up until the point where it interfered with their work.

The reality was that each team needed to stay out of each other's way as much as possible and try not to be a distraction.

Tanya, for her part, looked like she took this job seriously and didn't seem to enjoy it very much. The grim expression on her face told Taylor that she was pushing herself into the dark little place she needed to go to in order to be good at this.

She wore some body armor—ceramic plates from the looks of it—that covered most of her torso and thighs and connected via wire with her boots. It looked like the kind of power armor the army had distributed to the troops who weren't expected to head into an alien jungle. It was completed by a helmet and a facemask that lit, which indicated one of the more rudimentary HUDs.

Her weapons consisted of an M5 assault rifle with a small scope and an under-barrel shotgun with two shots. They were effective enough while still purchasable at the average gun store. Well, maybe not in California, but definitely somewhere in Texas. She also carried what looked like a Glock sidearm and a Bowie knife.

For Hector's part, the only armor he had elected to wear was a helmet. It had the same HUD as Tanya's and like her, he also had a gas mask apparatus that was easily removable if he needed to talk without sounding like he was underwater. What he lacked in armor, however, he made up for in weaponry.

His main weapon appeared to be a Callahan Auto-lock assault rifle with a number of modifications, which included laser sights and a grenade launcher under the barrel. He paired that with a couple of Desert Eagles at his hips, along with a lever-action shotgun hung from his back. The belt holding the shotgun in place held a variety of grenades, both those that could be used by the assault rifle and thrown by hand, as well as more ammo than anyone would ever need.

The guy appeared to enjoy spraying and praying with all kinds of prejudice. Taylor merely hoped he had the good sense not to shoot the people he was teamed with.

"A regular Conan the Barbarian," he said aloud. "The Arnie version, anyway."

"Where's your gear, newbie?" the other man asked, although he appeared to enjoy the comparison to the former governor of the state they were currently in. "Or did you forget it? Maybe you left it at home and you need to go fetch it, but you'll be right back?"

"Not really. While I do think of Liz as a kind of home, now that I think about it, but she's not that far away."

He turned, opened the back of the truck, and hauled his crate out with a little mechanical help. Once it was in the open, he started to put the pieces on. The mockery began to fade from Hector's eyes as he watched him don the pieces of a fully functional and battle-hardened mech suit. Taylor couldn't help a small smirk as he finished off with the helmet and checked the weapons he had on board as he always did.

After a quick word with Banks, she had finally and begrudgingly agreed to give him a license to purchase the rockets that fit into the launcher on his back, as well as the grenades that could be fired from under the barrel. These teamed well with the powerful sidearm at his hip and the machete-sized knife right next to it.

"*Tengo que conseguirme uno de esos,*" Hector whispered under his breath, the lust very clear in his eyes as every syllable was clearly heard through the suit's speakers.

"I should warn you, they don't sell these babies in your average military surplus store," Taylor said but he understood the sentiment behind the man's words. "Although, if you are looking into getting one of your own, give me a call. I know a couple of guys."

Those couple of guys were himself and Bobby Zhang, his partner in business—well, technically his employee but there was no need to belabor the details.

"Like I said," he continued as he moved to where his two new partners stood. "I'm the real deal."

# CHAPTER FIVE

F or possibly the first time, he truly realized how lucky he was that his suit had its own air scrubbers. The closer that they got to the fire, the thicker the air became with the smoke it gave off. He could smell it through the filters, of course, but at least he was able to breathe. The others appeared to manage as well. Their purchase of gas masks had apparently paid off, although they didn't seem overly talkative as they trekked through the tough terrain.

"So," Taylor said in an attempt to break what he felt was an awkward silence. "I have to ask since I don't think I've ever pictured anyone actually choosing this kind of work without being somewhat loose when it comes to the brain screws. Why would the two of you get involved if you didn't spend time in the Zoo, anyway?"

The other two hunters exchanged a glance.

"You know, we still don't believe you were actually in the Zoo," Hector said. "Even with a fancy mech suit like that."

"Yeah, because who wouldn't be able to pick one of

these babies up at a police auction?" Taylor asked and let the sarcasm drench his tone.

"True, but they're not impossible to acquire," the other man pointed out. "You have the right connections and the right kind of money, so you could be able to be outfitted for it. Not only that, you look like you were in the military. That's the way to get connections for stuff like that so there's no reason why you wouldn't be able to get your hands on one of those without having been in the Zoo."

"I guess that makes sense." He shrugged because he could see the man had already made his mind up and there was no point in continuing the discussion with him. "How about you, Tanya? Or will you still not get anywhere near this conversation?"

The woman shrugged and adjusted her grasp on her weapon. "You two can bicker and gripe all you want as long as you get your acts together when it's time to kill beasts. For the record, I don't really care if you went into the Zoo or not. Having that kind of equipment in the field will always be an advantage, even if an untrained ape uses it. You are trained though, right?"

"I wouldn't have been able to walk in this thing if I wasn't. They have a couple of the mech suits in the FBI and hand them out when deemed appropriate. Banks actually needed to be trained to use them. She put herself into a damn wall, she said."

"Oh yeah, she did say tell us that story once," Hector said. "She told me why the FBI didn't help us with equipment. Basically, you need to be qualified and cleared for the use of anything they give you, and it's not like they hand those courses out."

"And they don't have training camps for this anywhere in the US," Tanya said. "Not unless you join the military, anyway."

"Even then, they're careful to train only those who they know will be equipped with the mech suits," Taylor said. "I needed to be cleared before use and they told me they wanted me to get a degree in engineering with my GI bill if they trained me to use it."

"Give it a rest. We still don't believe you." Hector laughed but it was one of mockery rather than humor.

Tanya looked a little less skeptical but didn't appear to fully believe what he said either. He honestly didn't care what they thought of his credentials since Banks was really the only one he needed to convince, and he moved past it.

"So why do the two of you do this for a living?" he asked. "I can't imagine that it's because of the perks. Unless you guys get dental because I can tell you that I don't."

"It's not really about the perks, no," the other man said with a chuckle. "The money's fairly good, so I'll give them that at least, but it's mostly because... Well, who the hell gets to talk about doing this kind of thing for a living, you know? There are numerous dumbasses we need to keep off these kinds of jobs because they want to be a part of history so badly, but we're paid by the government to do it?"

"So, perks then."

"Sure," Tanya replied. "Being able to say you hunt monsters for a living is one hell of a resume booster."

"I got the job at the beginning because the FBI was still trying to learn how to kill the bastards," Hector said. "They weren't sure how to go about it, of course. The beasties they tracked ended up in my backyard and on the business end of my shotgun, so Banks asked if I wanted to get paid to do what I'd done. There was no other answer than yes."

"They actually headhunted me," she said. "I worked as a wildlife consultant in a few universities across the country to help researchers get in and out of dangerous locations without being shat out of your average lion or tiger. Banks was doing some headhunting at the time as the budget for the task force had expanded, and she thought someone who could handle regular animals would know a thing or two about handling alien animals."

"Was she right?" Taylor asked.

"Well, I'm still here, aren't I?" She grinned but it wasn't entirely one of amusement. He had the feeling it was part of how she handled this.

"I guess. But that means about as much as my claim to be from the Zoo. Talking about how you've been in the task force long enough really doesn't help me establish the kind of talents you have."

"Hey, fuck you," she said.

"Yeah, you guys called me a liar when I told you about my credentials, so don't think I'll give the two of you any benefit of any doubt." He narrowed his eyes to study the hills above them. "So, if we want to find the creatures, I'd say we can work on heading a little to the west and follow the hill line while staying inside the fire."

"Why do you say that?" Hector hefted his weapons. To his credit, for all the weight that he carried, he looked a long way from being winded. Stamina was something Taylor liked to see in the people he headed into the Zoo with—especially those who didn't go in with guns in hand.

Of course, he wasn't going into the Zoo and Hector seemed like his motivation was to shoot everything he ran into and chew bubblegum. Although he might be all out of bubblegum, from the looks of it.

The woods around them appeared to have not seen any rain for the past five years or so. He wasn't sure if that was the case, but while the larger trees looked like they had some green to them—possibly from tapping deeper wells of water—everything else looked brown and dry. It seemed like they were ready and waiting for the fire to burn through them. The blaze would move quickly, and their current trajectory guided them directly into the teeth of the flames.

"Why are we moving this way again?" Hector had obviously noticed that their path led them to where the firefighters were guiding the flames away from the nearest population centers. Given how many towns and cities were spread across the whole of the state, Taylor was surprised there were woods available to be burned at all.

That aside, there were enough problems for them to deal with in this area. Diving virtually into the fire was not something he looked forward to, but it felt like it was necessary at this particular juncture.

"We're moving toward where the creatures actually are," he explained. "They don't appear to be attacking the humans and are as afraid of interacting with them as the rest of the wildlife. So they'll do what the other animals will and head away from the fire and this way."

"And you're sure of that how?" Tanya asked.

"I'm not. However, the moment the beasts decide to attack the firefighters, it'll be all over the comm lines and we'll have a specific location we can hurry to. Otherwise, the only place where we'll find anything useful is where all the humans aren't."

"That makes sense," Hector acknowledged. "But don't think having a good idea makes you anything like a pro. It only means you have a brain that works."

"That makes one of us," Taylor said softly.

"What was that?" the man asked, although he'd obviously heard the comment clearly.

"I said we need to keep moving," he said a little louder. "If those monsters decide they are done dealing with the lesser creatures and the humans here, they'll push into the nearby neighborhoods. I don't think modern Hollywood can sustain losing all the stars living in the hills and around Malibu."

"Because keeping the film industry in this area up and running is why we're here," Tanya said and rolled her eyes.

"Do you think they would have brought all three of us into this job if there weren't serious political machinations behind it?" he asked and gave them each a hard look. "The people around here have all kinds of leverage on the folks in Washington, so you can bet your muscular asses that the reason why the folks up top have overreacted and are willing to pay through the nose is because calls were made and careers threatened."

"Whatever you say," she replied off-handedly. "We're still on a heading that will take us directly into where the fire is tearing through this place. If my experience dealing with wildfires is in any way accurate, we are about one wrong move away from being encircled by the flames and left with nowhere to go but up. I assume that suit can't fly."

"Not this one, no," he said. "Some of the lighter ones can, though. The light mech suits meant to be more mobile and less for defense in the Zoo do too—or maybe it's more accurate to say they can simply jump really high. I'm not sure that the difference matters. There's only so much fuel that can be carried in these bad boys so they're not built with that in mind."

"I guess," Hector said. "Are there any that don't need any fuel to jump? I'm thinking like…springs and shit."

"There are people doing interesting work with magnetic coils, if I recall, but that's mostly in the private sector."

"Can we focus?" Tanya snapped. "My point is, if we are trapped in the flames, how the hell will we get out?"

"Well, I should be fine," he pointed out and looked around.

"Even if the suit had fire-retardant capabilities, you'll still have to deal with enough heat to cook you alive in there," she retorted. "The kind of stuff people like to make armor from tends to convect a ton of heat."

"True, but there is padding in there to delay it." He paused as he stepped over a fallen log. "It would buy me enough time to get the hell out of Dodge, maybe with one of you, before the oven gets too hot."

"Which one of us?" Hector asked.

"That depends on which of you is the nicest to me," he replied with a small grin. "That, or whoever is the closest, because I won't loiter while you decide who deserves to live the longest."

"Whatever you say." She sounded distinctly unimpressed as they headed deeper into the wooded hills.

The flames built up to his right and left to climb higher into the hills, chew into the trees around them, and cut off the direct path along which they had come. There wasn't anything they could do about that now except head deeper into the woods in search of where the rest of the animals would most likely do the smart thing and run from the growing blaze.

More and more animals could be seen rushing past them as their fear of the humans was overwhelmed by the fear of the fire that appeared to have a life of its own. The inferno pushed harder as the wind from the coast filled it with oxygen to drive it faster than before.

"I'm serious," Tanya said. "One mistake from any of us, and we'll be barbecue. And not the good kind of barbecue either. We'll be incredibly well-done. Burnt, I'd say."

"Damn it. Now I'm fucking hungry," Taylor said.

"That's not normal," Hector pointed out. "Actually, when I think about it, there's nothing normal about you. Seriously, how many redheaded giants do you know?"

"Well, that's plain hurtful. Still, I could do with a medium-well done steak and a whole mountain of fries. Just…a whole pile of them. Maybe some endless shrimp too."

"Seriously, he's right. You're not normal, man." She shook her head.

"I'm not a normal person. If people talk about barbecue when I'm hungry, I think about food."

"Whatever," she said.

Hector didn't answer and seemed focused on the animals that scurried around them. They were mostly smaller creatures. Raccoons, skunks, and foxes joined the chittering squirrels and birds in the trees above them in the mass exodus to escape from the flames. A couple of the larger animals were present as well, and the man aimed his rifle at one of them through the smoke.

"Don't—" Taylor was cut off by the sound of the three-round burst. An animal's shriek could be heard above the crackle and roar of the fire that approached.

Taylor used his HUD to zoom in and get a better look at what lay on the ground, killed instantly by the pin-point accuracy of the man's shooting.

It looked like a coyote with its grey and brown fur already a little singed. At least it was a quick death, he noted but scowled. Senseless killing always rubbed him the wrong way, for some reason.

"That probably wasn't your best idea ever," he said with a grim look at Hector.

"I thought it was one of those alien bobcats," the man admitted. "And why not? Don't tell me you're one of those bleeding-heart liberals who can't see an animal die without throwing a fit?"

"Okay, I admit, it's never cool to watch an innocent animal die a meaningless death," he replied caustically. "But I merely thought that in this particular case, you would want to conserve your ammo."

"Why?"

In lieu of a reply, he pointed silently toward the top of the nearest hill.

# CHAPTER SIX

It was interesting to see the creatures move. Taylor almost missed it at first, but they climbed through the trees with surprising agility that made their movements difficult to describe at first. They looked like bobcats in their build but always used their tails to swing from branch to branch. This allowed them to move much faster than any cat but made them resemble simians more than felines.

They were also far larger than most bobcats tended to be, which made the trees heave and groan under their weight as they moved away from the fire. They seemed to realize that the humans they had encountered wouldn't simply allow them to pass without adding considerably more heat of a very different nature.

A handful of them approached but remained in the trees to stare at them. It was as if the three humans were being studied, monitored, and observed before the remainder would be allowed to approach. An odd chattering very clearly didn't come from the forest around them or the advancing fire. It appeared that the beasts were actually communicating with each other.

Taylor didn't like that. He had always hated the monsters that were more intelligent than they were supposed to be. While he had come to expect that kind of intelligence from the mutants in the Zoo, he had a feeling it had more to do with the goop than the location in question. Of course, it meant he shouldn't be surprised to encounter more or less the same thing here, but he didn't really want to have to delve deeper into the situation or its implications. The fact remained that the creatures were intelligent enough to possibly discuss some kind of strategy and he had no intention to wait for them to decide on the best way to deal with the humans. Time was not on their side, of course, with the fires still moving inexorably in their direction.

"Oh," Hector said a little stupidly. He looked into the trees around them, ejected the magazine from his assault rifle, and tucked it into his belt before he retrieved a fresh one and shoved it into place. "Well, let's say we believe you know a thing or two about killing these things. What do you think we should do next?"

Taylor wasn't entirely sure, but he found that more and more ideas emerged the more he thought about it. He grasped the assault rifle in his hands and made a note on his HUD to identify all the animals they needed to eliminate and keep track of them. There were at least three dozen of them spread between the trees, and there might have been more out of range.

"What? Where did all your bravado go?" he asked.

"Maybe it evacuated your body along with everything else that was in your bowels."

"For fuck's sake, can the two of your stop your petty bickering for one minute and come up with a plan?" Tanya snapped and aimed her weapon at the creatures that now began to surround them.

They circled above the three teammates to get into better positions while the sound of their chattering slowly faded. Taylor couldn't be sure if they no longer felt the need to communicate—which meant they already had their fucking plans made—or the fire was close enough that its roar was more or less the only sound he could really make out.

Either way, things would take a turn for the worse sooner rather than later, and he would not sit around and wait for that to happen.

"Move behind me, both of you," he said and motioned with his free hand. "Give yourself enough room to shoot around me, but make sure the armor is always closer to you than the monsters, got it?"

His companions nodded. Insults and barbs were all well and good and could be a fun way to pass the time, but when it was time to focus on what readied to kill them, he had to concede that they responded appropriately. The change from playful to professional happened quickly and at precisely the right time.

"I have a count of at least thirty-six of them." It was the closest to actual Zoo-like attacks that he'd encountered since leaving the damn place, and while they had usually dealt with monsters that numbered in the hundreds there, it had been with a team of at least five who were well-armed, well-armored, and ready for this kind of situation.

Oh, and there had been no fire then either.

Taylor brought the launcher on his back up to his shoulder. He only had four rockets in the tubes, which would be enough to eliminate a small number of the creatures, Unfortunately, they needed considerably more effect than that. He would have to think tactically.

"When I start shooting, save your fire for when they approach," he instructed. "As they move closer, they'll bunch up tighter and you'll be able to kill more of them in a shorter period of time."

"We know how to hunt these fuckers," Tanya retorted.

"You don't know how to hunt them in large numbers," he snapped in response, in no mood to deal with any sass. "Now get behind me and watch for your shots."

Their protests ceased and he aimed the first of the rockets at the closest tree, which also had the largest number of monsters in its branches as they were moving about before they initiated their first assault.

A streak of white cut through the smoke and a sudden explosion shredded most of the trunk. Chunks of wood and shrapnel from the rocket itself erupted and a handful of the monsters were destroyed in the blast. The tree fell, accompanied by the shrieks and screams of the mutants in the branches. Some managed to escape unscathed, however, and emerged once the damaged trunk settled.

The beasts immediately realized they were under attack and surged forward as he launched the other three rockets still in the tube. The missiles decimated those that advanced faster than the others and went on to fell another tree nearby that sheltered a large number of them.

Hector, of course, wasn't one to wait like he had been instructed to do. It wasn't long before the man's under-barrel grenade launcher fired behind Taylor, and a quarter of a second later, the blast detonated among a group of the creatures that pressed into the attack. A small number fell, none of which got back up again, but there were many that remained.

More than enough for all of them.

Once the last two rockets were fired, Taylor called up the targeting reticle for his assault rifle and settled into a steady rhythm. Of those that had been pinpointed on his HUD, a handful were already close enough that his companions could take care of them as they approached.

They selected their targets well and eliminated the creatures while he found those in the trees and killed them before they could find a way to circle above them. The methodical gunfire gave the three of them the space they needed as he began to back away.

The two hunters soon realized the position they were in. A wall of flame advanced steadily to where they held their ground against the mutants. The beasts moved quickly and leapt lightly from the ground to the trees to move away from the fire as well. Their distraction gave the trio the targets they required, but it wasn't long before the groups were forced in closer to one another.

Taylor honestly would have taken the Zoo over this bullshit in that moment. The fire aside, while his team-mates were armed sufficiently and trained well enough, they weren't able to keep up with the pace the bobcats pushed them into. Ammo was wasted with rounds fired into the air, and he honestly didn't trust them to not accidentally shoot him in the back.

At least in the Zoo, he could trust the people he went in with. These two were decent enough hunters, he could give them that much, but dealing with Zoo monsters required an entirely different kind of expertise. They didn't move like regular creatures, and their thinking process made them all kinds of different and dangerous to people who weren't ready for them.

Not everyone in the Zoo died during their first time in. He wasn't sure what kind of statistics anyone had to support a claim as to how many people actually survived the damn jungle, but in those cases, there was always the caveat of having a group that already knew what they were doing before they headed in. It wasn't a perfect system but as systems went, it was certainly enough to satisfy the average statistician.

This was new territory, however. Only one of the three was properly armored for this kind of encounter and properly trained and experienced in dealing with monsters like these. Their skill and experience in the hunting field notwithstanding, he was the only one who knew the next five or six steps they needed to take if they wanted to avoid being savaged to death.

When he was the only one who satisfied all the above criteria, it didn't sit right with him. It put all the responsibility on him—not only that of dealing with what they faced but of protecting the others too. At the very least, he should be there with people who knew what the fuck they were doing.

"Keep moving," Taylor called and adjusted his sights hastily to keep up with the mutants that surged around them. They were practically flanked by those that were above and around them already. He wasn't sure if the creatures would attack them if they got past or if they would simply run away. Both were terrible situations, of course, and he was surprised to discover that he hoped they would stick around and fight.

Not that he had much say in the matter, he realized. These were goop-spawned, after all.

"Reloading!" he called when the assault rifle ran dry and drew his sidearm to maintain fire while the other two continued to retreat. Both looked like they were willing to turn the hell around and run but didn't feel comfortable with the idea of abandoning him to the creatures.

Maybe they recalled all their tough talk from before and wanted to back it up, or maybe they had a mind to actually have his back. He honestly wasn't sure if he would be able to handle these monsters on his own.

The one positive thing was that it appeared neither of them doubted his credentials anymore.

With the assault rifle reloaded, he switched weapons and glanced at the trees above them while Hector launched a grenade into those in front. Taylor released a sustained barrage of automatic fire to clear anything and everything above them, tear through the trees as well, and send it all plummeting to the ground before he turned again. The rifle needed to reload and he yanked his pistol free to repeat the process.

One of the creatures had noted his direction and

launched up as he swung around. Its jaws snapped over his wrist and tried to drag the sidearm away.

It was barely a second's worth of distraction and didn't cause any panic. With the fire moving closer, he knew they had the time to spare since the monsters were, in fact, trying to escape rather than focused entirely on killing them.

This was why you didn't head into the Zoo with a group of amateurs, he couldn't help thinking as Hector pushed in front of him. He held his shotgun in one hand and the assault rifle in the other as ten of the surviving beasts attacked.

"Get some, you sons of bitches!" the man roared and opened fire to annihilate as many as he could while his teammate struggled to free his hand from the creature that tried to gnaw it off. It wasn't long before the assault rifle was reloaded, and Taylor swept the weapon around and fired twice at the assailant on his arm. He whirled again and reached out to grab Hector and drag him back behind him.

Unfortunately, two of the monsters had made it through the hunter's barrage and lurched toward him before the man realized how close they were. Taylor tried to reach him but the needle-like stingers on their tails punched into his teammate's unarmored chest. The man grunted and his lungs suddenly emptied as he looked at his chest as if confused and unable to fully register what happened.

"Fuck!" he roared as the hunter staggered. He holstered his sidearm and yanked the machete out. It took considerable force to hack through their tails before both stingers were severed. The beasts screamed in pain and fell back. They hissed and bared their teeth at the two men before they were gunned down.

Even if the stingers hadn't been poisoned, it looked like the physical wound they had inflicted would have been fatal anyway.

They were poisoned, however, and clear fluid already drained from Hector's chest as he collapsed, gurgling around the blood that seeped into his lungs through the wounds.

It was a rapid reaction and one he would never recover from even if he wasn't already unconscious. Taylor undid the belt across the man's chest, pulled it clear, and scowled at the mutants that gathered for another assault.

A quick tug yanked a pin from one of the grenades and he lobbed it into the middle of the creatures. He didn't even pause to look at the explosion as the fire suddenly rushed to fill the vacuum created and pushed toward them. As Tanya had said, he could already feel the heat radiate through his armor to generate a stream of sweat down his back.

He turned and handed the belt to her as more of the beasts thrust forward. The desperation he saw in them was easily recognizable but this time, it wasn't driven by something in the Zoo. Nothing told them to attack manically at the expense of their own lives except perhaps for whatever survival instinct was in them.

In all honesty, he might have felt bad about killing them if not for the undeniable fact that they would kill many, many more people if unchecked. They'd already started with Hector.

"Hector—shit." Taylor growled his frustration as he twisted to empty his magazine into the last of the attackers that had managed to escape the grenade. There weren't too many of them left, and those that had managed to survive this long were cut down quickly by the two teammates.

It didn't feel right to leave a body behind like this. Even if the guy had been something of an asshole, he was still someone who had stepped into the metaphorical breach with them. Not only that, while the intention had been a foolish one and had ultimately been unnecessary, he had still tried to cover for him while he was distracted.

But he wouldn't be able to carry the body and Tanya back and needed to carry her if they both wanted to get clear of the rapidly advancing fire.

He moved to the body and paused only long enough to yank the dog tags from the man's neck before he turned back to the woman.

"Get on my back!" he called and she complied without argument. There were a few crevices for her to catch hold of and hang on as he pushed into a sprint. The heat of the flames licked at his suit as they raced forward.

An odd thought occurred to him to throw the grenades at the fire in the hope that they would slow the flames but he didn't want to test the theory in that particular situation.

It was best to simply get the fuck out for now, and he didn't stop until they finally reached one of the roads, well away from the flames.

# CHAPTER SEVEN

Once the inferno was a safe distance behind them, Taylor realized that he had begun to slow. The mech suits had been designed to carry the person inside, the weapons, and the ammo and not much else, especially not the full weight of another human being. That wasn't to say that it couldn't, but he could feel that the bulk of the weight had settled on him to carry.

The strain on the hydraulics and power functions of the suit as well made him suck in long, deep breaths and his muscles burned with the effort to get them both out of the Zoo.

No, not the Zoo, he reminded himself as he helped Tanya off his back and onto the road. This was merely a random forest in California that happened to be on fire and happened to have Zoo monsters in it.

"Are you okay?" he asked and gave the woman a cursory scrutiny. There didn't appear to be any overt injuries, but that didn't mean that she wasn't hurt.

"I'm fine," she said and shook her head. "I have a couple

of bumps and bruises here and there and a couple of first degree burns, I think, but nothing a little aloe vera cream can't fix over the next couple of days."

"It seems like you'll be able to afford more than enough of it," he said. "You watch movies and TV series and get a kind of warped view of how much money is worth these days, and people don't realize how much money a hundred and fifty grand is."

"What will you do with your part of the money?"

"I'm starting a business and putting my degrees, experience, and contacts to use. My time in the Zoo gave me a decent amount of money—enough to get me started—but you know what they say about seed money."

"What?" she asked.

"Something about how you can never have enough, or something," he replied and shrugged. "Actually, I'm not even sure if that's a saying. I don't know much about running a business aside from the basics."

"Okay, well…sure." She sat on the abandoned road and clearly needed a second to catch her breath. He couldn't sit, but he removed his helmet for a little fresh air outside of the recycled stuff in his suit. Everything still smelled of smoke, though.

"What will you do with the money?" Taylor asked.

She looked at him a little warily. "Would you believe me if I said I had a kid and I'm putting money aside for him to go to college?"

"No shit?"

"Yeah," she replied. "His dad's a lawyer, so when we parted ways, he got full custody. Not that I fought it too hard. I wasn't a great mom, so I decided the least I could do was put money aside for him to go to college later on in his life. The chances are, though, if the jobs get more like this one was, I won't survive that long anyway, so it won't really matter what I do with the money for myself."

"That's a depressing way to look at things," he pointed out. "Fair enough, things will be tough, but if you push yourself hard, there's an equal chance that you'll make it to embarrass the kid in his graduation pictures."

"So, you believe me?" Tanya asked and pushed to her feet when they saw a few SUVs driving down the road toward them. "I could be lying, you know."

He smirked. "Sure you could, but I don't see why you would. When you put yourself through an experience like this, lying suddenly seems like a pointless endeavor. If you do it often enough, you learn to see the effect in others. We call it a thousand-yard stare, usually associated with people who just went through a traumatic event."

She looked at him, her head tilted as if she studied him anew. "You really were in the Zoo, weren't you?"

Taylor nodded. "I went in there once and liked it so much I decided to go in another eighty-two times before I called it quits."

"Shit."

"Fun times were had, but in the end, I think I had my fill of that damn place."

"Then why did you decide to hunt the monsters here?"

"I decided that I want to make sure I'm as far away from the Zoo for as long as possible. I agreed to this so I could do my best to make sure it doesn't spread to my back door —and believe me, the place has a tendency to spread where you don't want it to."

"Huh." She grunted but made no real reply as Banks disembarked from one of the SUVs and jogged over to where they stood. "Thanks, by the way," she said quickly

"What for?"

"For…talking, I guess," she replied. "I had a hard time pulling myself out of that forest. Mentally, I mean."

"Yeah, sure." He patted her gently on the shoulder. "Of course, I needed to pull you out physically too, but that's neither here nor there."

"Let's say that I owe you a drink and leave it at that," she said and laughed.

"That sounds fair." He turned his attention to Banks who had slowed her approach and looked around with a frown, probably for some sign of the third member of the team.

"Well, it's good to see the two of you are out of there, anyway," she said. "I saw a large group of the firefighters had converged on the area you headed into, which made me worry in all kinds of ways. Can I assume the job is done?"

"Well, I don't think we'll be able to collect any of the bodies until after the fires are under control," Taylor said. "But yeah. There were about forty of the critters in there. We handled them as well as we could have, under the circumstances."

"While I do trust the two of you, I will need some kind of proof to show to the folks at the home office to keep the bean counters happy," she said, pulled her phone out of her pocket, and pressed one of the quick dial numbers on the device.

"Desk, hi. I don't suppose you would be able to track

some evidence of the bodies of the animals they killed in there?"

There was a pause on the line during which he assumed Desk reminded the agent that his suit recorded essentially everything it encountered, which meant it was all the evidence she would need. Of course, there would probably be a few search parties sent into the forest to find the bodies, but that didn't mean they needed to hold off on paying the two of them their due in the meantime.

Banks nodded at him, which basically confirmed that their conversation followed his reasoning.

"Okay, thanks, Desk." She hung and turned to face them. "So, Taylor, could you send the footage you have to my address?"

"Already done," he said.

"And…Hector?" He had the feeling she hoped he would be a little farther behind, perhaps checking on something, and would join them shortly.

She wasn't stupid, however, and had to know the dangers they would face out there. The chances were she knew precisely what he would say next.

"He didn't make it." He kept his voice firm and to the point but still allowed the statement the somber tone it merited. "He… Well, he stepped in to cover me while I was reloading and dealing with a critter that tried to chew on my arm. He managed to kill a number of them but two got their stingers into him."

The agent nodded, her expression deadpan. "That's… well, that sucks. I'm sorry to hear that."

"We weren't able to get the body out," Tanya added.

"The fire was closing in too fast and it was all we could do to not be caught up in it as well."

"I understand that, of course." Banks looked surprised when he stepped forward. Hector's dog tags hung from the ball chain he'd had to break to pull them clear.

"Huh." She grunted and took them from him. "I guess that covers it, but then… Well, I didn't know he'd been in the military."

"I don't think he was," he said. "Well, he might have been, but long before we ever started dealing with the Zoo, anyway. Either way…well, there you go. There's the proof of his passing if you need to talk to family or whatever. There is enough footage in what I sent you to cover that too if you need it."

She nodded. "Well, I appreciate that you made the effort to take his tags."

"It's the least we could do. It's common courtesy for when you can't take a body for a proper burial—get the tags and make sure anyone involved with the person has some closure. You owe them that much."

"I can understand that. Let me get all this squared away with the folks upstairs and we can talk about how the two of you will be paid."

They nodded and Banks headed to one of the SUVs, where she likely had a way to contact the people who handled the task force's budget to clear the payment. If his experience told him anything, it was that it would take them a couple of days to get the money cleared under the best of circumstances. With a disbursement this large, he was willing to bet that it would take almost a week before they saw the six digits added to their collective bank accounts.

"Do you think they'll still pay Hector?" Tanya asked.

"How do you mean?"

"I mean, like... Well, of course they can't pay him directly, him being dead and all, but do you think they'll transfer the money to his family or whoever might have been close to him?"

Taylor paused and thought about it for a moment. "It would depend on the kind of contract he had with the FBI. Mine states explicitly that no cash will be paid out in the event of my being unable to collect it, which covers dying or not having the kind of evidence to support them being able to pay me. With that said, though, they do need to keep good relations with their freelancers, so I don't see why some exceptions can't be made. Especially in this case."

"I'd say this is the kind of case in which they wouldn't make an exception," she replied. "Like you said, a hundred and fifty grand is a ton of money, and if I know anything about the people running missions like these, it's that they don't like to part with cash when they don't have to."

"Banks does seem to have control of the money spent, though," he said. "I'm not sure if she'll exercise it in this case, but I wouldn't be surprised if she did."

"Is this because you feel a little guilty?"

"Why would I feel guilty? If anything, the guy was a massive, prolapsed asshole to me at first, so my returning the favor would be completely and utterly justified."

"Well, that's not what I meant," the woman responded and chuckled. "I only meant that...well, you said he died while covering for you while we were in the middle of it. Maybe you feel like he should be paid because he died helping to save your ass."

"I suppose that's not entirely untrue," he admitted. "Although I think my sentiment is more along the lines of…uh, well, we were all in the middle of that shit-show together. If I had died, I'd like to think you guys would have put some effort into making sure I got my dues, you know?"

"I can't say we would have, but I can understand the sentiment. Go on."

"Anyway… I guess I do feel a little off about it. Not because I feel like he saved my life or anything. The critter that tangled my arm up was a couple of breaths away from being swiss cheese anyway, so there's not much I care about there. And my armor would have protected me from taking too much damage anyway."

"Really?"

He pointed to his arm and a couple of dents where the bobcat had sunk its teeth in, along with a few higher up the arm and into the shoulder. "Believe me, these suits were designed to deal with attacks from monsters about three or four times the size of those we faced today. I would have been fine if he had done what I told him to do and stuck behind me. He could have maybe shot at the animals while they tried to chew through the plates, but he should have stayed with you. That and the fact that the guy went in with no armor to start with…I have to give it to him. It takes serious cajones to do that but doesn't make it any less stupid."

Tanya laughed and shook her head. "That's about as

fitting a memorial speech as I've ever heard. You should go to his funeral."

"Yeah, I don't do funerals. All that reverence and paying respects crap like people refuse to admit the bad things someone's done because they want to make themselves feel better or assuage their own guilt? I'll take raising a glass and moving on any day over dressing in black and lining up to look at the corpse."

"Hell, I'll drink to that." She motioned with her head to indicate that Banks was returning from the SUV.

"Well, I cleared it with the folks in the office," the agent said. "Everything is good for you guys to get paid. A portion of the money owed to Hector will be given to his sister and a portion will be added to both your paychecks too as a bonus for getting the job done as quickly as possible."

"I'll take that," Tanya said with what might have been a sheepish chuckle.

"I'm not sure how much yet, so I wouldn't go on a yacht shopping spree yet," the woman continued. "But it should be a good amount. At least enough to cover a couple of nights of tabs at...what was that place you like again?"

"Jackson's Bar and Grill," Taylor said with a smirk. "It sounds like you don't need us around here anymore."

"Nope. I will pass through Vegas, though, so maybe I'll see you there? I'll take Tanya here back home too, so we could both stop in and raise a couple of glasses."

"That sounds good to me," Taylor said. "I'll see you ladies there once I get back to my truck."

"We can give you a ride up the hill." Banks gestured toward one of the SUVs. "Hop on in."

# CHAPTER EIGHT

The drive home somehow felt a great deal longer than the drive to LA. Taylor wasn't sure that it made any sense, but he couldn't deny the way he felt about it. It wasn't enough to fully quell the general sensation of enjoyment he took from putting Liz on the road, of course, but it somehow felt a little less meaningful and a little shallower.

He knew what he was feeling, of course. It had happened far too often for him to not realize what was happening, and while he wasn't really able to ignore it, there was also no reason for him to wallow in it. Knowing was half the battle, and he'd come up with a kind of defense mechanism and a few rituals that helped him through it.

The technical term for it was depression, although he doubted that it was how most people understood the term.

It was what many professionals called post-adrenaline blues, although that probably wasn't the term used in textbooks. In his case, it had less to do with coming down from the adrenaline high after a mission and more to do with dealing with the sudden realization of how mortal he was.

Maybe it exacerbated the sudden plunge after an adrenaline high. He wasn't sure if there was more to it than that, although he had a feeling that any discussion would inevitably lead people he asked about it to suggest he might need therapy.

It wasn't that he didn't think he needed some kind of professional help but at this point, he was tired of being poked and prodded like he was one of those damn Zoo monsters. Moving on with his life would be difficult, and if people tried to hold him back out of professional curiosity, he wouldn't hang around and let them.

Lost in a muddle of thoughts, he actually wished the drive would come to an end. He needed time for food, drink, and a long night of sleep before he refocused on the work that tended to take his mind away from depressing realities.

With that said, now that he was technically not on any kind of a clock, he needed to make sure he didn't rack up any tickets—which would definitely come out of his paycheck. Desk wouldn't handle anything for him until he was needed to hunt monsters again.

Taylor's eyes narrowed when his phone rang with no number displayed on the dashboard. He had come to identify that as a sign that Desk was trying to reach him, but he hadn't expected her to call this soon after a job was completed. Was there another emergency that needed his attention or had one of the mutants escaped?

He sighed. *I suppose I should answer it.*

"McFadden here," Taylor said once he'd pressed the button to accept the call.

"Hey, Taylor, Desk here," the woman said on the other side of the line.

"I assumed so. I'm still not sure why you don't use a regular line like the rest of us."

"Because I need to maintain anonymity."

"Fair enough. So, how can I help you? Are there more dastardly monsters you need me to take care of?"

"I'm sure there are but none of have come up in the recent reports," she said. "I'll keep you apprised, though."

"So why are you calling me?" he asked. "Did you merely want to hear the sound of my voice?"

"It's nothing like that, although I do enjoy talking to you. No, I'm letting you know that Banks said she and Tanya are on the flight to Vegas now and they'd like to have a drink there while they're waiting for their connection. There's a place near the airport called Jessie Rae's BBQ. Do you think you can meet them there in…say an hour, maybe an hour and a half?"

"Sure thing."

Well, at least that was something to raise the spirits. There were few things more depressing than drinking alone, and while his first choice was obviously Jackson's, it was still a little early.

He wasn't that far from the city itself and it wasn't long before he eased Liz to the right off the 15 to W Russell and waited at the light to turn left. The stadium for the new Las Vegas Raiders was being refurbished. It had been completed in the early twenties and the bonehead company hadn't done their damned job. As a result, they had to pay to fix it.

Perhaps other cities would have argued in court. He assumed someone had a late-night "discussion" with the owner of the company and they agreed to fix the issue.

It seemed the Raiders might have picked a city fit for them to play in.

He headed over the bridge to the west side of the 15 and turned right on S Valley View. The location was on the left and a couple of blocks down. Only a few seconds later, he pulled into the parking lot of the barbecue joint.

It wasn't too much to look at from the outside, and this early in the afternoon, it appeared that the lunch crowd had recently finished and they were preparing for the dinner rush, although it was still open. Cars were parked outside and people inside looked to be enjoying themselves well enough.

Taylor entered and paused to breathe the refreshingly cool, air-conditioned air that contrasted with the scorching heat outside. He gave himself a moment to study his surroundings and noticed that Banks and Tanya already waited for him at one of the tables near the wall. The red-and-white checkered plastic top was still uncluttered, so it didn't look like they had ordered any food or if they had, the order was still on the way.

At least he wasn't overly late, anyway.

Banks was the first to see him and raised a hand to call him over to their table as one of the waitresses returned with a couple of bottled beers.

"What can I get you?" she asked and smiled politely when he reached them.

"I'll have what they're having for now," he said. She nodded and beat a hasty retreat, more from being busy than anything else.

It was a nice establishment, he noted. The smell of food cooking swamped the whole seating area, which made his mouth water as he took his seat. The interior had a homey feel, the kind of location that people came to for a comfortable meal of fantastic food.

"How was the drive over here?" the agent asked when the silence between the three threatened to last a while.

"It wasn't too exciting," he replied. "No wannabe biker gangs I needed to beat up and no trouble caused if that's what you're asking."

"It wasn't, but that's still good to know." She chuckled. "It was a short flight to get here, of course, but driving all the way to LAX and waiting for the flight to take off was what took most of our time. That alone was about three hours in total."

"It almost took less time to drive." He grinned. "And was definitely cheaper, I have to say."

"Well, we didn't have much of a choice since we're on connecting flights," Tanya replied. "I'm heading to Philly, while Banks here is—"

"DC," Banks said. "We'll work on squaring the budget for this year. You've all been very productive in the business, so we need to get it in place again for the next quarter to make sure none of you deal with not being paid."

"Sounds like...fun." He grimaced and shook his head.

"Yeah, it's not." Her scowl added emphasis. "People who run budgets in the government tend to have the largest sticks in their asses—right up until they set their own salaries, of course."

"That sounds about right." He leaned back in his seat as the waitress returned with his drink and placed it on the table.

"Can I get you anything else?" the woman asked and glanced at each of them.

"I think these two are heading off shortly—flights to catch, right?" he asked, and Tanya and Banks both nodded. "But I think I'll have…the Belt Buckle with waffle fries."

"Coming right up, sugar," she said and swung on her heel to return to the kitchen.

"Sugar?" Tanya smirked.

"Don't be jealous. I'm sure she didn't see herself getting too many tips from you two and she's fishing for a higher percentage with the only dude in the ranks."

"Whatever," Banks said.

"So, what are we drinking to?" the hunter asked as she raised her glass.

"We could always drink to Hector," Taylor said. "You know, respect for the man who died alongside us on the job. I didn't know much about him but he wasn't an asshole at the last. I'll say that he was the badass he imagined he was to the very end."

She nodded and the agent shrugged. It seemed like neither of them really knew much about the man, and while it was a sad thing for him to die on the job, they really didn't know what to say at this point.

All three raised their glasses.

"Hear, hear," Tanya said softly and lowered her head a little as they all took a swing from their beers.

Taylor looked around. "I don't know...do any of you have some words to share about the guy? I only met him today so there's not much I can say."

"Well...sure," Banks said. "Umm...he was the first specialist freelancer we brought onto the team. His credentials for the job didn't include Zoo experience, of course, but in the end, he knew what needed to be done and he did it well. He has family I need to contact about his death—his parents, a couple of brothers, and a sister who's listed in his will. That's...more or less all I know about him. I really hope he's in a better place, though."

He narrowed his eyes, although he made no comment about how it seemed she had put far more effort into vetting him than she had with Hector. Admittedly, from what the man had said, it had seemed that he had been recruited as something of a spontaneous response, but he still would have thought she would have put more research into his background. She hadn't even been sure if he had spent time in the military before.

It was an interesting thing to note but not really relevant to the current conversation. He would bring it up with her later.

"On the bright side, I think I can say with some certainty that your payments will be approved soon," the agent said after another moment of silence. "Losing a member of the team will never be easy, but in the end... Well, I think we need to move on. Keep it going."

Taylor nodded. "You're not wrong, but... I don't know, I still feel a little depressed after the mission." He looked out the window for a moment at the traffic light since there wasn't anything happening at the stadium. "It's not the kind of thing you can really rush. You have to let it take its course, usually with booze, food, and a little conversation. Before you know it, you're past the downer part and one can move forward."

"True," Banks said and looked a little abashed as though she felt she had pressed them when it wasn't required. "Although I have to say, I'm not really comfortable with you being so...uh... Well, for want of a better word, sensitive. I was way more used to dealing with you when you are light, loose, and despicable. You know, the way you introduced yourself to me." She took a sip of her beer. "That was the guy I could simply cringe and move on from. Now, I'll have to try to decide if I might have misjudged you, and I don't like that."

He couldn't help a small grin as she spoke. "Oh, I'm still the light, loose, and despicable person you met before so there's no need to get philosophical on my account. My point is that sometimes, even the light and loose need to take a break in view of the need to...well, I hate to describe it as pondering my own mortality, but that seems about right to me."

"Oh, good, all's well in the world again." The agent smiled and took another swig of her beer before she checked her phone. "Well, it looks like the payment has already been processed and you two should see it in your accounts over the next couple of days. With that done, I think we're clear to head on out and catch our flights. Will you be good to drive, McFadden?"

"With the way I feel," he replied, "I intend to have more than one of these. I have Liz with me, though, so if I drink too much, I'll call Bobby to come and pick me up. Don't let me make you late for your flights."

Banks nodded as he stood, took Tanya's extended hand, and shook it.

"It's been nice to meet you, Taylor," the hunter said while Banks moved over to give a tip to the waitress. "I look forward to working with you again someday."

"Right back at you. Good luck with dealing with your kid."

She smiled. "Thanks. Good luck with…" She waved a hand vaguely in no particular direction. "All of this, I guess."

CHAPTER NINE

Drinking alone was depressing.

It wasn't that Taylor didn't enjoy his own company because he did. But when he was drinking, it was usually to help lower his own inhibitions and that was best done with someone whose inhibitions were also lowered. Most people never understood that the therapeutic benefits of drinking had little to do with the drinking itself but rather the lack of societal filters that kept you trapped inside yourself.

You could do that at a bar with a barman. *Or woman. Preferably a barwoman.*

When you were drunk, you did what you wanted to do, said what you wanted to say, and in the end, when everything that was pent up was released, you moved on. That was the beauty of socially accepted self-medication. Obviously, people over-medicated. They did it alone and they wallowed in it.

That was when things took a turn for the worse, which was why he tended to not drink alone. He knew it would only make all his problems worse. And, like many others, he had enough to make his entire life a real problem if he let them.

He had long since chosen to not let them, which was how he had been taught to deal with things and so far, it had worked out great for him.

*Absolutely fucking great.*

Besides, he wasn't drinking alone. He was eating alone and having a drink with it. There was nothing wrong with that. He could enjoy his own company in these situations while he enjoyed the brisket and waffle fries, as well as his third beer.

The place began to fill up again as the dinner crowd moved in and headed deeper into the room to leave him in peace at the small table in the corner. There wasn't much reason for him to interact with them, and it appeared that most of the folks didn't mind leaving him to his own devices.

It wasn't long before he picked his phone up and called Bobby's number. It wasn't a terrible thing to do, but the guy was probably not working at this point. He would be wrapping things up at the shop and contemplating a drink before he returned to his apartment.

"Zhang here."

"Hey, Bungees, how's it going?"

"Hey, Taylor," Bobby replied. "How's Los Angeles?"

"Well, there were tons of fires but aside from that, it wasn't too bad."

"Wasn't?"

"Oh, yeah, I'm back in Vegas," he said.

"So it was a short trip, eh? Did you get paid?"

"I did, and the largest bounty they've paid us yet. I've hung around this place near the stadium called Jessie Rae's BBQ since I got into town. The problem is that I've had a couple of drinks, so I don't think I should drive Liz to the shop."

"Oh, I get that." Bobby chuckled. "Were you celebrating?"

"Something like that," he agreed and lifted his beer to see how much was left at the bottom.

*Shit, that's low.*

"Anyway, I wondered if you might be able to come over and pick me up—and drive Liz to the shop? I obviously don't want to leave her here."

"Oh, sure. I guess I'll need to take a cab or something out there so I can drive Liz back."

"Sure, and I'll pay you back."

"You'd fucking better. I'll be there in…thirty minutes? It's kinda a distance from here."

"That sounds good. I appreciate it."

There was a pause on the other side of the line. "Anytime, man. I'll be right over."

Taylor hung up, finished his food, and ordered another beer while he waited.

Enough people had arrived to make him feel they might pressure him to give the table up. He shrugged and decided to deal with that when it happened. Twenty-five minutes ticked by before he finally called for the check and finished his beer when Bobby came through the door.

"Hey, man," his friend said and they shook hands quickly. "Is everything okay?"

"Yeah," he said as they moved outside and wandered to

where Liz was parked. "Well, kind of. I think I'll be all right in a while. There's no need to worry about it."

Bobby eyed him closely as they climbed into Liz and he started her without saying anything.

"Was it a bad job, then?" the man asked once they were out on the road again. He turned right on S Valley View, then left to go to the 15.

"Yeah. One of the guys died. I don't think I was ready for that shit and it hit me a little harder than I thought it would."

"What, that people die?"

"No, that the Zoo's killing people here in the States. Well, I guess there's an element of truth to the people dying too. Shit. It reminds me of all those others, you know?"

"The person who died," Bobby said. "Was it anyone you know?"

"Not really," Taylor replied. "It was only the one. The guy was an asshole at the start, but he got in the middle of the fight and died. So yeah, he was an asshole and I didn't really know him, but it wasn't pleasant to watch. I'm still dealing with it."

"Huh." The other man let the silence linger for a moment before he spoke again. "Okay, I kind of get it. Folks in the middle of a dangerous place and fighting side by side kind of develop a camaraderie that's difficult to lose."

"And yet it's the kind you lose the most often," he agreed with a shrug.

"Yeah, I suppose. Did you manage to get his body out?"

"Nope, we were in the middle of a wildfire by then and had to make a run for it as soon as the job was done. I did manage to nab his dog tags, though, so…" He looked off to the left and barely noticed the airport as they drove past. "It was the least I could do."

"When you're in the middle of it, the least is all you can do sometimes," Bobby said with a firm nod, and he couldn't help but agree.

Thankfully, the drive to the shop didn't drag as he'd been afraid it would. Bobby's car was still parked there.

It was almost six in the evening, and while the two of them had never gotten around to actually discussing what kind of schedule his employee would work to, it was generally accepted that they would start between eight or nine in the morning and finish work sometime around five or six in the evening.

The fact that the man had still been in the area when Taylor had called meant that he was either about to leave or he had intended to work a little later than usual.

Either way, he had a feeling he would have to give him a raise before too long. He could afford it now that the FBI had decided to pay more than they had before.

"How were things around here today?" he asked as Bobby put Liz in park and they slid out.

"Oh, nothing too big," his friend called over as over his shoulder they shut the doors. "The suits we'll work on next came in—and, oh yeah, there are five of them."

"What?" he snapped and stared at his companion as they reached the back where they had set their shop up. "Is that what you call nothing too big?"

"Nope, but I do call it me being facetious, though," Bobby said with a grin. "The guys liked our work on the other suits so they sent us more, and there are a couple of other merc teams in the Zoo that want our help, too."

"Shit," Taylor said and his gaze settled on where the suits had already been put up on racks to give them a full view of the damage.

None of them looked like they had taken too much of a beating, but if he knew anything about anything, he could tell they would be riddled with issues inside—electronic, hydraulic, and basically everything between.

"I thought you'd be happy to see the business we're getting," Bungees said and watched him closely.

"It is great, don't get me wrong. But all things considered, those suits will take a while to restore to working order, even if we work on it nonstop every day and even a few weekends. While there's the whole supply and demand scenario which gives us a little leverage, they'll need these suits back as quickly as possible."

"We can work them one at a time and bill them individually."

"Sure, that would work, but it would be a temporary fix, at best. Besides, that will mean they lose the saving they get on the bulk shipping." He scratched his chin and frowned in thought. "We'll need some help in here."

His friend nodded. "That's up to you, of course, but having a couple of extra hands here with us couldn't hurt."

There was a short moment of silence before he stepped up to the closest rig. He ran his fingers over the suit. "What do you think? Should we get recruit extra talent?"

"Talent on hand would be nice," Bobby agreed. "Having people who actually know what they're doing would be best, though." He thought for a moment. "Honestly, finding them would be a serious pain in the ass. You would have to do the same kind of headhunting Banks did when she found you, and... Well, I'm sure you can attest to the fact that it'll probably be hit and miss."

"The folks she hired aren't too bad," he pointed out. "Sure, not the cream of the crop, but when you think about it, those are dying in the Zoo anyway, so she had to find the best talent available."

"I was talking about you." The other man raised an eyebrow.

"Oh...ouch." He chuckled. "Although, with that said, it should be noted that it's a fair comment. What do you think we should do in this case? Simply look for people with some kind of experience in mechanical engineering?"

The other man joined him and they examined the damaged suits. He noted a few spots of dark liquid, obviously someone's blood. "I suppose that's one route you could take if you wanted to. Maybe if you have any buddies from your time in college?"

Taylor considered his contacts and recalled one or two names that might be worth reaching out to. "Sure, I can do that. I didn't really stay in touch with any of them but I could always locate them, I suppose. People like to be told that there's a good, paying job available for them these days with this economy."

"Sure." Bobby yawned and covered his mouth. "And I could reach out to some of the people I used to work with in the garage to see if they'd like to make the same kind of move I did, and we decide what to do later. But with that said, we don't necessarily need someone with experience. Even having a couple of extra hands on the job would go a long way, and you wouldn't have to pay them as much. Like…you know how you would hold the flashlight while your dad repaired the car? Something like that."

"I don't know what the fuck you're talking about." Taylor grinned, retrieved a wrench, and began to take one of the suits apart to try to get a feel for the kind of damage they were looking at. "Whenever I worked in the garage with my dad, he held the damn flashlight while I worked on the car. It also didn't help that he yelled at me the whole time to not get anything wrong. Or that I was under four and a half feet tall at the time either."

"Your dad was weird," his friend pointed out. "Well, except for the yelling part. My dad would yell at me for holding the flashlight wrong, so maybe that's kind of normal for all dads."

"Damn, I hope not. That aside, you made a good point. If we bring in someone who lacks the qualifications but wants to learn and doesn't mind putting in the same hours we do—besides taking a lower salary—it would probably work for us. We can train the newbie to the point where they start taking more responsibility on in exchange for pay adjustments."

"That sounds all business savvy." Bobby's grin faded. "I…well, the only problem is that no one who fits those characteristics really comes to mind."

"Well, plan A was always for us to find someone we knew could put in the hours and had some expertise to join us. Finding a glorified intern would always be plan B. Or…maybe even C. I don't think I can afford to take on more than one new employee at this point."

"I'll make a couple of calls and get a couple of resumes in front of you by tomorrow."

They worked together to store the pieces of the suit he had tinkered with where they'd be safe.

"Can we pick this shit up tomorrow?" Bungees asked when they were finished.

"Yeah, sure," he replied. "I can lock everything up for the night if you're in a hurry to get out of here. Sorry for keeping you and…well, again, thanks for coming to pick me up."

"Again, it wasn't a problem." Taylor pulled his wallet out, then handed him the money owed for the taxi he'd needed to take. "I look forward to continuing this work of ours tomorrow."

"Same here." They grinned before the other man headed out.

Taylor heard the car start and accelerate away but hung around in the shop for a while.

The suit he had partially taken apart had mostly taken internal damage and the outer armor looked intact. There were a couple of bumps and scrapes here and there but that was to be expected when you were dealing with the Zoo.

It was intact, but the problems inside promised to be interesting to deal with. The hydraulic functions had been damaged, and that usually meant you would need to be dragged out of the Zoo or carry about a ton of mech armor out on your own. In this case, it appeared that while some of the systems had been damaged, none were at the point where they rendered the suit useless as a whole.

Once that happened, it was almost cheaper to merely buy a whole new suit.

The extensive damage to the inner layers was interesting, though. It seemed that whoever had been in it had taken quite a beating, and from the looks of it, had come out alive.

The memory drives would have been wiped, as was protocol for the mech suits that left the Zoo area, which was a pity. He was a little curious to see what had happened to leave the armor in this state.

With that said, it wasn't something he would be able to start on tonight. It had been a long day, and while he didn't feel quite like heading directly to bed, he wasn't in the mood to work either. That would have to wait until the next morning.

For the moment, he simply decided to square away all the materials and necessities, lock up, and go out to find something to drink—hopefully, something stronger than a beer.

# CHAPTER TEN

Taylor took a little longer than he had originally intended to lock the shop as he was sidetracked in an attempt to think of a couple more names he very likely wouldn't actually use. It was a good thing he was at least still considering the options and hadn't simply stuck with what he had and hated, but in the end, he would need inspiration to come up with something he really liked.

Until that happened, he was stuck with what was on the paperwork an included his name. It wasn't the best but it would do as a placeholder.

At one point, he wondered if he shouldn't simply call it a day and go to bed but the thought of spending hours alone in his room held little appeal.

He hadn't fully dealt with what had happened in LA, and if he tried to sleep now, it would mean that either he'd simply remain awake for hours or what sleep he did get would be the kind of restless bullshit that never helped anyone.

Of course, there was no certainty that drinking would help either, but at this point, it couldn't hurt.

*I might as well give it a shot.*

The effects of the alcohol that he had imbibed during the afternoon had already faded from his body.

He felt comfortable driving but he doubted that he was would feel the same by the end of the night. It was best to go somewhere Liz would be safe until he could return to pick her up.

There was only one place in the city he knew of that would pass muster. Jackson's had a bartender and a bouncer whom he trusted.

Besides that, it was open twenty-four hours a day, which meant it would never be abandoned even if Marcus was off-duty. Constant activity tended to keep the carjackers at bay. While the AI installed would create a ruckus if anyone tried to drive it who wasn't cleared by them, it would still be an annoyance to have to track a missing vehicle.

The biggest issue, though, was that he didn't know what dumbass joyriders would try to do to his baby and so wouldn't risk it. It didn't take too much thought for him to decide on Jackson's and he set off without further delay.

As much as he liked driving Liz, there were certain issues with steering her through the tighter corners to be found in a few areas of Las Vegas. She wasn't the most agile of trucks, and when it came down to it, her weight made her almost as bad as a semi to manhandle through the roundabouts.

He needed to find something smaller and easier to maneuver through city streets. The idea of a motorcycle still held appeal and it would fit the look of the suit Bobby had made for him. What was the point of looking like a biker if you didn't have a bike to go with it?

Thus far, he had been too busy to look into that. It might well be that the best choice for his situation might be a business lease since he would be able to deduct those expenses from the taxes he'd have to pay on the business. He wasn't too knowledgeable on that side of things, however, and he reluctantly accepted that the expertise of an accountant was very necessary when it came to any larger decisions.

Maybe Bobby would know someone he could use.

The parking lot at Jackson's was fairly empty, which wasn't surprising for a Tuesday night with no major sports event happening.

It was for the best—for him, at least, since he didn't need the intrusion of a crowd of people all yelling at screens. It wasn't that he felt antisocial but more that the people he wanted to be social around were on a very short list.

One of the members on the list happened to be at work and stood behind what didn't seem like a very busy bar. She looked at her phone as most of the patrons were seated at tables and booths around the bar.

They were mostly regulars who were in for a drink and a chat with friends, which left little for the bartender to do between refilling their drinks.

Alex saw him come in through the doors and her face lit up. The response to his arrival triggered a warm and comfortable feeling—like they said, it was always pleasant to go somewhere you knew you were welcome. The way she waved him over helped to raise his spirits.

"Taylor!" She leaned over the top of the bar when he approached and stretched both hands to pull him in for a tight if somewhat awkward hug. Her voice carried and caught the attention of a handful of the nearby patrons. Fortunately, none were overly concerned with a simple meeting between friends and decided to return to their drinks.

*One large male with red hair in a bar. It's something you see every day, right?*

She certainly seemed happy to see him, and he returned the hug carefully. It seemed important to not knock anything over but also spend enough time in the hug to let her know that he had missed her too.

"Are you working hard or hardly working?" Taylor asked with a vague gesture around the semi-abandoned bar and grill as he took his seat at the bar. She recalled his beer of choice without prompting and poured it quickly before she slid it in front of him.

"Amazingly, a little of both," she replied with a small smile. "When things are slow like they are tonight, my bosses pay me more to restock the bar and get everything clean and ready for the busier nights. It's better than having to do it when the bar is mobbed and you have to get the busboys to do most of the restocking."

"I'll have to take your word for it. At least you make extra money when the tips aren't plentiful."

"Sure." She shrugged. "It's not as good as the tips on a busy night, of course, but it's better than not getting paid at all. Time and a half on the hourly rate is enough to make up for it, though."

"Well, if I were you, I would ask them to simply pay you a regular wage so you don't have to rely on tips to make a living, but that's a whole other issue."

"Yeah, anyone who talks about a living wage without including tips can expect to not keep their job for very long," Alex explained. "There's nothing we can achieve on our own and well...at this point, it's more of a cultural thing, so I don't see it changing. Kind of like the gun control issues. People can talk about the problems but in the end, there are too many people who are willing to take the problems with the benefits, so nothing will ever change."

"That's interesting. Is that the kind of stuff they teach you in college?"

"They cover the basics but we have to come up with the details," Alex said. "How about you? I'll be honest and say you looked like you came in here looking to have your mood lifted—like someone killed your puppy and you were about to go on a rampage that ends with seventy-seven Russian mobsters dead."

Taylor thought a moment, his lips pursed. "I don't think I get that reference."

"Oh, it's not important, only the best action franchise from the 2010s and early 2020s." She shrugged and grinned. "I'd think an old fart like you would be tuned into those kinds of movies."

"I'm not that old," he protested and narrowed his eyes. "Not that my folks were the kind of helicopter parents who kept their kids from watching violent movies. I guess I simply didn't know about it and was caught up on the renewal of comic book movies that happened during my formative years."

"Well, if you're ever in the mood, I think they show the John Wick movies in some of the smaller theaters around here from time to time. Sometimes, they do a marathon of all five of the films, so you have to set aside the whole night, but it's totally worth it."

"That sounds like you're asking me out," he said with a small smile.

"Well, I might be but I'm also telling you to watch those movies." She laughed. "And you can take that however you like. I do have to push, it seems, since you seem determined to deflect my question about your current mood."

"Damn, I thought I was successful in that."

"Well, you almost got it past me, especially with me talking about John Wick which is something I like. However, the fact remains that something's bothering you, and it looks like you came here to either drink your way through a bottle or two or be talked out of it." She folded her arms. "So, do you want to talk about it?" She scrunched her arms a little tighter and her cleavage responded impressively. "Or be distracted from it?"

Taylor chuckled. "I've said it before and I'll say it again —you're very intuitive. You should be a therapist."

"Don't change the subject." She leaned forward on the bar. "Do you want me to ask what's bothering you, or do you need to be distracted from it?"

He finished his drink before answering but the woman instantly knew it would be another way for him to deflect and already had a glass waiting for him before the empty one touched the bar.

A smile formed immediately on his face. Alex was sharp and on the ball when she wanted to be. He was tempted to ask her if she was looking for another job so they could maybe get someone like her on his team.

But that would have to wait. He had a feeling she would be pissed if she thought he was deflecting again.

"I don't think I can talk about it," he said finally. "I wouldn't mind talking about something else though if you'd like."

"Okay." She nodded. "Can you talk about what you do for a living, or is that something you'd rather not talk about?"

Taylor shrugged. "I guess I can talk about it. I own a business here in town but it's only starting up." He raised an eyebrow, "I think I've told you that already."

"But that's not what's bothering you."

"Nope, I guess not." He sighed. "The whole issue that has me a little down is my part-time job."

"What do you do for your part-time job?"

"Honestly?" He looked both ways down the bar. "A whole ton of stuff. It's not the kind I'm really allowed to talk about, but it's many different things all over the country. The work involves a fair amount of traveling, meals on the go, and in the end, getting back can be a little difficult."

"I can see that." Alex looked thoughtful. "So, this part-time job that has you dealing with traveling and different things...does it pay well?"

"Funnily enough, yes, it has so far," he replied with a nonchalant shrug. "Not enough to retire on, but it's enough to help keep me and the business afloat during the opening stages. Why do you ask?"

"Well, I wanted to ask why you keep a job that has you depressed like this when you have something else going on. But I guess solid remuneration is enough of an answer for me. Money is the reason why I keep this job, after all, and you don't see me traveling around the world for it."

"Well, there's always the upside that you have the opportunity to be around interesting people like me." He grinned but she didn't seem to see the humor in it.

"Human interaction is nice but it's also a little over-rated. Especially when the humans you interact with are drunk and you're sober."

"Oh, fair enough."

"But I think I do know of something that will help you with your low spirits. It'll also help me with the fact that I've been bored to tears all damn day." She took a moment to clean the bar's bench.

"Now that's an ambitious statement." He drained his glass. "Continue."

"Well, it starts with the fact that my replacement has arrived and my shift is about to end," Alex said and waved to another woman who entered the bar section from the kitchen. "Part two involves you letting me drive since you've been drinking and I haven't. There's also the fact that I know where we're going and you don't."

"And where are we going?" He raised an eyebrow. While he already had an idea as to what she had in mind, he wanted her to confirm it.

"Back to my place." She stepped away from the bar.

"Meet me outside in the parking lot in…shall we say, five minutes?"

"Will do." He pushed to his feet, withdrew a couple of fifties from his wallet to pay his bill, and left a generous tip as she disappeared into the kitchen. Damned if she didn't know a thing or two about this kind of thing. Now that she mentioned it, heading to her place did seem like it was exactly what the doctor would have ordered in this kind of situation.

It had been what his actual doctor had ordered when he was still in therapy. Well, technically, it was when he had finished therapy, but the result was the same.

Alex waited outside in the parking lot in what looked like an older model Honda but one she had put considerable effort into maintaining.

"Where are we headed?" Taylor asked as he pushed the front seat back before he slid inside.

"Like I said, my place," she replied. The gears ground for a moment before the vehicle lurched forward and onto the street.

"Okay, that would be more or less the same answer you would give me if you were taking me out to some kind of murder dungeon too," he pointed out.

She chuckled. "Sure, but do you really think I would be able to overpower you and somehow manhandle you into a murder dungeon?"

"I've learned never to underestimate people, no matter what my size or theirs. After all, we're dealing with people who have access to all kinds of modern amenities, so no assumptions."

"Well, if it will put your mind at ease, my building is just up the street…here." She slowed and turned into an underground parking lot, then brought them to a halt near the elevator.

The overall look of the building was similar to her car, he noted. Both were a little long in the tooth, but there were signs that a fair amount of work was put into making them useful to those who needed them.

If nothing else, the elevator worked and took them to the fifth floor without incident. Alex took his hand and guided him through the hallway toward apartment 506, unlocked the door, and pulled it open, then stepped inside first and turned the lights on.

It was a small studio apartment but indicated that considerable effort had been put into making it livable. Movable partitions separated the kitchen, a small living room with a TV, and a bedroom. It was clean, organized and tastefully decorated. Any number of people would kill for an apartment like this, and she had made it more of a home than merely a place to crash after work.

"It's a nice place," Taylor mentioned as he looked around.

"There's no need to flatter me. I know it's small and a little dingy."

"It's better than what I have right now," he replied. "Although, in my defense, I would say I'm still working on improving it."

"Well, I'll have to take your word for it." She yanked her shirt over her head and threw it onto the small sofa in front of her TV in the living area before she turned her back to him. "Help me with the clasp?"

"Sure." He undid her bra and she pulled it off to toss it

beside her shirt before she turned again and stood on her tiptoes to place a light kiss on his lips.

He returned the kiss, a little surprised by her forward nature. She pulled away.

"No foreplay, then?" he asked.

She shrugged, took his hand, and guided him to the bed. "Maybe later."

# CHAPTER ELEVEN

He surprisingly still needed a little while to catch his breath. It wasn't to say he was out of shape or anything, but he had drawn on every ounce of physical conditioning to keep up with Alex, who looked to be in spectacular shape herself.

In his defense, however, she seemed to struggle to keep up with him as well. Currently, her perfect breasts rose and fell at an equally rapid pace while she recovered.

It was a gorgeous and hypnotic sight to behold, and Taylor couldn't stop himself from staring.

It took her a few moments to notice his gaze. She laughed softly as she turned onto her side and traced her fingers lightly over his chest.

"Do you like what you see?" she asked coquettishly and leaned in to place a light kiss to the left side of his chest.

"Yesss," he admitted. "I don't think I'll ever get tired of seeing it, either."

She laughed, a soft, beautiful peal, and turned to lay on

her back again and stare at the ceiling. "I'll be sore tomorrow, but damn if it's not worth it. Fuck me."

"Sure." He turned to look at her again before he glanced at his crotch. "But...uh, give me five to ten minutes."

She chuckled, pushed herself closer to him, and pulled his arm around her shoulders. Her other hand guided his to rest on her breast. She turned her full focus on him and her fingertips explored the body she had touched, grasped, and scratched lightly only moments before.

Now that she was in less of a hurry, she allowed herself the luxury of studying what she touched and her touch quickly found the myriad scars that adorned his bare skin.

"So, this side job of yours," Alex noted and leaned in to inspect the old wounds a little closer. "Does it get you into the kind of trouble that earns you these, or is this from a past life?"

Taylor looked at the scar in particular that she currently inspected with her fingers. That one was fairly unique since it had been caused when one of the larger monsters had fallen on top of him. The weight and force had damaged his armor and a chunk of his breastplate dug into his chest.

He hadn't been able to remove it and it had taken two days to get out of the Zoo before he could remove the chunk of metal buried in him. An infection had forced him to stay in the hospital for a few weeks while the doctors worked to keep him alive.

Once his time in the hospital was over, he was quick to head into the Zoo again. He was a sucker for punishment like that, even though it meant having a thick, ugly scar around his ribs.

There were many more of them spread across his body.

Bullet wounds could be seen here and there but they were outnumbered by what could only be described as injuries from claws and teeth. There was even a small burn scar on his left shoulder from when one of the acid-spitting lizards had gotten a little too close and winged him. It had mostly been absorbed by the armor he had worn but some had penetrated. He almost hadn't even felt it and only noticed a bright red welt when the suit was removed later in the day.

"Well, with regard to your question," Taylor began and weighed his words carefully, "you'll have to understand that the answer would be both. Yes." He thought for a moment. "Both is a good answer. I've left a life where I got most of these behind me." He looked at his chest and touched a few of the larger marks. "But my part-time job has me getting some too, although at a considerably slower rate. This one, for instance"—he pointed out a small scar on his left arm—"is from less than a month ago."

"You're weird." She chuckled and leaned in to place a light kiss on the scar near his ribs. "I like that, although you should probably note that no job is worth putting yourself in this kind of physical danger for, no matter how much it pays."

"Well, when I joined the military, I was paid jack shit and still put myself in this kind of danger, or worse," he pointed out.

She looked at him with a small smirk. "I guessed you were in the military, remember?"

He pulled himself into a seated position so she could see his back and a tattoo of a skull with a knife through it, under which the words *Semper Fidelis* were written. "Jarhead, right here."

"Huh." She frowned as she studied the tattoo. "I'm genuinely surprised that I missed it, although in my defense, I was focused on what was happening a little to the south of that region."

"Fair enough." He chuckled and dropped onto the bed again.

Alex pushed herself slowly to the edge and stood, stretched gracefully, and walked to the bathroom. Taylor didn't want to overstay his invitation, and while most of his trysts had a fairly secure timeline, he was actually unsure as to what he was supposed to do next.

Leaving while she was awake simply felt like bad form and leaving while she was asleep would mean her door remained unlocked until she woke up. That left her vulnerable to being burgled.

*And it's also a massively dick move.*

He usually didn't put too much thought into these situations, but given that he genuinely liked being around Alex and had every intention to have a drink at Jackson's in the future, he was at something of a loss.

"Hey, so," she called from inside the bathroom, "do you mind if I ask you something?"

"Ask away." He stretched to gather his clothes.

"What is it that you do, precisely?" She stepped out and moved to a closet from which she selected a shirt that was a few sizes too large for her as well as a pair of light shorts. "I know, you said you couldn't really talk about it and I get that, but considering that you're former military and you look like you're getting ready for your fifth season with the

NFL as a defensive end, I'm simply not sure what kind of work you could be involved in."

Taylor watched in silence as she climbed onto the bed, shifted to the side he was seated on, and draped her arms over his shoulders. "Would you believe me if I told you that I was a mechanical engineer?" he asked.

She shrugged. "Sure, the GI Bill can do all kinds of things for you, but not if you say that's all you do. All things considered, I don't think a career in engineering would result in these kinds of scars. Just saying. And especially not this recently."

"Well, it's difficult to say, honestly. I do have a job working as an engineer at a business that is getting up and running thanks to the connections I made during my time in the service. I actually like doing it, and it's a job I'm good at."

"So I guess your part-time job is the one that gives you all these." She stroked a recent scar that was intersected virtually in the middle by a couple of very recent nail scars.

"Something like that, yeah."

"I honestly don't understand why someone who has a job he genuinely likes would go out of his way for a part-time gig that gets him all battered." Alex leaned down to place a kiss near the mark like she wanted to help to make it better.

*Okay, that felt really nice. She could continue that with a few more.*

"Well, you have to believe me when I say I have my reasons," Taylor said. He turned to look at her and ran a finger lightly over her cheek. "Like you'll have to believe me when I say there is a whole pile of legal paperwork that prevents me from telling you all about it."

She nodded. "I suppose I understand, although you can't expect me to not be curious."

"I wouldn't dream of it." He chuckled, kissed her lightly on the lips, and pushed himself from the bed. It was time to change the subject. "I think I need to head out for the night."

"So you won't spend the night with me?" She smiled and raised an eyebrow.

"I don't think I will, no." He began to put his clothes on. "Is that a problem?"

"I was joking," Alex said and laughed. "Okay, I wouldn't have kicked you out but if I'm honest, I do sleep better when I'm alone in bed. And after tonight, I'll need all the sleep I can get."

"Are you working tomorrow?"

"Unfortunately, yes."

"I have to say that your easygoing nature about this is refreshing," Taylor said once he'd hauled his shirt on. "Most women I meet would rather not be a part of the whole 'wham bam thank you ma'am' situation."

She shrugged expressively. "You'll come back to Jackson's so I'll see you again. And all things considered, I have a feeling this kind of thing will be a regular occurrence. You fuck like a man possessed so you'd better believe I'll come back for seconds." She studied him and the trace of humor in her eyes faded. "But let me be clear when I say I'm using you for sex." She tilted her head to the left to emphasize her point with a stern expression. "Terrific sex, sure, but still a good hard fuck."

Taylor stared at her in silence for a moment. He hadn't expected that but he hadn't been lying when he said that it was a refreshing change of pace.

"Well, I can't say I disagree," he said. "And you'd better believe that I'll be back for another round."

"I know." She winked and climbed off the bed to walk him to the door. "And I'll be waiting."

He couldn't help the grin that slid onto his face and remained in place as he made his way to the elevator. It lasted until he was out of the building and halfway to Jackson's in the Uber. Liz needed to go home as much as he did.

---

Stakeouts were the absolute worst.

There wasn't anything in the world Jon hated more than being stuck in a car, waiting for shit he had no power over to catch up with his need to get the fuck out. He had felt that way when he was a kid waiting for his mom to finish the shopping and her conversation with the neighbor, Denise.

And he felt that way now seated outside what looked like a dingy apartment building while they waited for their target to exit. Word of his return to town had reached them a couple of hours before and he and Mike had been lucky enough to catch him driving away with a chick he'd met at the bar.

Their paperwork told them that Taylor McFadden was living in the strip mall he had purchased less than a month before and not this apartment building. It meant that this was her home, and from the looks of it, they had no plans to look at her snow globe collection.

Some people tried to make stakeouts better with good, guilty pleasure foods like fried chicken or pizza. Others brought board games or had games on their phones and chargers that made sure they never needed to worry about their battery time.

Unfortunately, none of that changed the fact that they were stuck in their car until this McFadden guy had finished poking some chick, which would allow them to continue to follow him around the city.

As he shifted in the seat yet again to try to find an elusive comfortable position, he considered the way things might play out. The first prize was that this was a hit and run booty call. Unfortunately, the guy might also decide to spend the night, which meant they would have to do the same. That led to the even more unpleasant realization that he and his partner would have to set out a sleeping schedule, and that meant neither of them would have enough sleep or even restful sleep.

*Trust the annoying fucker to screw that up too.*

He reminded himself that they were being paid forty grand each to do this. While he could agree that it was worth it for the monetary compensation, it didn't change the fact that waiting around in a stakeout sucked hairy rat balls.

Mike looked equally miserable. Both had been in this kind of situation before. The best missions had been when they were with a team that included someone who knew their way around computers. It entirely avoided scenarios like this one since they could mostly track the person's movements through cameras around the city.

Unfortunately, they couldn't count on that being the case every time and every once in a while, they needed to dust off their stakeout skills and put them to the test.

"Do you want to play a game?" Mike asked finally to break the silence that had settled over them.

Jon couldn't understand what kind of game could be played at this time of night, but at this point, he really didn't care. All that mattered was something could be done to alleviate the boredom.

"Sure." He straightened in his seat and growled irritably when something cracked in his neck. "What did you have in mind?"

"I...fuck, I wish I had something in mind—and that wouldn't be a distraction." His companion shook his head. "Even I Spy would draw our attention off where it has to be, right?"

He shrugged. "At this point, I would play fucking tic-tac-toe simply to give us something to do. But you're right. The only game we have going is Spot The Target. Seriously, are stakeouts not the fucking worst?"

"Agreed, but only when you're not able to occupy yourself. If we could only use some of those phone games that can wrap up three or four hours without us even realizing it."

"Yeah, but if you're distracted with a game, you don't pay attention to the subject of the stakeout," he pointed out.

"Sure, and even though there are two of us, it's not how we

work." Mike sounded as morose as he felt. "We both know that it's all too easy for something to slip by the both of us even while we're watching. We can't afford to mess this one up. It could be our ticket to a whole new and very lucrative future."

"Good point." He couldn't help a long, protracted sigh. It occurred to him that sometimes, being a professional might be a pain in the ass. Things had been so much easier when he'd mainly had to rely on muscle and the ability to follow instructions. He thought of all the wannabe private dicks who seemed to make a living out of half-baked surveillance and shoddy investigative skills.

Unfortunately, men like him and his partner needed to establish and maintain their edge if they wanted to advance in their industry. Professionalism would be what set them apart from the riffraff and they wanted to be set apart. It was the pros who got to dictate terms, and although they still had a shitload of learning to do, this was a good short-cut to a bright future.

Still, they would have to survive a potentially long fucking night if he had nothing to do that could keep his mind occupied without drawing his attention away from the target.

"Well, well, things are looking up. I don't think we'll need to pull straws for the first sleep shift after all," Mike said.

"What makes you think that?" His partner's sudden change in perspective brought a surge of hope.

"Because he's leaving the building." The other man inclined his head slightly in the direction of the apartments.

Jon leaned forward in his seat to peer across the street

where, sure enough, their mark now stood. He grinned and his mood eased considerably. Hit and run McFadden might or might not have satisfied the girl, but he'd damn well satisfied his watchers.

The tinted windows of the sedan they had rented made sure the man had no idea he was being watched, but any sudden movements from them could change that. It was best to remain calm for the moment.

"Do you think we should tag the girl as potential leverage?" he asked and made a mental note of the address.

"A less than one-night stand?" Mike shook his head. "Probably not. Still, it can't hurt to keep tabs, right? Keep her on the radar, just in case."

"Right," Jon agreed as an Uber pulled up to give McFadden a ride.

# CHAPTER TWELVE

Although Taylor wasn't sure at what point in the evening his spirits were actually lifted, there was no changing the fact that they had been.

Either the conversation with Alex or the sex—or maybe both—had done the trick. He only realized it during the ride to Jackson's to pick his truck up, though.

He paid the driver, collected Liz, and headed to the strip mall in what essentially amounted to a blur. It all culminated in him falling asleep quickly in the bed he had set up in the area he had assigned as living quarters in the building. It might have been a better option to stick around at her apartment and sleep in a real bed, but he'd no sooner formulated the thought before he nodded off to sleep like a baby.

The next morning arrived quicker than he would have liked and gave him about six hours of sleep before his alarm blared.

He grumbled softly and fumbled for his phone so he could shut it off and maybe sleep in a little. Didn't he deserve that shit after the long day he'd had the day before? He'd made enough bank to justify calling in a personal day on a Wednesday.

*Like, what'll HR do to me?*

It took him longer than he would have liked to realize that he hadn't set an alarm the night before and the warning that blared from his phone told him someone was approaching the strip mall and had been picked up by his security system.

"Fucking…goddammit," he grumbled, pushed up on the bed, and remained seated for a moment while he inspected his bare chest. There were more than a few signs of the rough kind of sex Alex enjoyed and which he had rather liked as well. Scratch marks were quite visible all the way up his chest, and from how raw the skin on his back felt, he could only assume the situation was worse there.

"She'd fucking better hope she's sore today," he muttered under his breath. "I hope she has a weird but incredibly noticeable hitch in her step, too."

That last hope had little to do with retribution, however. He yanked a shirt and pants on before he headed down to the shop where Bobby had already turned the security system off and settled on one of the tables with a couple of coffees along with a box of donuts.

"Morning, sunshine," his friend said, as chipper as always. "I hope I didn't wake you."

Taylor responded with a grunt that ended in a sigh. Basically, anyone who had spent any time in the military knew how to be functional from one second to the next when waking up early in the morning, no matter how much sleep had actually been enjoyed. Despite that, it didn't make them all morning people. That was especially the case for him and he honestly wouldn't have minded spending most of the morning in bed, even if it meant having to catch up on work for a few hours later in the evening.

Unfortunately, Bobby was infuriatingly and enthusiastically a morning person.

He represented the really special kind of asshole who preferred to be up early instead of late at night. Seeing someone as cheery and upbeat as the stout Jet Li-looking motherfucker was definitely something to piss Taylor off. The fact that he knew he was annoyed for no damn reason only made it worse.

"How are you feeling, boss?" his friend asked and put one of the coffees in front of him, sensing his foul mood.

Taylor paused and looked at the coffee for a moment before he took a sip. It was black with a ton of sugar, exactly like he had gotten used to while in the corps.

It was the kind of coffee that carried a kick to it too, and he sighed, a little refreshed after a couple of sips.

"I'm feeling marginally better if I'm honest," he admitted. "The blues from yesterday have passed and I feel like a brand-new man."

Bobby narrowed his eyes. "You got laid, didn't you?"

"As a matter of fact, yes, I did," he replied with a smirk and a wink.

"Yeah, well, that'll do it. Getting some of the hormones out of your body does tend to help when you feel down in the dumps. The only problem is that most women don't think a depressed man is attractive."

"Well, that's simply because you're doing it wrong. If

you pull it off right, it looks less like you're depressed and more like you're dark and brooding. Women start losing their panties when they find a guy who's dark and brooding."

"I guess so." The other man chuckled. "I was never able to pull it off, though."

"I'm not sure if it's something that can be taught or if it's something you're born with." Taylor took another sip. "If it's the latter, I'm fairly sure I'm with you in never being able to pull it off. With that said, it was needed and damned if it didn't work."

His friend snickered, took a sip of his coffee, and wolfed one of the donuts. "Well, moving right past your sex life and to the matter at hand, I was able to collect a handful of resumes from folks I've worked with before who could use a job here. I'm not saying I know any of them well enough to vouch for them, but I did select those I knew to be hard workers." He glanced at his boss. "That was what we were looking for, right?"

Taylor nodded. "We can teach someone who has a mind to work and learn. We can't teach someone if they don't want to work, no matter how smart they are."

"Agreed. I've already emailed you the resumes. Why don't you give them a look while I start on the suits and let me know if you like any of them?"

"Okay, that sounds like a plan A." He picked up his coffee and a couple of donuts from the box and headed to his living area. After a quick wash and breakfast, he looked through the resumes he had been sent.

He could hear his friend's Latin music playing in the

shop where he was working. That man would listen to anything.

*And like it.*

Bobby had made sure Taylor knew he wasn't vouching for any of the names that were presented, and he could see why. None of the group looked overly promising. They were all mechanics who had some time in the field, but the group had no experience working with the mech suits.

That wasn't too surprising, but the fact that none of them had a single reference to their name was a little alarming.

Admittedly, he didn't actually have high expectations for the first people they looked at. Those who were readily available would never be the first choices, although they were likely to be employed. They were skilled labor, after all, and there were businesses in the area that could afford to take the risks involved with hiring people they didn't know based on corporate needs.

Well, he assumed so, anyway.

Still, if he had to choose one of them, it would be the youngest of the list. Mark Rollins, age twenty-four, had gone to a couple of vocational schools and had degrees from both of them. This at least showed that he was capable of starting something and sticking it out to the end. It also meant he had the kind of credentials they could build on.

Most people experienced in working on the suits tended to already be snapped up by the larger companies that manufactured them. Helping Rollins to learn the trade would mean lucrative job offers for him down the line.

Mech production and repair was a growing industry that would go only one way and that was up.

Having set the kid's resume aside, he headed to the shop where Bungees had already started work on one of the suits that had been sent in for repair. The man turned and lowered the volume a little when he heard his approach.

"So, did find anyone you liked?" Bobby asked.

"Well, they were slim pickings."

"I know. It was the best I could do on short notice." The man shrugged and turned back to the mech. "I have put feelers out for a couple of the guys I know better and can actually vouch for, though, and should hopefully hear from them in a couple of days."

"Thanks for the effort, though, and let me know." It didn't need to be said that he was ready to trust anyone his friend was willing to vouch for. "In the meantime, I found one kid who might be interesting. Mark Rollins. He doesn't have much experience, but he has a couple of vocational school degrees and that's at least something in his favor. He clearly has the brains for this kind of work, so there's nothing to say we can't try him and see if he's a good fit."

"That sounds good to me. Do you want to give him a call?"

"Sure, but I'd like you to be in on it since you know the kid."

"To say I know the kid is a little strong," Bobby glanced at him for a moment. "We worked in the same shop for a couple of months and that was it. You should also know it's actually the same place you hunted me from, so…keep that in mind, I guess."

"Sure, but still." The other man shrugged again as Taylor

punched the number on the resume into his phone and let it dial.

It took about twenty seconds of ringing before a voice answered.

"Hello?"

"Hi, is this Mark Rollins?" he asked.

"Speaking."

"Hi, I'm Taylor McFadden. You don't know me, but your resume was given to me by a mutual acquaintance, Bobby Zhang? He told me you might be looking for a job and I'm actually looking to fill a couple of vacancies at my shop."

"I...hey, sounds cool, man," Rollins said. "Do you want me to come in for an interview or whatever?"

He narrowed his eyes and the two men exchanged glances. It appeared as though both had come to the same conclusion at the same time. The sluggish tone and the drawn-out vowels of the kid's speech indicated that he was as high as a damn kite. While weed was legal in the state of Nevada and had been for decades, being baked this early on a Wednesday did strongly suggest a habit that could bite them in the ass later on.

"Ah...yes," he said but suddenly regretted having made this call. "When do you think you would be available to come in?"

"I only need a...like, give me a couple of days? Maybe more if you do like...random drug testing or whatever. I think some of my stuff was laced, you know?"

"All right, then. Let us know when you're available," Taylor said before he hung up.

MICHAEL ANDERLE

"Let us know when you're available?" Bobby asked with a chuckle.

"The guy's baked to the point where I doubt he'll even remember we had this conversation. And if he does, we might actually be able to use someone with that kind of mental acuity." He grinned. "You know, man?"

The other man laughed and shook his head. "Well…you win some, you lose some. At least we found out what the guy was like upfront. Anyway, I'll keep looking."

"Yeah, me too. The problem is that many of the folks I studied with were potheads too, so the chances are we won't do much better than Rollins."

"It's truly good to see you keep your hopes up in situations like these," his friend told him with a small grin as he returned to work on the mech suit they had inspected the night before.

It would require a fair amount of work, but if anyone knew what they were doing, it was Bobby. He was already pulling pieces out and laying them on a nearby table in the order in which he would need them.

Say what you wanted about the man, he was a methodical worker and when he fell into a rhythm, he could go through repairs at an astonishing speed. Taylor had seen it happen.

He was about to join him when his phone buzzed in his pocket again. The initial suspicion that it might be Rollins calling him back was quickly put to rest when the caller ID told him it was Banks. He wondered why she would try to get hold of him and hoped like hell they didn't have another fucking monster that needed to be eliminated.

"Give me a second. I'll be right with you," he told Bobby, who nodded. "I have the FBI on the line."

"Take your time." The man waved dismissively over his shoulder and made no effort to look away from his work.

Taylor took a couple of steps away from the work area before he accepted the call but put it on speakerphone. "Special Agent Banks, to what do I owe the pleasure? Do you have another job for me so soon?"

"Not really, no," she replied and sounded less passive-aggressive than usual. "I hate to say this—and I know you will probably love to hear it—but…uh, I need a favor."

"Look, I know we've talked about this and we might have joked around about it too." He grinned. "I knew this day would come, but not this soon. Anyway, as long as we skip all the foreplay and you do all the work, I'll throw you a bone, no problem."

"What?" she demanded and suddenly sounded annoyed. "No, you asshole. Dammit. I now have that image stuck in my head and, in case you wanted to ask, the mind can indeed vomit."

"Well, if that's how it'll be, I'll accept you returning the favor in the form of a blowjob. No teeth, though."

"Will Zhang perform it?" she snarked.

"No! " Bungees answered quickly.

Taylor smiled.

"Well then, I invite you to quite literally fuck yourself," Banks said. "But I still need the favor. Do you mind if I come over in a couple of hours?"

"Wait, I thought you would be in DC, talking to a huddle of bean counters."

"I'm afraid an emergency arose that required my attention," she replied. Given the favor she needed, he could only assume it was a personal emergency and that left him a little uneasy. He much preferred to avoid anything personal in his professional relationships, despite the jokes. They were, in fact, his way to avoid any kind of non-superficial engagement.

"I've had some of my people do the presentation, so all should be well," she continued. "Back to the topic at hand, do you mind if I come over and discuss this with you—and maybe Zhang too—in person?"

"I don't suppose this emergency that required your attention has anything to do with the favor you want to ask of us?"

"It does," she confirmed. "It's put me in something of a bind, and…well, I know you don't owe me anything, but I could still use a solid."

She was wrong on that, at least by his count. He did owe her a fair amount, even if he would never admit it.

"I guess you can't tell me what the issue is over the phone?" he asked.

"Sorry, no,"

"Then come on over," he agreed. "We'll see you in a couple of hours."

The click when she hung up was, thankfully, much more her style. The real Banks still lurked in there.

# CHAPTER THIRTEEN

When Taylor really thought about the call from Banks, it unsettled him considerably. He'd known right away that it was far from usual for her to call this soon after a job was completed and his first worry had been another clusterfuck that needed his skills to resolve. If she made contact, it usually meant she had another job in the pipeline for him, but she had other freelancers to feed this kind of work to as well so it would have to be something exceptional for her to call.

Still, in retrospect, another job might have been preferable. It would probably have been a damn sight better than the even more unusual impossibility that she'd asked him for a favor. For all his teasing, she did appear to be the kind of woman who could handle herself in most situations. She was tough, rugged, and hard to keep down and could come up with solutions to virtually any problem that was thrown her way. That the solution sometimes involved getting someone with more expertise to deal with it in no way diminished her competence.

What niggled at him most was that he knew she wasn't the kind of person who asked for favors, especially from the likes of him. She trusted him to get the jobs she sent his way done, and he trusted her to be on his side when it came to releasing the money into his account. He'd had some doubts about her in the beginning, but she'd largely allayed those when she sided with him and avoided a possible dispute involving the serial killer in Georgia.

Now, she broke the mold and turned to him for a favor?

That seemed like the kind of shit she would involve friends in—people she trusted to keep secrets and be understanding and all that crap. Admittedly, she didn't seem like the kind of person who had too many friends, but she would, without doubt, trust those she did have with her life.

What really annoyed him, he realized, was that Banks might actually consider him a friend or at least a confidant. He didn't like it when people trusted him to do things for which he didn't want to be held accountable. Favors simply felt like they would ruin the professional relationship the two of them shared.

It was a nagging pickle that remained on Taylor's mind even though he tried to put it aside while he worked alongside Bungees. He'd hired the man as a specialist in repairs, while he mostly ran support. Bobby focused on taking the suit apart and identifying the issues that needed to be fixed while most of what he currently did was to prepare the pieces to be replaced in the suit. The work itself was merely fixing what needed fixing and cleaning the parts while he thought of ways to make it better.

More complicated repairs would come later when they

had to examine what might have been damaged in the electronics. Bobby would also list the possible upgrades they could install and everything they would need to perform those. He'd give his boss a list that he, in turn, would send to one of the nearby manufacturers to ship to them posthaste.

The work was what he could usually count on to keep him distracted in these kinds of situations, but his mind couldn't help but wander back to Banks. What kind of favor would she ask for? And what could be so compelling that it had prevented her from heading to DC to handle the task force she spent so much time taking care of?

He might as well call it her baby.

It seemed like she cared about it about as much as he cared about his business, even if he couldn't think of a name for it.

The only reason he could think of for leaving something like that to trusted co-workers would be a family emergency or something along those lines. But that personal emergency now required a favor from someone she could only tolerate in a work environment. That told him it was more than your average emergency.

He had already decided to help her. But if she expected it to be met without at least some form of mockery on his part, she was in for a rude awakening.

It was almost midday and around the time when both men began to wonder whether lunch would be early or late when Taylor's phone buzzed.

It alerted him that someone had tripped the security system. Bobby had turned it off, of course, but that didn't mean he wouldn't be warned about anyone who might arrive.

He'd learned his lesson before. There were many dangers involved in living in this neck of the woods, and while he had taught the folks who wanted to extort him for living in the area a lesson, he wasn't the type to give career criminals too much credit for their ongoing long-term memory and learning capabilities.

They would probably be back at least once if not twice more before they realized he had the FBI on his side. There were many people whom organized criminals were willing to take on, but everyone knew that you left the feds and the IRS alone—for separate yet interestingly similar reasons.

"We have visitors," Taylor said and wiped the grease from his hands.

"Banks?" Bobby asked, his head still buried inside the mech's chest.

"If not her, then probably those extortionists back for another can of whoop-ass." He tossed the dirty rag on a bench. "There isn't really much reason for anyone else to visit at this time or day of the week."

"Is there reason any other time or day of the week?" His friend twisted to peer at him.

"I assume there are probably teens or local college kids who like to party in abandoned buildings. But I think that's mostly my bias against college kids and teenagers."

"Whatever you say."

His phone buzzed again, and a quick look told him Banks had texted him that she was outside. The press of a button opened the doors of the shop to allow the special agent to drive her SUV into the converted garage.

A few things about her arrival immediately attracted Taylor's attention.

The fact that the SUV, while dark and tinted, did not have the usual federal plates meant this was a private vehicle. He also noticed someone in the passenger seat. It was hard to make the person out, but he could assume it was a younger woman from the build of the shadow cast against the tinted windows.

Banks stepped out of the car, told the person inside to remain there for the moment, and waved at the two men as she moved away from her vehicle. She walked quickly and purposefully toward them as if she'd made up her mind that this was something she had to do and so had best get it over with as soon as possible.

"Hey," she said with a small, embarrassed smile. "Thanks for talking to me. How are you doing?"

"Never better." Taylor nodded toward the SUV. "Who's riding shotgun?"

"That's Victoria Madison or Vickie," she explained. "And I'm sure you've already guessed that she's the one this whole favor thing is about."

Vickie looked like she had no desire to wait around for Banks to finish as she slid out of the vehicle and stretched. She looked a little older than what he would normally call a girl but not quite a woman yet, although that opinion was challenged by her dark hair being cut short and the horde of metal on her ears, as well as a nose stud and a lip ring.

She resembled a character straight out of a Stieg Larsson novel, and from the looks of the tattoos, the Swedish author did appear to be an inspiration for her style of choice.

"Fucking...dammit." Banks took a deep breath to calm herself and jerked a thumb over her shoulder. "Anyway, that's Vickie."

"Is she a family relative?" Taylor asked.

"Yes. Not that close but still close enough to get me uninvited from the family Thanksgiving dinner if I don't bail her ass out of trouble, which is kind of what I had to do."

"Hence the emergency, I take it." He nodded. Vickie did look like she was the kind to get into trouble but again, that was based more on the bias her personal image created. For all he knew, she could be a PhD and had simply chosen that look because she was in the middle of an identity crisis.

"Anyway," the agent continued, moving right along, "she has something of an Attitude problem—with a capital A—and the kind of personality that regularly puts her at odds with people in positions of authority over her."

He'd guessed that much already.

"As a result, she landed herself in trouble and while people like her are generally given the option to either serve hard time or be shipped to the Zoo, I was able to use what little clout I have to get her on probation."

That immediately dragged his attention away from his ongoing anxiety over the favor. "Wait, that's what they're doing these days?" he asked, his eyes narrowed.

"Unfortunately for some, yes, depending on the crime," she confirmed. "There are some shady practices run by the companies that need numbers boosted in the Zoo. I've even heard a rumor of someone being shipped out because their contract was bought out by the State Department, but that's a whole other issue. The point is... Well, I need to get her involved in some kind of job to keep her probation officer happy. I was alerted to the fact that you're looking for someone to work for you here, so...that would be the favor."

Taylor raised an eyebrow. "You want me to hire a member of your family who has committed a crime that you don't appear to be willing to expound on because her probation requires her to have a job? I merely wonder if I have all the details you're willing to share with me. Not that it appears to be all that much, to begin with."

"She's a computer specialist," Banks admitted. "That's more or less how she got in trouble in the first place. Those are in short supply around the Zoo so they try to pick up as many of them as possible."

"Don't mess with me, Banks," he said, his voice a little lower than usual in an attempt to keep this part of the conversation private. "She's a hacker who broke in somewhere she didn't belong, and that meant she was signed off to head to the Zoo until you stepped in. Now, you want me to employ that special kind of annoying menace in my little fledgling company? She doesn't even have the right kind of skill set."

"She knows computers," she retorted and made a visible effort to match his low tone. "I know for a fact that the suits you work on have a ton of development put into the electronics, and she would know a thing or two in that area."

He stepped back a little, surprised by the response. Then, he glanced at the girl and rubbed a hand through his hair. "It's more or less in the ballpark, but there's a considerable difference between being able to break through a bank's firewall and writing the code those firewalls need, much less keeping track of the top-of-the-line coding that went into designing the software that runs these suits."

"And I'll guess that neither of you knows how to work or tinker with the software in the suits," Banks asked him and raised an eyebrow.

"Be that as it may, we don't know if she does either." He wasn't willing to concede the point yet.

"Hey, guys. You know it's rude to talk about someone behind their back, right?" Vickie called from where she leaned against the SUV and inspected her fingernails. "I'm not saying I can hear what you're saying but I obviously know it's me you're talking about."

"This is what you want to put on my team." He gestured to Vickie.

"I merely thought that since I have to keep an eye on you, I might as well do the same with her while I'm at it and I only have to look in one place."

"Yeah, because that shit puts me at ease," he replied and shook his head as he strode to the SUV. The newcomer merely watched his approach with an expression that was both defiant and a little curious. He noticed that she made no effort to straighten her casual pose, though.

He wasn't at all sure what he wanted to say and sure as hell hoped the right words came when he needed them.

She didn't have the look of a petulant teenager, despite that being how he pictured her at first. There were none of the traditional signs of any substance abuse, although that was easy to fabricate. She was short and barely reached his chest, and her lean build and pale skin would normally have suggested a sense of fragility she would have fought to overcome.

Surprisingly, though, she exuded a calm confidence. He couldn't put his finger on what it was in particular about her that gave him that feeling, but it wasn't something he could simply shrug off.

Vickie seemed to be sizing him up in the same way he scrutinized her, but he couldn't tell what she thought as her face had now settled into an emotionless mask.

Maybe that was what made her seem so damned sure of herself.

"I'm Taylor McFadden." He extended his hand to her. "I own these premises and the business that operates here. I've been told you're looking for a job."

She straightened from the SUV, squared her shoulders, and took his hand in a surprisingly firm grasp. "Nice to meet you, McFadden. Niki over there had a fair amount to say about you on the ride over, not much of it nice."

"I'd be disappointed if I heard otherwise." He glanced over to where Banks stood and scowled fiercely.

"You own this place, huh?" the woman asked and made a show of examining the shop with a critical expression. "I really hope it's a work in progress because it looks like shit."

"That's hurtful"

"It's fair, though," Bobby interjected. Taylor turned his head to give his friend a sour look before he faced his prospective employee again.

"Sure, it's fair, and yes, this is all a work in progress," he admitted. "But it's still hurtful."

"Yes," Vickie continued from her previous point. "Niki

did me a solid by getting me out of the mess I got myself into so I'm really not in a position to turn down any offers from her. If you'll have me, I'd be willing to work with you."

"For me," he corrected. "We work repairing mech suits that merc companies use in the Zoo, so it'll be a taste of what you avoided, thanks to Banks. I'm not sure what you know about the mechanics of mech suits—"

"Not all that much," Vickie confessed but showed no inclination to back down. "I've never worked with the suits, not even the software they've developed for the modern ones, but I am familiar with the basic principles and am willing to learn."

"Good," Taylor said. "We work hard around here, which means there's a huge demand for the kind of work we do. Almost too much, honestly, which is why we're looking to boost the employee count around here. Regarding salary… I think somewhere along the lines of forty-two thousand a year, plus bonuses for jobs done and room for improvement."

"Oh, there was another thing I wanted to ask about—" Banks started but he raised a hand to stop her.

"Let me guess, she also needs a place to stay, right?" He directed the question to Vickie.

"Yeah," the woman said. "I was staying with a friend, but when the feds trashed the place…well, let's say I'm not welcome there anymore."

"I have a couple of rooms upstairs you can use," he said. "Like you pointed out here, they're still in the process of improvement and are a little under-furnished, but it's a roof over your head and you'll have electricity, running and warm water, and a bed. Oh, and Wi-Fi."

"I was about to ask," she said with a smile.

"That's the only offer you'll get. And it's not negotiable."

"Those mechs look cool and I'd like to learn to use them." Vickie honestly looked like she meant every word. "Considering that it's this or the Zoo, you won't regret having me on board."

"I don't think I will. But you're not hired yet."

"If we're taking a break, how about lunch?" Bobby asked.

"Lunch," he agreed, nodded, and turned to her. "What are you in the mood for?"

"Pizza?" she asked, her eyes narrowed like she thought it was a test.

"Pizza it is."

# CHAPTER FOURTEEN

B obby was put in charge of placing their order with a nearby restaurant that made excellent pizza and had distributed a couple of free delivery coupons to celebrate their use of an app. His decision was, predictably, three large pizzas since Banks had elected to stay for lunch.

The selection of meat lover's, pepperoni and olives, and ham and mushrooms meant Vickie would have to settle for one of the free salads that were included with the order if she was a vegetarian, along with one of the sodas that were ordered in.

It was a generous lunch and thankfully, neither Vickie nor Banks was vegetarian and attacked the food with as much gusto as the two men. There were some initial doubts that they would have enough food to feed all four of them, but by the time they were down to half a pizza, most of them were content to merely sip the cool beverages and enjoy being out of the raging heat outside the building.

If there was anything Taylor really liked about prefab

buildings, it was that they provided great natural insulation against the elements, either heat or cold. A simple AC system had been installed and it was enough to keep the whole work area livable.

That had been his experience with buildings in the Zoo as well. They had probably redesigned the prefab material with the heat of the Sahara Desert in mind and the new specs would be rolled out to all other users across the world. The material was cheap and easy to transport basically anywhere, which was why it was the first choice when it came to buildings that needed to be put up quickly in difficult locations.

The only downside was that, as Vickie—and everyone else—had pointed out, the boring gray blocks of prefab buildings tended to look like shit. While his property was too old to have the latest improvements, it still did a damn fine job in his opinion.

There hadn't been much talking about the business at hand during the meal, of course. All four appeared to realize that this was a break from work and they made no effort to talk about anything work-related while they enjoyed the food.

It was something Taylor had learned from his father and also from his first CO. People tended to work better when they didn't think about what they had to do all the time. Regular rest and downtime were important.

Of course, he would have to address the situation that had brought the two women there eventually.

He still wasn't sure that Vickie would be a good fit. She had said all the right things but he couldn't tell if she had merely done so in response to the pressure that was put on her by Banks. He needed to find a way to read her more accurately.

"So," he said finally and took another sip of his soda. "Vickie, you mentioned that you knew a thing or two about the software they use in the suits we work on, right?"

"Well, I think I said I didn't know much about it," she replied quickly as if she had anticipated the question. "I know the basics since the root of the code is in many of the modern VR devices that they've sold for gaming, but I'm sure you're aware that there's a difference between gaming and real life. When they work on the design for mech suits, they change it to be more functional at the expense of the user interface, while the VR gaming pods are designed to be all about the UI, so…you have to look into that first."

Taylor leaned forward slightly as an idea began to play at his head. "Do you think you could find a way to work some of the UI upgrades from VR pods into the suits we work on to be able to make them more user-friendly?"

The woman fiddled absently with her nose stud and tilted her head, lost in thought for a moment. "It would take considerable work and I can only guess that you would need to tweak it for each individual mech suit but sure, it's possible. It wouldn't be particularly easy, though."

He nodded. "Well, let's be honest, I don't know anything about this kind of thing and I don't think Bobby does either. We're knowledgeable on how these suits are physically built and, of course, the electronics to keep them working, but we don't mess around much with the software, mostly because it's what the users are used to. If someone who knew what they were doing were able to design a more user-friendly interface for the mech suits…

Well, believe me when I say that the guys in the Zoo need all the help they can get."

Vickie regarded him with a small frown. "What are you thinking—that I would design the software for the suits you guys work on?"

"I think that if you were able to overcome the difficulty of adapting the software to the mechs, you would be able to put your copyright on it and sell it to us and anyone else you please for a profit," he pointed out. "It's not a huge market, but it's starting to grow and as of right now, no one I know of has really explored it. This would be a cutting-edge advancement and it's yours for the taking."

She thought about it for a long while, her expression cautious. "I think I could do that. The biggest issue would be to find a way to keep the suit from getting in the user's way while still providing as much functionality as possible. It can't work like training wheels—you know, good to help beginners learn but gets in the way of the pros who know what they're doing."

"That sounds like something to think about."

"So, I have to ask," Vickie said and leaned forward. "Your hesitancy in hiring me…does it have anything to do with the whole look?"

Taylor studied her closely before he answered. "No. I'm fairly sure you're past the phase in which it would simply be rebellion against what people might expect of you. I think it's some kind of statement that helps you feel more comfortable in your own skin but wouldn't get in the way of your work ethic."

"What kind of statement do you think I'm making?" she

asked him. Banks, he noticed, kept her head down and mouth chewing.

There was a long pause as he weighed and considered his words carefully. "To me, it seems like you have the brains of your average high-powered businesswoman or lawyer and the will to get it done, and you decked yourself out to go against the look people expect from the stereotypical powerful and successful woman. You don't want to be a pinup or an example to little girls around the world. My guess is you want to be your own person with no one dictating who or what you need to be."

Banks shook her head and muttered as much to herself as to the table. "I still don't like this new, sensitive side to you."

"He's not wrong, though," Vickie interjected. "Well, it's a little more complicated than that but he does have the gist of it."

He shrugged. "Look at the likes of Marie Curie. She never let a single facet of herself be the definition of who she was and instead, demanded to be accepted for the full package of who and what she was. Of course, in her case, that happened to include being a woman and a brilliant physicist and chemist, as well as a winner of the Noble Prize twice. Although she did die from exposure to radiation, so I would hold off on that if I were you."

The woman nodded. "I'm not a physicist or a chemist, though."

"That's not the point," he countered. "You know your way around computers in ways that would run circles around Bobby and I, as well as Banks here. I think Desk might have you beat, but that's neither here nor there. My point is that

MICHAEL ANDERLE

looks are a problem that ends up being a weight around the necks of women who want to be recognized for their accomplishments like researchers and specialists like you. Guys are programmed from a very basic level to react to the looks of a woman first and foremost. I'm not excusing us, but it does explain much of the shit that happens."

Vickie tilted her head and narrowed her eyes like she followed what he was rambling about.

"You'll have to deal with that burden for your whole life," he continued. "The question is whether you will accept the reality of it, rise above it, and learn how to accept it as a part of who you are as a whole. The other option, of course, is to bitch about being pretty and be eaten by non-figurative animals that, ironically enough, won't care about your looks at all other than how much your piercings will add or subtract to your nutritional value before they eventually shit you out."

Banks smirked and Vickie stared at him like she hadn't thought of it from that perspective before.

"The best part, of course," he said, "is that when you have the whole manic pixie dream girl thing going for you, people will consistently underestimate you. If you have the brains for it, you can take advantage of it and them."

"That seems a little dishonest to me," she replied dubiously.

"Sure, that's true. It is in one sense. Or you can think of it as taking advantage of your natural talents. Whichever you choose is up to you, of course."

She nodded, although their attention quickly turned to Bobby. The man had lost interest in the conversation and

144

began to watch something on his phone. It had started out at a low volume but it quickly began to build. Taylor suspected that he had done it on purpose to bring their conversation to an end.

It was also very evident what he was watching without even needing to see it. The sounds were fairly indicative of the monsters of the Zoo—he would never forget those— although he couldn't tell if this was a video that had been uploaded from one of the Zoo bases or if it was one of the so-called real Zoo pieces that involved people putting a ton of CGI on regular animals.

It was odd how those had become more and more popular these days. It was like the world wasn't weird enough already and they needed to add a little something to make it special again. What really bothered him, though, was how people appeared to think of the Zoo as old news and accepted the fact that alien goop had created a jungle full of horrors simply because it was too far away for them to care.

Truly, humans were a weird breed.

Banks inched over to where Bobby sat and tried to catch a glimpse of what he was watching. Lacking Taylor's experience, she had no idea what the sounds could possibly be until she finally saw the screen. Her eyebrows elevated before her eyes narrowed like she tried to process what she was looking at.

"Is that real?" she asked incredulously. "I know insects are kind of the go-to when it comes to horror movie monsters since so many people have a dread for them anyway. But honestly, something that looks like a giant grasshopper but with a scorpion's tail doesn't seem realistic."

"It's a locust," Taylor said he gathered the pizza boxes, plates, cups, and bottles strewn over the table in the common area. "Not a grasshopper. They were the critters that set all of this in motion from the beginning, to hear it told, and they were the first creatures the goop messed with. They've mutated any number of times and grown worse with each one."

"But with scorpion tails?" she asked, genuine disbelief in her tone.

"Yes. They call it the scorpion locust. You watched the footage of what we killed in LA so it shouldn't really be that surprising to you." He walked around to see the creature in question. It looked like it was filmed from an angle as if a researcher attempted to study it from afar. "Oh yeah, that one's real. I've killed a whole shit-ton of those in my time there."

"You were in the Zoo?" Vickie asked.

He glanced at her, then Banks, and finally met her gaze again. "Yeah, didn't Banks tell you about that?"

"It's not like I had time to fill her in on your whole fucking history," the agent replied with a scowl.

"Fair enough. But it does seem to be the kind of thing one would mention, considering how we know each other and what it is I do for you."

"She actually didn't get into that either," the woman said cheerfully. "She merely said she knew a guy she trusted, more or less, who might have a job open."

"She said she trusted me?" Taylor turned to stare at the FBI agent. "That doesn't sound like you."

"That isn't what I said," Banks retorted. "I said that since I could keep an eye on you I would be able to keep an eye on her too."

"I distinctly remember the word trust being used," Vickie argued.

"Moving right along," Banks said and shook her head. "So, is that a real Zoo monster or do they simply come up with new shit to keep people interested in the jungle th—Oh, shit, did he—"

"Yeah, they tend to attack with the tail first," Taylor explained. "Their venom won't necessarily kill you if you can treat it immediately, but the anti-venom doesn't always work. Besides, there's no guarantee because the Zoo constantly mutates, so what works today might not work tomorrow. It's incredibly painful, though, and a fucking slow and brutal way to die. I'm no doctor but I've heard medics talk about hemotoxins and neuro-toxins and shit, so yeah, it's something you want to avoid."

"Fuck yes," Banks said.

"Nicely put," Bobby agreed.

Vickie frowned. "What are you guys look—oh, wow."

The woman came around to see what it was that they were all watching, which happened to be a video of the researcher attacked by the scorpion locust. The tail had come out and it now used its jaws, the bottom half of which split down the middle. The mutant savaged the armor and bit into the flesh beneath while the man screamed in sheer agony.

"Oh, he dead." Taylor grimace. "He really, really dead."

"I don't know, if someone can...nope. Nope, now he's

dead," Bobby confirmed. "That's his liver coming out of the hole there."

"Liver?" Vickie asked. "I…hate liver…"

"I bet you Jiminy the killer scorpion locust feels differently." Taylor turned to look at the woman and realized she seemed a little green in the face.

"I do not like," she said and covered her mouth with her hand.

"Don't you dare throw up on my floor," he ordered, scowled, and pointed over her shoulder. "The bathroom is that way."

She spun a little desperately and all but ran to the bathroom and slammed the door behind her.

"Well, thanks for that mess," Banks said and shook her head. "You're both assholes, by the way."

"You say that like this is new information to you," he retorted. "Now, both of you get off your asses and help me clean up."

# CHAPTER FIFTEEN

I t took about ten minutes to complete the cleaning. It should have taken far less time, but Bobby resisted the idea that he should be expected to help and instead, watched more of the ZooTube videos. That, of course, distracted them all very effectively until it looked like Banks would be sick too.

Taylor drew the line at that point. With no other bathrooms nearby and within bolting distance, he wouldn't risk her throwing up on his floor. He knew he would have to clean the mess, and he said so in no uncertain terms—and threatened to make his companions do it instead, at gunpoint if necessary.

With that incentive, Banks and Bobby joined him with sudden enthusiasm and so avoided making a bigger—and way nastier—mess.

When they had finished, he realized that Vickie was still in the bathroom.

"Shit. Did I turn the water on for that bathroom?"

"Yep," Bungees said. "I happened to check when we first cleaned up after you moved in and it was already on."

"How do you not know what's happening in your own building?" Banks asked.

"It's not like I have full control over the whole premises," Taylor protested. "Well, I do, but that doesn't mean I exercise it. My priority is those sections I need for the business and the living quarters. Besides, there are busted pipes everywhere, so if I leave the water on in the entire building, my water bill will go through the goddamn roof. It only makes sense to turn certain sections off when I'm not using them."

"Back to the topic at hand," Bobby said, "it does seem like Vickie is taking a little while in the bathroom. Maybe she needs help."

"She'll call us if she needs us," he replied. "Especially when it comes to the water."

The agent stared at him with a critical expression and raised an eyebrow.

"What? I haven't been in there, and it's not like we were prepared to have a lady on the premises. You should know we didn't expect you to be around since you said you would be on the other side of the country. And we certainly didn't think you would bring company."

"Okay, that's a good point," she admitted. "Although I would add that you still don't have a lady on the premises. She's female but not a lady by the strictest definition."

"Well, we're not ready to have a member of the British nobility over for a visit either since we're being all technical for some reason." Taylor rolled his eyes.

"True." Banks grinned. "And it's not like I would call the two of you gentlemen, to be honest."

"Right, because a gentleman wouldn't tell you to go eat a whole bag of dicks," he retorted. "But me being merely a regular dude who makes money off the sweat of his own brow can say that—and mean it—because my money doesn't come from the fact that... Shit, I actually don't know how lords and ladies make their money." He looked at his friend. "Probably like...investment banking, right? Or maybe owning land?"

"Maybe a combination of both?" Bobby suggested. "Besides, I heard they don't even pay taxes, so that's always a plus."

"No, that's only the royal family," Banks said.

"Which constitutes about a solid half of the gentry." Taylor grimaced in disapproval. "Those guys have inter-married and bred enough over the past three or four centuries that I'm surprised they aren't all genetically horribly related by now."

"They are," she said. "And it's been for much, much longer than the past four hundred years."

Bobby shuddered. "How did we get to talking about the British royal family again?"

"Who the fuck knows." Taylor shrugged dismissively as the door to the bathroom opened.

Vickie stepped out and looked a little ashamed when she saw the three of them staring at her.

"I'm sorry I took so long," she said softly and kept her head lowered.

"Don't worry about it," Taylor said. "Are you feeling okay?"

"Yeah." She didn't look it, however, and definitely appeared a little paler than she had earlier. "Seeing that stuff is a little hard on the stomach, especially since we had barely finished eating."

"Yeah, sorry, my bad," Bobby said and owned up to his mistake with a cheerfulness that diminished the effect somewhat.

"Unfortunately, when I get going, everything from the smells and the appearance of things around me tend to make it a vicious cycle for a little while, so I usually want to make sure I'm done before I come out. I'm seriously fine, honestly. It got rid of most of the pizza I ate, though, so that sucks. It was good stuff."

"True," Taylor agreed. "Those guys make good food. I think I'll order from them again. It sucks about the waste, though."

"I know." She looked around and craned her head to the side to see behind him. "There was still some left over, right?"

"Yeah?" Taylor replied warily.

"It should take me a couple of hours to get the taste and the memory out, but I'll be famished then. Is it too much to ask to save the pizza for me until then?"

"I won't make promises, but I don't think we'll eat anytime soon. Anyway, now that we're done with lunch and…uh, getting rid of lunch, what say you we talk business?"

"Okay." Vickie found one of the half-empty soda bottles, took a swig from it, and swished the sweet liquid around her mouth before she swallowed. "Have you decided if you'll hire me yet?"

"Yeah, I have," Taylor said. "I'm not great at first impressions, though, so we can call it a test period to make sure we work well together. That goes both ways, of course, for you and me. I can probably have contracts written up if you want, and your first paycheck will come through next week or whenever you can open a bank account."

"I have a bank account," she confirmed.

"Cool, we can get the paperwork started tomorrow morning, then. Once that's done, you can start work and take time to decide if you want to stick with us for the long-term or if you prefer to head out somewhere else. With no hard feelings, obviously, and I could probably give you a reference too since your probation requires you to have a job, right?"

"Yes." The woman scowled. "It's bullshit if you ask me. I tend to prefer the freelancer life so there's no steady paycheck. Unfortunately, the people in the government love them their steady paychecks and the ability to pull the taxes out before a person gets their hands on it." Banks sent her a hard look and she added hastily, "Or so I've heard."

"Right." Taylor grinned at the agent's glowering expression. "Oh, and I can show you to your room if that's still the idea. Again, it's not the Ritz or anything, but you'll have a bed, food, a working kitchen, and running water and electricity, so you'll be able to live here until you find someplace better. Besides, since you probably don't have a car of your own yet, you don't even need to drive to work. In exchange, we'll start work at nine tomorrow morning. That's my offer and like I said, it's non-negotiable."

She hesitated and glanced at Banks who now showed

no indication of her opinion or any emotion on her face. This was Vickie's choice, and hers alone.

"Okay, let's go with that," she said when she realized she would have no help from that quarter. "How do I know you won't change the terms of the arrangement when you want to?"

"Because you could always call your…aunt?" Taylor glanced at Banks.

"Not even close," the special agent replied with a chuckle.

"You'll be able to call Banks, and I have the feeling that she can suddenly fill my life with a slew of problems. Since you guys have a personal relationship, I have the feeling she'll enjoy making my life a living hell. Well, that and the fact that she'd probably not mind simply being a bitch to spite me."

"He's right. I would enjoy that," Banks confirmed smugly.

"There you go." Taylor gestured at his new employee. "You have the whole of the FBI as a guarantee that I'll hold firm to our deal."

Vickie paused, thought about everything he had told her, and appeared to come to a decision.

"Okay, I'll take the job," she said.

"It's not like you had much of a choice anyway," Banks grumbled under her breath.

"She did and she chose here," Taylor said in a stern voice. "I'm sure you would have been able to find some other form of employment, but I promise you this is the best choice given that your other option would probably be to flip burgers in a local restaurant. Admittedly, there are some nice places around here, but from what I hear, the pay is terrible."

"I get it. You're the best of a bad bunch," Vickie said and rolled her eyes. "Anyway, I have conditions."

"Conditions?" Taylor asked.

"Yeah, I was about to ask too," Banks said. "What do you mean by conditions?"

"Nothing you'd disapprove of." The woman put a hand up to halt further questions. "I only want to make it clear that our relationship will be one hundred percent professional. We'll work together and maybe even be friends. If that happens, it happens, and there's no way to control that, but I need to say up front that I'm not on the market, as it were. We won't be fucking, so don't even try any of your...charms."

"Charms?" Taylor looked at Banks, who shrugged.

"Yeah, I was about to ask," Bobby interjected and laughed. "What do you mean by charms?"

Vickie pointed to Taylor. "I don't know, exactly, but a big guy with bright red hair and beard who looks like an Irish Jason Momoa...well, he's the type of guy who has charms."

"I'm not a fucking leprechaun," Taylor protested. "I'm not even Irish."

"Not lucky charms, moron," she countered. "I mean, like...plays. You have tricks you use to get women to sleep with you. I merely need to know that you won't ever try to use any of those tricks on me. I'm not saying they wouldn't work, but at the moment, you aren't to try them, understood?"

"Now is not the time to mention that tricks are for kids, right?" Taylor said and looked at the others for support.

"Answer the fucking question," Banks snapped.

"I understand that you will not tolerate any advances on my part," he said with a firm nod. "And that any advances on my part will be rebuffed and result in you leaving. I will not use any…tricks or charms or anything like that on you for the duration of your employment here."

"Good." Vickie mirrored his nod with an even firmer one of her own. "As long as we're clear. Don't even try to get all charming on me."

"Don't worry," he said with a small smirk. "You're not really my type anyway."

"Nor you mine," she retorted. "So, I think we're done here, right?"

Taylor nodded.

"Awesome." I think I'll start on giving the bathroom a deep, deep cleaning." She looked around. "Where are the mops and stuff?"

"Down the stairs in a little closet to your right," he said, and she sauntered away as he turned to Banks.

"Thanks," the agent said. "She won't let you down, and if she does… Well, give me a call."

"As long as you know you owe me one now," he replied with a grin.

"Right," she said. "I'll head out. You guys have a great day."

"You too, Special Agent. Let me know when you have more work for me."

"Will do." She waved to the two men, her demeanor much closer to the Banks he knew and… Well, not loved, of course, but certainly respected despite their exchanges that might suggest otherwise.

---

"I fucking hate this car," Jon said and glared as he once again scrutinized their sedan. The abusive heat of the sun beat down on them despite having the air conditioner on at full blast.

"What's wrong with it?" Mike asked. "It's perfect for this kind of mission. No one notices a nondescript gray sedan like this, and with the tinted windows, most people won't even realize we're here."

"It's so cramped. I feel like we've been stuck in here forever and I think I'm about to go fucking crazy."

"Well, what would you suggest?"

"Think about it. The car of choice for a stakeout is always a van, right?" Jon asked. "It has enough room and gives you space to work with. Not much, but some. More than this fucking car at any rate."

"Yeah, these days, when anyone sees an unmarked van outside their place, they immediately know someone's watching them," Mike said. "We might as well scream our position to the people inside. No, believe me, the sedan was the better choice."

"I don't dispute the choice." Jon tried to stretch but banged his hands on the roof instead. "I know you made the best choice at the rental place, given our options. I only wish this was something with a little more space. Like an SUV or something."

"Jesus Christ, stop complaining," his partner snapped

irritably. "It's not like we'll be here for too much longer. We already have the guy's place of residence and most of the people he knows and interacts with regularly, so it won't be long before we can make our move. We merely have to be careful. That goes against the grain for both of us, I know, because we've been spoilt. We're used to the quick in-and-out operations that make the best use of our skills. But we've talked about it and both want more, and we won't get far if we stay stuck in the same old routines. We have to be flexible and learn new skills. Besides, from the reports, it looks like this guy has friends in high places and it won't do to piss them off."

"Why not?" He knew the answer, of course, but he hadn't worked with the man before so wanted his take on the situation. It was always good to find out where their reasoning might diverge.

"Because they won't retaliate against Rod fucking Marino. They'll target us for retribution," his partner pointed out.

"You're right." The agreement was given a little begrudgingly—not because he didn't actually agree but because it was a very effective handbrake on all his instincts that clamored to simply do the fucking job in the way they knew best.

Their attention was drawn away from their cramped vehicle and what was essentially a meaningless debate when someone exited the building driving an SUV. Of course, it would be the kind he thought would be perfect for their situation except for the undeniable fact that a big black SUV parked outside a building was about as subtle as the unmarked van. Only one woman was inside, which meant the one who had been in the passenger seat when they arrived had stayed.

"That's one of the friends in almost high places, right?" Jon glanced at his partner for confirmation although he'd already scanned the information they had.

"Niki Banks," Mike confirmed and consulted the file they had been given for a moment. He'd also done his homework but it was good to refresh one's memory and besides, it helped to pass the time. "She's a special agent with the FBI and probably the go-between for McFadden and his friends in high places, I assume."

"We haven't been able to confirm that, though. She might be exactly the kind of leverage we might need in case plan A falls through. It's always good to have a plan B."

"I agree that we need a plan B," Mike said. That was a no-brainer, especially in their line of work. They'd already discussed it when they formed the tentative plan A but as yet, hadn't found what they considered a viable option. "But you have to be the special kind of crazy if you think we can use someone from the FB fucking I."

"I have been called crazy on occasion," Jon admitted. "But yeah, I get your point. Leave Banks off the list."

"On the other hand, there is the girl she left behind. I don't have any names or ID on her as yet as she's obviously a new player here, but she might be what we're looking for. We'd better do our homework. Get on the phone."

Jon nodded and dialed the number of Marino's people who ran research on the case for them.

## CHAPTER SIXTEEN

The day passed quickly. Taylor showed Vickie up to her room, which constituted a small kitchen, a military cot, and its own bathroom but still managed to have more square feet than most apartments in the city. He left her there to start getting her shit together.

She had brought a couple of bags in Banks' SUV and needed to unpack. He'd suggested that she start the next day so she would have time to settle in.

It would also give him and Bobby the chance to get some work done in the afternoon while they adjusted to the concept of having a new member on their little team. He felt sure she would fit in well enough, and even if she didn't, Banks had left it open for them to call her and pull the plug on the whole deal.

If that happened, Bobby still had the word out with his friends that they were looking for workers and the position would probably be filled again quickly and without too much difficulty.

There was an odd moment when he heard Vickie move

around in her little apartment. He was used to the relative quiet in the area without having to share it with anyone, but he accepted that he would have to adjust to having the woman in the same building as him.

He had acclimated to sleeping in a barracks with almost thirty other men during boot camp, so this would be a breeze by comparison.

A little uncomfortably, he stared in the general direction of her area. For all he knew, this was a new and sneaky way for Banks to keep tabs on him. With a rueful grin, he shook the thought aside. Honestly, that was an entirely convoluted alternative to the obvious solution, which was to simply bug his phone lines.

The next morning saw him up and ready to go by nine. He had managed to get an early night as all the sleep he had missed out on the night before rushed back with a vengeance. As a result, he was rested and refreshed, if still a little grumpy by the time he needed to head down and start work for the day.

Surprisingly, Vickie was up as well and was apparently already in the garage. He could hear her tinkering with the equipment down there.

Ordinarily, he would have been annoyed that someone messed with his stuff, but she had to get used to her surroundings eventually and might as well get started sooner rather than later. It wasn't like she would find textbooks on their particular field of work. Besides, the fact that she was early for the day was a promising sign that she did, in fact, take this opportunity seriously.

Once he reached the garage area, a few changes were instantly apparent. Her hair had already been short when they first met her—six or seven inches long, in fact. It appeared that she had taken his advice regarding appearances to heart, however, and had applied a trimmer to her head and given herself a buzz cut. It looked like she had just arrived at boot camp.

Ordinarily, he would have found the choice a little odd but interestingly enough, it looked natural on the woman.

Taylor dropped into the seat beside his workbench and began to adjust the security systems for the morning to only detect and alert. He made no comment at all on her choice of hairstyle.

She had obviously expected something and moved over to where he sat.

"What do you think?" she asked finally and ran her fingers over the short hair.

He nodded. "You're rocking it, and it is one way to make your looks your own, I guess. It's not the usual way to go about it, but I have the feeling you're not one to settle for the usual, so I guess it is fitting."

"Thanks." The woman lowered her head. She probably wasn't used to positive reinforcement when it came to her antics and likely didn't know what to say next. "What are you working on?"

"I'm bringing the security down for the day," he explained and rubbed his eyes. "We've had problems in this part of town and since Bobby and I know a thing or two about security systems, we set one up for the building."

"It looks fairly extensive." She tilted her head and studied the network he was working on.

"Yeah, I guess you could say that. Don't worry, I already added you to the exempt list so you shouldn't trigger anything.

Although, having said that, it would be a little tricky to get any of your…shall we say friends through the system late at night. Not only that, I won't be pleased to have to wake up and do it for you so I'd suggest you spend the night at his or her place."

"His," Vickie corrected him. "No offense to the chicks who dig other chicks, but guys are what work for me."

"That's not really my business." He turned as the garage doors began to open to reveal Bobby's truck waiting outside.

As had become something of a custom, the man had brought coffee and pastries for them to have as breakfast.

"So, for starters," Taylor said once they were ready to work, "there are these pieces here." He indicated one of the metal tables that held a number of pieces from one of the mech suits spread on it. "We'll put the suits back together, so you can probably start by taking some of that blue spray over there and using it and some of the paper towels to clean off the green marks—like you see here."

She leaned in close and narrowed her eyes at the splotches of green that appeared to be mixed in with the grease. "What the hell is that?" she asked.

"No one's really sure," Taylor said. "Specialists have tried to identify it, but all we know is that it's present in the Zoo, and it quite literally gets everywhere. It's a mild corrosive and if left, will damage the armor. We need to clean it off before we can start putting the pieces back together."

"Okay. "

He didn't think he would need to double-check her work but he did anyway, at least for the first couple of pieces she attended to. Sure enough, she was deft and methodical, and her thin, nimble hands were far better suited to the work than either of the men's were.

"It looks like this green stuff gets into the circuitry too," she noted after almost an hour of cleaning. "But it doesn't look like it mixes well with the electronics and almost stays away from them."

"Yeah, it mostly only sticks to the joints," he agreed. "It doesn't like electricity."

"You talk about it like it has a mind of its own."

"If you are around the Zoo for long enough, you'll realize that essentially everything in the jungle has a mind of its own. It gets to the point where you kind of have to assume that everything does until proven otherwise. Seriously, even the trees can swoop down and take you if you don't pay attention."

"You seem to know a lot about the Zoo."

"Some might say there aren't many who know it better, except maybe a handful of the researchers," Bobby pointed out.

"Were you in there?" she asked him.

"I went in a couple of times," the mechanic replied. "It didn't agree with me, so I stuck to fixing the mech suits of those who were stupid enough to head in time after time like this one." He pointed at his friend. "I cycled out after about a year and stayed away."

"Believe it or not, that is the smart thing to do." Taylor inspected one of the pieces and studied the damage that had been done to the circuitry around one of the reloading mechanisms.

"Which I guess makes you a dumbass for heading in

there eighty-three times, right?" Bungees told him with a grin.

"I'll not disagree with that," he responded. "Although there's something to be said for having survived the damn place so many times."

"Eighty-three?" Vickie stepped over to him and took the piece from his hand.

"Yeah…it starts a kind of addiction when you head in there the first time." He paused when he noticed she wasn't acting like he thought she would. "What are you doing?"

"It's a simple mechanism," she replied, pulled the devices apart, and reversed the polarity. Her eyes narrowed in focus, she fiddled with the wiring before she applied a little electricity to confirm it was now working. "It's not that complicated but sometimes, when something goes wrong, it's hard to see."

"Well…I would have found that eventually." Taylor pushed aside the feeling that he'd been outdone by a damned rookie. "The damage must have jarred the wiring together."

"Sure, you would have," Vickie said with a small grin before she returned to her work.

She was still a beginner, and while he didn't appreciate having his skills challenged so openly, it was still good to see that she was picking up on what they were doing so quickly.

It was refreshing, really, and his irritation aside, he began to think their new employee would prove an asset.

"So, what I'm doing now…" she said once he began to assemble the pieces of the suit again while Bobby worked on the hydraulic system. "It basically amounts to busy work, right?"

"Well, you're not wrong, but that's also not entirely accurate," Taylor explained. "Getting to know the individual pieces and components these mechs work off is never a waste of time, of course. And yes, we do need to clean that green stuff off before we can put it back together."

"So, what is this mechanism supposed to do?" she asked as she watched him put it together. "It looks simple but it also looks like it's seen a ton of work."

"It's an automatic reloading mechanism." He put two pieces together and reached for a third. "It connects to a series of magazines in the chest, and the chain rolls them forward across the arm and to the weapon that's being held —usually an assault rifle—and reloads it."

"Why don't they keep the ammo stored in the arm?"

"Unfortunately, it's because the chances of losing an arm are too large to ignore. That and the arms are the most likely to be impacted during combat, which causes something to break. If the mechanism breaks and the ammo's stored on the chest, you can always reload it manually. If it's in the arm, it would be trapped inside the armor, which means you need to destroy the suit to get to the ammo inside."

"I guess that makes a morbid kind of sense." Her expression seemed both fascinated and disapproving. "It still seems like it's a process that needs more efficiency, though."

"Well, think about it," Taylor said once he'd fitted the necessary pieces together and connected them to a power source to make sure the mechanism worked correctly. "Again, a ton of money goes into improving these suits, and they're making new and advanced models every year. Oh, and remember to trademark your ideas. You don't want to be fucked over by a company that gets their hands on it while it's still in development."

"Do you have any ideas for improvement?" Vickie asked.

"Well, they're not my ideas, but many suits have issues with relying on hydraulics and mounted rockets to move faster," he explained. "Especially the heavier ones. A friend of Bobby's came up with a system that works with magnetic coils instead. It takes much less power to function and delivers far more bang for your buck, so to speak."

"Ummm…" she said thoughtfully as she returned to cleaning the remaining pieces. "But it would be an issue with diminishing returns. You would need larger and larger coils in the boots the heavier the suit is. The coils would make it heavier and heavier and bring it to the point where it no longer works."

"Yes," he agreed. "But it does work for the lighter suits like the ones you see here, so we're working on installing them on all those it would work on efficiently. The clients have said they approve of the changes and that it helps them move faster, more lightly, and with less power consumption."

"I wouldn't think you'd need to worry about that with a nuclear-powered mech suit," she said. "I'll be right back. I'm heading to the ladies' room."

"Take your time." He waited for her to be out of earshot

before he turned to Bobby. "Did you tell her the suits we're working on have nuclear power packs?"

His friend shook his head. "Not many people figure that out. Too many are scared of that kind of thing these days."

"Huh. She's a smart kid and picks the details fast up too."

His friend grinned. "Maybe too fast?"

"Nah, nothing like that." He ignored the grin and refocused on his work.

# CHAPTER SEVENTEEN

"What are you working on?" Taylor asked when he returned from his lunch break.

Vickie looked up from the device she was working on and didn't seem like she was overly embarrassed to have been caught fiddling.

The whole idea of her joining their crew was for her to learn about the suits so she would be more of a help to make the shop function efficiently. Most of her work thus far had been the smaller jobs that needed to be done but required far less technical expertise.

Any knowledge or experience she gained meant that eventually, she would become skilled enough that she would need an upgrade from intern to apprentice and with higher pay. In turn, this obviously meant she'd spend less time cleaning up and more time actually working on the suits. That was the eventual idea, of course, but it meant they would need to find a new intern. Or maybe they would simply have to divide the damn jobs between them.

*No, it's better to find another intern.*

MICHAEL ANDERLE

"I'm trying to find out how these motion sensors are supposed to work," Vickie explained and showed him the processor she was tinkering with.

"You've been around for almost a week now. I'd say you should know what they do already."

"I know what motion sensors are but that's not the point." She shook her head. "I'm saying that… Well, the whole system is far more complicated than it needs to be. It's supposed to simply transfer the data to the HUD, but there are a ridiculous number of loops that feed it into this processor here."

"Oh, that's because it's supposed to handle data from other sources too," he explained. "You have a couple of inputs from the motion sensors and a handful from the night vision in there, as well as a couple of other sensors spread across the suits." He touched a point on the part she was holding. "All feed into this processor here and are transferred into a program in the HUD that gives the pilot a live feed of basically everything that's happening around them. It was made because there are some parts of the Zoo where the tree cover is so dense that it might as well be night. The people in there need to be able to operate with as much of a view of their surroundings as possible."

"Huh." She frowned and took another look at the part in her hand. "But what if the processor is damaged? Doesn't that leave the pilot blind?"

"Not really." He shook his head. "First of all, there's a reason why it's placed this deep inside the breastplate. That's to make sure it doesn't get damaged and if it did, you probably wouldn't give a shit because you'd be dead. There are a couple of redundancies spread through the rest of the suit, and if all those fail and you aren't dead, you can still access the data and have it brought up to your HUD. It'll work that way, but it won't be all...uh, plugged together. Anyway, I would have thought someone with your particular set of skills would at least know something about electronics."

"Sure, I learned a thing or two," Vickie said. "It's hard not to when you spend so much time building computers and stuff like that. I can't say I enjoyed it, though, and when my brain became cluttered, I did a Sherlock Holmes and cleaned the clutter out of my mental attic."

"That's not how brains work."

"It's how my brain works," she replied and shrugged.

"Whatever. We'll work on soldering the pieces together that need it, including that processor there. I'm not sure how closely you want to watch, but if you want to be close, you'll need glasses. They should be in the desk over there."

He gestured toward his left and it seemed that Vickie did, in fact, want to help but the shop's phone rang. There weren't too many places with a landline these days but given that he needed to be in contact with folks outside the country, it was cheaper to call them from that than from a cellphone. It was easier for them to call him too, although it meant someone needed to be around the physical location of the device. If they weren't, a message could be left and if it was urgent, they could use his cell phone as a last resort.

This was how he'd set things up until he managed to route the landline to his cellphone, which would allow him to answer it from wherever he happened to be. He wasn't sure if that was the best idea, though, since he didn't want to answer a call from a potential client if he was drunk. That would deliver a blow to his reputation he didn't think it would recover from.

With that said, there were still kinks in the business they needed to resolve.

"Vickie, would you mind answering that?" Taylor asked, his soldering gun already in hand and glasses in place. While it was only soldering and he wouldn't have to worry about the dangers something like welding would present, he was always strict about eyewear in the shop.

"Sure," she said and picked the receiver up from the cradle. "Who the hell has a landline these days?"

"We the hell do. Answer the damn phone."

He could almost hear her eyes rolling as she pressed the receiver to the side of her head. "McFadden's Mechs, how can I help you?"

It wasn't a great name, but he had yet to use his frustration over that to generate a more impressive alternative. He pushed the irritation aside and focused on his work but also listened to the only side of the conversation he could hear.

"What?" Vickie demanded. "No, I'm not a secretary. Why, are you a janitor? Yeah, all janitors are men, right, so all men must be janitors... Are you kidding me right now?"

He raised an eyebrow. Maybe work could wait. He wanted to hear what she had to say to whoever had called.

"Yes, it was a sexist question, thanks for asking," she snapped. "Now, do you want to try again? Hi, this is Vickie from McFadden's Mechs, how can I help you to not be a sexist asshole this afternoon?"

Well, that was one way to go about it.

Taylor was close enough to hear the man on the line laugh, which was better than them being offended and hanging up. Still, he might need to step in if things escalated. He suppressed a grin and pushed up from where he was working to move beside her.

"Sure, you can probably get your suit to us for much-needed repairs, but if you want it to be a rush job, it means you're asking us to put the jobs we already have lined up on hold to get yours out first, right?" she continued. "So, you can go ahead and ship it here, but if you want it to be a rush job, there will be a fee for that... Ten thousand... Yeah, that's our protocol. All right, then. If you can get it to us next Tuesday, we can ship it back to you the Friday after that for the regular fee plus the rush fee which will be added to the invoice... All right. I look forward to working with you."

He sat across from her and raised an eyebrow. "What was that?" he asked.

"Oh, the guy wanted it to be a rush job, so I thought he should pay us more if he wanted his suit faster than everyone else," she explained.

"We don't have that kind of policy."

"You should."

"Yes, and as a matter of fact, we do now." He grinned. "That was quick thinking, and upselling is something you'll definitely be rewarded for."

"What do you mean? What kind of rewards are we talking about?"

"Based on what we charge to repair suits of armor like that, adding ten thousand should get you a commission, right?" He paused to run the numbers mentally. "Let's say ten percent of the added profits, which would be a thousand dollars added to your paycheck once we've finished the mech."

"Can it really be that easy?" She looked decidedly cautious as though she expected a catch.

"You have a new job, now," Taylor said. "Upselling is always something that helps a fledgling business, as long as we're not too greedy about it. The guy on the line—my guess is that it was Collins from the Jokers merc company—took the news easier when it came from you, and I think that's something we can exploit."

"Exploit?"

"Maliciously," he confirmed.

"I… Well, thanks, I think." Vickie considered the whole episode and gave him a look of frank surprise. "Not many people I know would believe in a stranger like you do."

"Well, I believe you want to redeem yourself in Banks' eyes. And I believe that you believe her when she said your first misstep would be your last and that she wouldn't be able to save you from the Zoo after that. With all this in mind, it seems only fair to give you a clean opportunity at redemption and make sure you know your efforts are appreciated."

"Thanks. You know, again. It's nice to be involved in something I actually care about."

"Which reminds me," Taylor said. "What the hell did you do that made people threaten to send you to the Zoo for, anyway?"

She shrugged evasively. "Who the hell remembers?"

"You," he stated bluntly. "And especially because it only happened about two weeks ago?"

"Like I said, my head is an attic that needs to be cleaned regularly so it can store information that's actually relevant to my life."

It was clear that she was pulling his leg, and while he was curious as to what she might have done, he wasn't curious enough to continue to dig into her life. What she did was on her mind and her conscience, and she was already dealing with the consequences of it. If she wanted to talk about it, that would be her call to make, not his.

He at least had something to think about when he refocused on work. Bobby joined them soon after, and a productive day ended with one of the suits finished and ready to ship out. The remainder would most likely be in shape to ship out over the next week or so.

Obviously, they would have to focus on the rush order when it arrived the following Tuesday, but that was something they would address when it actually happened although they'd make the necessary adjustments to their timeframe once they received full details. The order email would come soon, and with it, the first acceptance of their changed policy regarding rush orders.

"Did you pick up the parts we ordered?" Bobby asked as he settled beside the mech they were finishing.

"What parts?" Taylor glanced at the man and narrowed his eyes.

"The parts we ordered," his friend repeated. "The ones we need to replace in the hydraulic system in mech number four?"

He could almost hear a clock tick inside his head. Everything he'd heard sounded familiar, but he needed a few seconds to put the pieces together.

"Shit, I really need coffee." He stepped away from the suit and cleaned the grease from his hands.

"You know the shop charges to hold the deliveries, right?" Bungees raised an eyebrow.

"Right, I know. I know." He checked his watch hastily. "And they should close in about an hour and a half, so I think I'll go there now. Are you guys good to work until I get back?"

The mechanic gave him a thumbs-up as he snatched Liz's keys up and headed out to where she was parked. Thankfully, the truck was large enough to transport the crates with the parts they needed, which meant they didn't have to rely on delivery drivers, whose rates were always too high along with the risk that the merchandise might be fucked up on the way.

Taylor pulled Liz out of the garage and into the parking lot before he drew his phone from his pocket to find the address to the shop in question. It was a business that sold parts for a variety of mechanical devices, and those they didn't have in stock could be ordered from manufacturers all across the country.

It was the only place locally that sold what they needed, and he was still adjusting to the way Vegas was built so relied on his phone to find his way around the city.

His gaze flickered upward, alerted by an inherent instinct that something was very wrong.

There was never much traffic on the street in front of the strip mall, and most of the cars that were parked in the area tended to be stripped for parts within days. Seeing an intact sedan out front was enough to secure his attention.

But the two men with the vehicle immediately

upgraded curiosity to concern. One carried what looked like a couple of coffees and his friend inside the vehicle gestured impatiently for him to hand one over.

He couldn't put a finger on what it was about the two men that bothered him, but there was something there that pushed a warning bell and it wouldn't go away.

The one in the car pointed at where he sat in Liz and watched them. After what seemed like a panicked exchange between the two, the one outside reached into his coat and drew a Glock from an under-arm holster.

Taylor could hear the protests from the man in the car —or maybe he only thought he could—but there was no time to think about what they might be discussing. They didn't mean well, that was obvious enough. He ducked behind the dash a second before gunshots were fired from across the street.

The world around him exploded in glass and he covered his head instinctively. Adrenaline kicked into him, shoved his heart into overdrive, and filled his mouth with a foul taste as he stretched toward the glove compartment. He was licensed to carry in the state of Nevada but honestly, he'd never thought he would need access to a gun while on an innocuous trip to collect parts. Most of his shooting was done from behind a mech suit.

His weapon was an older model M&P but more than reliable from the company his father used to swear by, and damned if he wasn't happy to see it. He chambered a round from the magazine quickly and flicked the safety off with his thumb. For now, he remained where he was, hidden behind the bulk of Liz's engine while the volley continued.

His caution meant he wouldn't be able to see what they

were doing or if they had moved, but it was better than getting shot.

Not by a huge margin, but for now, he could live with it—and hopefully live as a result of it.

Taylor shifted to the passenger door and pushed it open while the shooting continued. He hadn't been able to see what kind of Glock the other man used. Being unsure of how long it would take him to reach empty was not a pleasant experience.

"They could both be shooting at you now, for all you know," he grumbled, frustrated by the sense that he was trapped. He knew better than to think Liz's door would be sufficient cover for him, but it would keep him out of sight and that was sometimes all one really needed.

A couple of holes appeared on the door and told him that he wanted to wait. He peeked up from behind the dashboard and when he saw that the man was reloading quickly, he pushed his arm up over the dash. It was his left arm and therefore wouldn't have the best aim, but it was about time he delivered a little suppressing fire.

"No, don't come out to see if I need help with the shooting," he snarked under his breath. "That would be too much. Seriously, let me handle all the fighting, as usual."

Maybe he should call Bobby for help. The guy had a shotgun in there somewhere that could help.

Unfortunately, he had no time for that now. The shooting was loud enough in the close confines of the vehicle that all he could really hear were his ears ringing after four shots. He could, however, see the other two men scramble for cover once they realized he intended to fight back.

"That's right, assholes!" he roared before he stepped out of the passenger side, slipped the pistol into his right hand, and pulled the trigger a couple more times. "I have a fucking gun too."

The shooting started from behind the car again as one of the men tried to cover the other while the second attempted to start their vehicle. A sharp stab of pain and a splash of red touched Liz's black paint job to confirm that he had been hit but at that moment, he didn't give a shit.

"You'll have to try a little harder than that." He held the gun in a two-handed grip before he fired again and grinned when the man fell and shouted in pain before he was dragged into the car by his friend.

"No you fucking don't. I ain't done with the two of you yet by a damn mile."

He continued to pull the trigger until it merely clicked and, enraged as he was, it took a moment for him to realize that his gun was empty. The sedan accelerated away and the tires squealed in the almost overwhelming silence in the absence of gunfire.

Although there were extra mags in the glove compartment, he wouldn't be able to retrieve and load one before the car disappeared.

"Fuck." Taylor looked at his shoulder and scowled. "Son of a fucking whore."

CHAPTER EIGHTEEN

It didn't look too bad although it stung like a bitch, but aside from that, there wasn't any indication that real damage had been done. The bleeding had already stopped, and while he didn't mind having a couple of new scars to impress the women, he was still too angry to think about this with anything other than a burning desire for vengeance.

It wasn't long before the garage door opened, but no vehicles emerged. He snagged one of the extra magazines from the glove compartment and readied his weapon.

While it was probably unnecessary, it would also be downright dumb to assume no one would return. Aside from the men who'd attacked him, he was a little surprised that the police hadn't already been called.

Instead, he was greeted by the sight of Bobby who stepped cautiously from inside the strip mall with his shotgun in hand. He turned slowly, obviously trying to find some kind of threat for him to fire at.

Having the man there was reassuring and he wouldn't

suggest he put the weapon away yet, but they were likely safe for the moment. He waved his good arm to call him over.

Vickie peeked out from behind the door but wisely stayed away from any potential gunfire, unlike Bobby— although he wouldn't criticize him for that, even though it maybe wasn't the brightest move. Of course, the fight had stopped, so he had probably thought it through.

"What the fuck is going on?" his friend demanded. His gaze continued to scan their surroundings to locate the source of the shooting. He scowled when he saw the gun in Taylor's hand and the blood. "You're hurt."

"It's barely a graze. As for the first question... I'd say someone attempted a drive-by but they were parked at the time. Besides, they weren't very good at it."

"It looks like they did fine." Bobby examined his shoulder.

"I'm fine," Taylor snapped and yanked himself away. "Liz, on the other hand..."

"Fucking bastards." The mechanic growled under his breath and shook his head in disgust. "Did you get a good look at them? Maybe we can call Banks to see if she can't look into, find out who they are, and pick them up before they return for round goddamn two."

He shook his head. "They were across the street and I only had a couple of seconds before they realized I'd made them and opened fire." He pointed. "They were parked over there in a grey sedan but I didn't get the make or model, though. And they had coffee."

"Coffee? Like...what? They needed to energize they went on a shooting spree?"

"I think it was surveillance. When they realized I'd noticed them, they panicked."

"Why would people case this place?" Bobby looked at the shop in confusion. "We're not exactly a prime target for robbery. Okay, the suits are worth a solid dime, but there aren't enough people out there who would want to steal second-hand suits. Or any of the other equipment you might have around here, for that matter."

"If you say so."

"Do you think they were associated with the criminal element you had to deal with before?"

"It's hard to say for sure, but I don't see any other explanation." He scowled in the direction in which the vehicle had disappeared. "The guys I dealt with before were low-level thugs, iffy street talent recruited to try to deal with me the first time around. The second group wasn't much better. These fuckers were… Well, I definitely wouldn't call pros, but my gut says they're at least a step above others. They were well-equipped and knew their way around a gun but weren't experienced enough to not panic." He sighed. "So…fucking hell, I don't know, but it looks like maybe whoever the boss is decided to up the stakes and bring in a couple of bottom-tier freelancers."

Vickie ventured out from where she had been hiding and had apparently decided that everything was clear and no one would actually shoot at her. It was a fair assumption, of course, but Taylor would still have preferred her to remain inside for the moment.

He didn't need the kind of hell Banks would throw at him if her pet project was wounded or killed in a gunfight.

"Are you okay?" she asked as she approached and noted

the bloodstains on his arm. "Do you need me to call an ambulance?"

"I'm fine, dammit. Who the hell are the two of you—my parents?"

"I hope my kid would be a little more appreciative of concern," she retorted. "You look like you're in pain."

"I'm not in pain, I'm pissed the fuck off."

"That's understandable." Bobby patted him gently on the shoulder. "Someone did take a shot at you, after all. Let's at least get inside and patch that wound up before it gets infected."

"People have been shooting at me for a while now and that doesn't piss me off," he snapped, although he did begin to walk toward the strip mall. "Hell, most of them had a good reason to do so." He waved the hand with the gun toward his truck. "No, I'm pissed off because they damaged Liz."

"Yep, people will die for that." His friend cast an offended look at the vehicle.

"Wait, you were shot at and what you're most pissed about is that they put holes in your car?" Vickie asked.

"Truck!" Taylor corrected sharply. "And she has a name."

"She does?" The woman paused for a second as she finally realized who Liz was and glanced at the other man for confirmation.

"We call her Liz," Bobby said with a nod as they covered the last few steps to the garage, where he began to rummage around for a first aid kit.

"That's….nice." Her tone said she really hadn't reached any real understanding but was willing to run with it in the circumstances.

Taylor shook his head, eased his shirt off, and inspected the injury more closely. "As far as I'm concerned, Liz is family, and if you fuck with family, you're asking to have your ass beat with a lead pipe until you piss blood."

"Okay, you really care about the car—"

"Truck," Bobby corrected as he returned with the kit he found and motioned for Taylor to take a seat.

"Right, of course. Truck." Vickie's expression finally settled into resignation. "You really care a lot about the truck, but shouldn't your focus be on calling the police?"

"They won't do us much good," Taylor told her while his friend set about cleaning the wound. It wasn't that deep at all, barely a graze, but it began to bleed again when a sterilized cotton swab was pressed onto it. He couldn't help a sharp intake of breath.

"We could always give the feds a call." The mechanic kept both his gaze and focus on what he was doing. "Although it probably isn't the worst idea in the world to let the police know about what happened. The chances are that people have already called them to report gunshots."

"And you're positive about that?" she asked and raised an eyebrow.

"What am I, a police monitor?" Taylor knew his tone was abrupt but decided the circumstances warranted it. "How am I supposed to know if someone called them? My point is, if someone did call them, they're already on the way. If no one did, we can deal with it ourselves without the local cops interfering. Or, more realistically, filling the criminals in question in on how we can be dealt with more efficiently."

"You're a little cynical, aren't you?" she said with a chuckle.

"More than a little. But that's not the point,"

"So if I were to offer you my services in using cameras to locate our attackers and hopefully identify them, would you have a snide comment about that too?"

"I—" He looked up. "Wait, can you do that?" Taylor narrowed his eyes. "That wasn't supposed to be snide. I'm actually wondering."

"Our cameras wouldn't have been able to catch much of anything across the street," Bobby said. "We tried when we first heard the gunshots, but they didn't show us anything other than you taking cover."

"Yeah, Liz is far more durable than I am. Speaking of which, we should probably think about what kind of repairs we'll have to put into her. I know the door, hood, and the windshield will need to be replaced. Did you see anything else?"

"I think the passenger window needs help too," the mechanic told him. "There are a couple of bullet holes on the body which will be a bitch to buff out. It might actually be cheaper to simply buy new pieces and set them in. All things considered, I would think about going with solid steel to simply armor Liz at the same time—maybe even bulletproof glass for additional protection."

"The added weight will fuck up the suspension and the mileage," he replied. "I never realized I would need to build me a fucking popemobile."

"Hey, so do you not want me to take a look through camera footage to find the assholes who did this?" Vickie asked to draw the attention of the two men. "Or will you simply sit around and wait for them to come back? Maybe work up a couple of gift baskets? A barbershop quartet?"

"I'm not sure what you're talking about," Taylor replied. "Didn't we establish that our cameras didn't cover the attackers across the road? I simply moved on from there to help the process."

"Well, yeah, your cameras don't cover the road." The woman rolled her eyes. "But there ain't no one talking about my cameras."

"You have a camera system?" He looked sharply at her, both offended and a little nervous. "When did you have time to install that? And how come I wasn't aware of it?"

"Oh, I didn't install them in the strictest sense." She grinned cheekily. "I...uh, might have kind of tapped into an existing network. You know, to help them to boost their efficiency while only using some of the data for my own personal benefit in exchange. It's a bargain if you ask me."

"What network?" Bobby asked. Taylor already had an inkling of what she meant.

"The city's traffic cameras."

"What?" The mechanic threw his hands up, exasperated, and stared at her. "Why would you do that?"

"I'm a little paranoid about my safety," she explained. "There are people who would still like to get their hands on me so I'd like to know if they come into the city, which would give me some time to bug the hell out."

"I...uh, guess I understand that," Taylor said. "It's still a dick move to do something like that without telling us. And I'm fairly sure that shit is illegal."

"You would have told Niki," Vickie pointed out reasonably. "I couldn't have that."

"True enough, and would I have been wrong to?" Taylor glanced around for his shirt before he remembered it was torn and bloodstained and he'd need a new one.

"Yes." The woman sat and folded her arms. "I'm a hacker, remember? Anyway, moving away from how I hurt your feelings over not telling you about hacking the cameras, do you want me to make it up to you by tracking the dumbasses who shot your precious car?"

"Truck, dammit. But yes, I would appreciate that. And if you do find them, I'll think about not telling Banks how you kept up with whatever you did that landed you in trouble in the first place."

"Are you blackmailing me?" She tilted her head and regarded him with a challenging expression. "Because that would be interesting."

"I don't like the term blackmail. It has too many foul connotations. Think of it as me being a good leader and finding ways to give my people the right kind of incentive."

"Right. Incentive has a far more positive ring to it." She grinned. "Let me get my laptop and I'll get right on that shit."

"You know I'm kidding, right?" he said, and she paused at the door and turned to look at him. "I would never sell you out to anyone, not even Banks. You're a part of this team and that means something."

"I know," Vickie said with a small grin before she sprinted up the stairs to her room.

"Are you sure about that?" Bobby whispered as Taylor inspected his bandage. "It might be useful to have something to hold over her if she gives you trouble."

"Okay, there is no doubt in my mind that she'll be all

kinds of trouble," he replied as quietly. "But I think it'll be worth it. She will be worth it, I mean. She has a tough exterior, but her center is…gooey and nice—maybe a little too gooey and nice but we'll work that out of her and mold her more to our specifications. In the meantime, I'm reasonably sure threats won't be the way to keep her on our side. People—or, at least, her type of people, respond far better to positive reinforcement than they do to negative."

"Is that something your drill instructor taught you?" His friend smirked and raised an eyebrow. "Or is it something you came up with on your own?"

"Let's be honest, our drill instructors were never people," Taylor responded with a grin. "And as long as we're being honest, neither are we, not really. We're merely…caricatures of the people we used to be who use coping mechanisms we developed to keep what we became under the surface. Just…trying to survive what happened to us in that fucking place."

"That is surprisingly deep and philosophical. Annoyingly deep, actually. I don't like you when you're deep. It's depressing and annoying at the same time. I definitely don't like it so make it go away. Say something about how you're here in Vegas to exploit the looseness of the female population."

"I'm here to exploit the looseness of the female population." He laughed. "Does that make you feel better?"

"A little, but the other stuff still left a bad taste in my mouth. Keep saying despicable things."

"I don't get involved with women. I sleep with them—although not too much sleeping actually goes on—and I'm gone by the morning without any emotional ties."

"Okay, that's better." Bobby relaxed and took a seat. "You had me worried there that you were actually a thinking, feeling person."

"My apologies for that. It was a temporary lapse in judgment."

"What was a temporary lapse in judgment?" Vickie asked as she returned, toting a laptop and what looked like a router, although he wasn't sure why she needed that.

"I was only… Never mind." Taylor shook his head. "What have you been able to find?"

"Nothing so far. I still need to get connected." She placed both devices on the table and booted them up. "Now, let's see if we can find the assholes who damage your c—truck, shall we?" She wiggled her eyebrows, but her smile was malicious.

CHAPTER NINETEEN

Niki Banks didn't enjoy being in Vegas.

The fucking place was either morbidly hot or artificially cooled, and there was no in-between in the entire city, at least until the sun went down. Then everything was too cold for her to handle. People honestly had too much ambition when it came to settling in the most uninhabitable places on the planet.

The other option was that they simply wanted to get as far away from where oversight could catch up with them as possible and settled in the most uninhabitable place possible until they became the oversight themselves. That was, essentially, the circle of life, over and over again. No matter how free people wanted to be, there would always be those who thought order was necessary—and that they, of course, were the ones who needed to be in charge.

Not that it was really a bad thing. There were people who needed to be kept in check.

People like Taylor, she reminded herself, although he was the best of a bad bunch. They needed law enforcement as a motivator to remain regular citizens, while others needed to know that those in charge were there to protect them and make them feel safe.

It was really the only reason that she had a job. She sighed and sprawled on her hotel bed. The FBI didn't like to set their agents up in nice hotels when it wasn't necessary. Even the apartments and houses they maintained around the country for when people needed a place to hole up for a while were shit-heaps.

Thankfully, she had managed to weasel her way around some of the stricter rules about where she could stay for her time there, supposedly to oversee her operation in the city. Although this particular trip was really only to make sure Vickie was all right.

She really did worry about the kid.

For now, though, she was able to worry in some style where she stayed at the NY-NY Hotel and Casino on the Strip. The rates were surprisingly low, although still higher than what the FBI preferred to approve for hotel stays. Of course, the price was meant to be low since the owners expected people to spend all their extra money in the casino.

Niki knew that there was only one way to beat the house, and that was to not play. She could enjoy the amenities available without additional strain on her spending budget.

If worse came to worst, she would pay for the excess out of her own pocket. It was better to have a decent place in which to spend her time than try to relax in a place that reeked of mildew and possibly dead hookers.

There were other reasons why she would have a hard

time relaxing, but it was nice not to have to worry about the damn sheets being clean. She had been over the room a couple of times with a black light, even though she knew from the start that she would probably regret it.

Thankfully, either she was lucky enough to book into the only hotel in the world where they cleaned the rooms with bleach on a regular basis, or she had encountered an exception to the rule. It could be that a party had gone a little too wild and created enough of a mess to force the management to break out the nuclear option and the purple stuff.

Either way, she didn't want to think about it too hard. All she really needed to know was that the bathroom was as clean as a whistle. Well, a new whistle, anyway.

She paused when she heard a buzzing in the room.

"Oh. fuck. If someone left a dildo behind, I'm so changing rooms." She hissed her annoyance and looked around, even though she'd already done a thorough search on arrival. At least if she had found someone's sex toy left behind in the room, she could have demanded a complimentary dinner or something. People always offered her things when she showed them her badge.

She grimaced when she located her phone, left on vibrate on the desk in the corner of the room. The number told her that Vickie was trying to get in touch.

"Huh, I actually expected her to call it quits a couple of days ago," she said, shook her head, and answered it. "Vickie, nice to hear from you again."

"Yeah, right," the woman scoffed. "What are you doing up this late anyway?"

"You called me," she said. "How late is late?" She glanced

hastily at her watch. "It's only eight in the evening. I don't know what you're complaining about."

"You regular people are generally asleep by now," Vickie said. "I merely assumed you were a regular person who needed to be up in the morning because you really cared about your pointless job."

"My job is important," Niki said defensively. "I'm in federal law enforcement. I save lives."

"It still sounds pointless to me."

"Says the girl who is an intern in a mech shop," she retorted. "How's that going, by the way? How are Oog Oog and Fat Jet Li treating you?"

"I don't even have time to address how offensive that is. I need your help."

"I knew that was coming." She grimaced and tried to quell the rising frustration so she'd be able to think clearly. "I can wrangle a reference from McFadden. Believe me, with a veteran's reference, you could probably get a job anywhere. Well, except most of the casinos. They have a problem hiring people with your particular...legal issues."

"I'm sure they'd rather have me on their side than against them," the other woman retorted. "But no, it's nothing like that. I need you to help me with something else. I'm sure you're already aware that someone tried to shoot Taylor, right?"

"I—what?" she snapped. "No, I haven't heard that. Who told you that? When did that happen?"

"Earlier this afternoon. Well, I guess that answers the question of whether or not someone called the police."

"No one in that area calls the police. They're all too afraid of the local criminal element—those who are being paid for so-called security in the area. They'll call someone if they personally run into trouble, but it'll be their protection, not the police. It's what they pay for, after all. Besides that, if the criminals are the ones who sent the people to do the shooting, they will definitely not do anything about it on the off-chance that someone nervous did actually call them for something that wasn't a direct personal problem. As far as they're concerned, the people who are shot at are the ones who haven't paid anyway. On that topic, why didn't you guys call the police?"

"We are, technically," Vickie said.

"No, I'm not the police. You will not lay this on me."

"Sorry, but I kind of am," Vickie said and didn't sound too apologetic. "Anyway, this is me letting you know there was a shooting around here. Oh, and I also kind of need your help to identify the people responsible."

Niki took a second to stare at her phone before she replaced it against her ear. "How the hell am I supposed to identify them?"

"Oh, did I not mention that I have their faces and fake names used at a car rental? Do you ever check your email?"

She rolled her eyes, crossed to her laptop, and opened the email she had been sent. The pictures of the men meant nothing to her, although she could push them into a database or two and have an answer spat back out at her, but that could wait. The car itself meant nothing either since it was a rental, and the names that were used to hire it were, as the woman had said, probably fake.

There was a name attached to the rental, however, that was familiar. Minosse Incorporated. She had run into the name long before when she had worked other cases with the FBI.

"Did you get the email?" Vickie asked.

"Yeah," she said. "Are you sure all of this is correct? Especially this name, Minosse Incorporated?"

"Yeah, I'm sure. I remember it being a weird name for a company until I dug a little deeper and found it was a shell corporation. Why do you ask?"

"Because I've seen it before," she explained. "La Cosa Nostra likes to hide their money in a number of seemingly legit shell corporations. They like to use Greek and Roman mythology for the names. Minosse is the Italian name for King Minos, and I've seen it tied to the mob before. They would have a fit if anyone else used that kind of naming process, so… Well, I can't be a hundred percent sure it's them until I do more research, but I do think it is."

"Why would the mob want to attack Taylor and Bobby?"

"Oh, well, countless reasons…uh, could apply." She decided to leave it there. "But I won't make any more conjectures until I know for sure. Tell them to be on alert out there."

"They're very alert already around here."

"Well, I guess that's all they really can do," Niki said. "I'll work on this. In the meantime, how are you doing, Vickie? Are you settling in?"

"Aside from someone taking shots at my boss?"

"Obviously."

"Well, it's not what I thought it would be," the woman said. "It's harder work than I expected, but that's not really a terrible thing. Taylor and Bobby are cool to work with.

You know, tough but fair. They have their own style of doing things that's not very orthodox, and... Well, you know me, I'm all about the unorthodox."

"So, you're having a good time?"

"Sure. Like I said, they are tough but fair. They appreciate the work I've done too. I think I'd like to spend more time here with them. Maybe get a place of my own too, but...you know, baby steps."

"I'm happy to hear that. But please, make sure I don't get any calls from someone to tell me you've been picked up while breaking in somewhere you're not meant to be. If that happens again, even I won't be able to keep you from being shipped off to the Zoo. Only the straight and narrow from now on, got it, cuz?"

"Yeah," Vickie said. "Will you call me when you find anything?"

"I'll call Taylor when I find something," Niki corrected her. "You'll focus on your work, understood?"

"Yeah, fine. But I'll talk to you later, right?"

"Yeah, I'll call you later to see how things are going," Niki replied. "Now get to bed."

---

"Fucking—watch it!" Jon snapped.

"You fucking stay still," Mike remonstrated roughly. "I won't be able to patch you up with you flinching like a little girl every time I touch you." The wounded man rolled his eyes and looked around the basement they had commandeered as a haven in which to lick their wounds.

Quite literally in Jon's case, and his frustration was exacerbated by his pain.

"We spent a week staking that place out," he said. "A whole fucking week spent watching, casing it, and trying to learn how that fucking security system worked, and the one time I head out to get coffee, the guy notices us. How the hell did he notice us?"

"You have to calm down," his partner said curtly. "We knew upfront that this guy isn't your ordinary average Joe. He was a fucking Marine, for fuck's sake, and had set something of a record with his Zoo trips. That aside, we were careless. It's not like we even tried to be inconspicuous." He patted the wound with a swab soaked with antiseptic liquid and scowled when his patient yelped. "Do you really think he made us?"

"Do you think I would have opened fire if I didn't think so?" Jon pointed out belligerently. "He looked directly at us, and I could see it by the way he stopped the vehicle so abruptly. And I knew he'd have a gun in the truck so what the fuck was I supposed to do?"

"Walk away? Look casual, get in the car, drive away, and come back in a different vehicle."

"And he would have been looking for us," he argued and shook his head vehemently. "He knew we weren't two guys who stopped in a random part of town for coffee and would have known if we came back, even if we used another car. I was… Well, it was an opportunity. Yes, it wasn't plan A and we were caught on the back foot but he was out in the open. If we could get to him there would be no need to find a way through that damn security system."

"And how did that work out for you?" Mike asked and readied a new swab for another attempt.

"Don't sass me," he responded sharply. "I made a decision and it was the right decision under the circumstances, even if it didn't work out in the end. It wouldn't be the first time we had to think on our feet and change tactics when something unexpected turned our plans inside out. This was bad but could be fixed, and that's exactly what I tried to do—turn it into an opportunity that worked for us. Either way, it didn't work so we now need to find another way to into that fortress disguised as a strip mall."

"How?" Mike countered. "He won't come out, not in any way that we'll be able to get to him. The big guy will be with him all the time to make sure he stays alive, and now they have the bald girl with them too."

"Other guys tried getting to him and failed, but he was alone then. The bald girl and the Jet Li-looking mother-fucker are clearly close to McFadden and are therefore the perfect way to get into his little fortress and take control. They're leverage, you see. We can use them."

"The chances are that it'll merely piss him off more." The man didn't look at him and focused on applying the bandage.

"Sure, he can get pissed off all he wants," Jon replied. "But if he's missing his kneecaps and maybe a couple of his fingers are broken too, he'll still get the message that you don't fuck around with Marino. Pissed or not, that's what we're being paid to do and I'm sorry, but I don't think I can stand being stuck in a car with you for any longer. We're operatives, not fucking PIs. Stake-outs are not our territory."

"No, no, I get that. I don't think I would be able to be stuck in there either. So what are your plans to get our leverage over McFadden?"

"The guy leaves the area every evening, but the chick doesn't. Maybe she's fucking McFadden but either way, it seems our weak link is the guy who goes home every night. The intel says he and our target go way back, so there's friendship there and the redhead will want to avoid anything happening to him. But he comes in every morning, so we can simply sneak in after him."

Mike stared at him in astonishment for a moment, then nodded. "That sounds like the beginning of a plan, anyway. If we get in quickly enough, they won't have time to do anything before we secure the hostages. But you need to have that gunshot wound closed first. Are you sure you don't want to go to a hospital to have this treated properly? I have some first aid training, but you might need an actual doctor for that."

"I'll be fine." Jon growled, shook his head, and pulled a fresh shirt on. "Doctors need to report any gunshot wound victim to the police and neither of us wants to have to try to explain this to them. Besides, it's barely even a flesh wound, although it felt worse when it actually hit me. Anyway, we have no time to waste, all right?"

"Fine. But I'm driving."

"That's probably for the best." He popped the vial of pills they had managed to find in the house into his pocket. "I don't want to be pulled over for a DUI."

# CHAPTER TWENTY

It was a long day and Taylor didn't like those. The work was supposed to be enjoyable and rushing about in an attempt to have everything done on a time limit was not pleasant.

There really wasn't much they could do to avoid the work, of course, even with his shoulder being too painful to move around much. Bobby had finally rushed out to pick up the parts they needed in his truck while Taylor and Vickie moved Liz into the garage to inspect the damage in a safe location.

Of course, there had been more than he'd expected. Rounds into the engine had caused considerable problems under the hood, and she would need far more work before she was functional again.

He'd cursed volubly during the inspection and wanted to start there and then. But Liz would have to wait because they still had orders that needed to be completed first. Once Bobby returned, the two men had worked for most of the afternoon and well into the evening. While the firefight and all its ramifications still weighed heavily on their minds, at the moment, there was nothing they could do but wait until Vickie had information for them.

If there was anything he had learned to do during his time in the Zoo, it was compartmentalization. Too many people obsessed over shit they had no control over, and that was the kind of thing that distracted you in the Zoo. Only idiots worried about shit they couldn't see and missed what they could see if they'd only remained focused on what was important. By the time they noticed, of course, the monster they should have worried about was already eating their ass…or hand, foot, arm…whatever.

The need to survive had quickly taught him how to set his feelings aside on a variety of topics at any given moment, at least until he could do something about them. For now, all he could deal with was working with Bobby to fix the mech suits.

Vickie had found considerable data in the meantime but none of it made sense to any of them and she decided to dump it all on Banks.

That woman would know what to do with it. For the moment, however, they wouldn't get much else done, the work was finished for the day, and he had a feeling they all needed a damn drink after the day they'd had.

"I'll need a new car," he said as they locked the shop.

"I thought your heart was set on a motorcycle." Bobby looked at him with narrowed eyes. "You know, to complete the look of your new suit."

"Sure, that was the plan, but now that we're dealing with people trying to kill me, I don't exactly want to be caught out in the open with nothing between the bullets and me but a motorcycle, you know? And it looks like Liz will be out of commission for a while, at least until I can spare the time to get her up and running again, which means that since we're heading out to get drinks, I need you to give me a ride again, Bungees."

"I kind of knew that was coming," the man said. "I still wasn't looking forward to it, though."

"Look on the bright side. At least you'll have drinking company. Although you might want to think about taking a cab when we're done. Speaking of which, how old are you, Vickie?"

She looked up from where she still studied her computer screen. "Why do you ask? Are you starting to rethink that whole not-your-type statement?"

"I…well, it probably wouldn't be in your dreams, but no. The answer to that is no. You're still not my type and I hope you take that as the highest of compliments. I'm asking because we're going to get sloshed and since you've been a part of this whole episode, you have an invite to come drinking with us. Oh, and because you've been helpful in trying to track down the assholes who shot Liz—"

"And you. Don't forget that," Bobby pointed out as they headed over to his car.

"Right, and me," he added and rolled his eyes. "Anyway, the point is, the first round is on me and that's much less likely to happen if you're not allowed to drink."

"Well, I'm twenty-two," she replied. "So, there's no need to worry about that. I have an ID and everything."

"Awesome. Houston," he called. "We have no problems. Now, let's go get us a drink."

"You sound very upbeat for a guy who narrowly avoided having his head shot off," his friend commented as they climbed into his truck. "Not that it's a bad thing, mind you, but still, a little upbeat."

"You know how it goes." Taylor settled into the back while Vickie climbed into the shotgun seat. "You get a little fearful for your life, the adrenaline pumps, and when all is said and done, you've survived and all that adrenaline needs somewhere to go. You celebrate having survived, then move on." He considered putting the seatbelt on but decided death could throw the dice. "Isn't that how everyone reacts to having a scrape with death?"

"It's hard to say." The mechanic eased out of the parking lot and onto the road. "For one thing, it seems like you've been involved in that kind of situation so often, you have dealing with the undesirable elements of escaping life-threatening situations down to a science. Which, you know, is great for you but probably doesn't apply to everyone."

"Fair enough. Vickie, how do you react to a near-death experience? Most people drink. Do you? Drink, I mean."

"Who doesn't drink?" she replied with a laugh.

Taylor shrugged. "Some people don't. It's a valid choice and I've learned not to assume anything. You never know when someone has a problem or they needed to quit, you know?"

"All right, that makes sense." She rubbed her fingers idly over her buzz cut. "And I've never had one, to be honest. I've never even been in a car accident before. Not that I'm complaining, of course. If we go with hypotheticals, though, I'd say that…yeah, it would probably mean a ton of adrenaline and feeling like you're immortal, so a drink with people who can bring you down if you go too far is probably the best scenario."

"Cool beans." He gave her a small grin. "I'm thinking Jackson's."

"Jackson's it is," Bobby said and continued down the still well-trafficked streets of the city. The nightlife in Vegas was something of legend and comparable only to the likes of New York, which meant it would be at least a handful of hours until the streets were more or less abandoned for the night. There was still a horde of sports cars and limos sandwiched in with the regular vehicles and trucks that needed to get from point A to point B.

Taylor wasn't a fan of the usual kind of nightlife. Even in his developing years, loud music and dancing had never appealed to him that much, although he pretended otherwise since it was what the opposite sex appeared to enjoy.

As of right now, all he really needed was a drink and company to ground himself again and all would be fine.

If Alex was working that night, so much the better.

It wasn't long before Bobby pulled into the parking lot and locked the truck before the three of them headed toward the door, where Marcus the bouncer was stationed.

"Taylor, it's nice to see you around again," the man said with a broad smile and bumped the proffered fist. "Bobby, right? And…I don't know this one."

"Marcus, this is Vickie, the newest employee in our little business." Taylor gestured to the large man. "Vickie, this is Marcus, the best bouncer in Vegas."

"I think that if you were in the business, you could give

me a run for my money," Marcus admitted. "Not an overly competitive run, but I'd still need to apply myself to it."

"That sounds about fair. Vickie, show him your ID to make sure you're cleared to drink in this establishment and we should be good to go."

She did as she was told and they were allowed to enter the building. He looked around and noticed more patrons seated than there had been the last time he'd visited. A baseball game played on the screens, which explained their numbers, and while he could see Alex behind the bar, it seemed like she was too busy to interact with them or do more than give him a simple wave.

"A sports bar?" Vickie asked and looked around. "Really?"

"It has great service, good drinks, and fantastic—okay, mostly good—food that tastes better with each drink." He pointed to the screens. "Sure, there's sports playing, but there's no need for you to focus on that."

They found a booth and one of the waiters came over to take their orders for drinks, which Taylor was paying for, and food. He chose the ten-ounce ribeye steak with mashed potatoes and gravy. Bobby stuck with the half-pound chopped steak dinner, while Vickie decided on the roasted salmon, which came with a side of sweet potato fries. A plate of fries was ordered for the table.

Bobby shifted impatiently in his seat. The man tended to get surly when he was hungry, and from the looks of him, he was famished enough to demolish the half-pound of steak he'd selected.

In fairness, it was on the late side and none of them had

eaten since lunch. It was odd how food was forgotten in situations like this.

Once their drinks arrived—beers for all three—the mechanic raised his glass and looked at his companion.

"What are we drinking to?" Taylor asked but had already raised his glass in response.

"How you dodged death?" Vickie suggested.

"Maybe how Vickie is actually one hell of a saleswoman?" he countered.

"I actually thought something along the lines of actually getting the business up and running, despite all the mishaps and, let's be honest, dangers," the other man said.

"How about all of the above?" Taylor suggested and all three shrugged agreement that all points deserved a little tchin-tchin.

"Wait," Bobby interrupted a second later. "What do you mean by Vickie is one hell of a saleswoman?"

"Didn't I tell you? Oh yeah, one of our clients called and asked for a rush job on a suit they will send next week. She told them that would only be possible if we added ten percent to the fee, and the guy agreed without so much as a pause."

"Ten percent is almost...what, twenty-five hundred?" the other man asked and frowned as he did the calculations in his head.

"More or less. I said she should get ten percent of the profits she made on that upsell."

"That seems reasonable. Nice work. It's not exactly retirement money, but you could always put the bonuses aside in a savings account or something and only live on your salary."

"What would I have to save up for?" she asked.

"Have you thought about going to college?" Taylor raised an eyebrow.

"Sure, I've thought about it but never seriously," Vickie replied. "I attended one near my hometown but I dropped out when I realized that I knew more about Information and Coding Theory than my professors did."

"Well, you should think about it again. In fact, I might even go so far as to make it a part of your job contract if you want to go to UNLV."

"What do you care if I get higher education?"

"That's not the point." He sighed. "Look, I might not make it. With an education, you could have your choice of jobs. The diploma might not mean shit to you, but it could be a ticket to a company you can't get into any other way. It's all a game, even out there in the Zoo. We seem civilized, but we aren't. We are simply a veneer over a group of animals that learned how to build a fire and write our words down. We are all animals at the end of the day. You don't have to hunt, but to get ahead in this new jungle, you still have to learn how to stay alive and thrive. So, your first task is to do the jobs around the company. Your second is a degree."

He half-expected her to roll her eyes and change the subject and was surprised when she leaned forward while he spoke like she was actually paying attention.

"Huh." She looked thoughtful. "I guess I never thought about it like that before."

They were interrupted when their food arrived on steaming hot plates, delivered by two waiters who each carried two plates. They placed the fries in the middle and the others were set in front of the people who had ordered them. Bobby looked like he had been taken over by a wild animal, and as soon as the plate and silverware were placed in front of him, he was quick to attack the food.

Vickie was similarly famished and tucked into her salmon with enthusiasm. Taylor started with the fries at the center of the table.

"It's something to think about, you know?" he continued with his previous point. "Besides, if this company needs someone with your kind of credentials, we might have to go ahead and borrow yours. There's always a benefit to hiring someone with a string of letters behind their name and hell, you could get a better salary if you had them too. If not from me, then from another company in the area that would kill to have someone with your brains on their team. Just saying."

"Ugh, fine, she gets the picture," Bobby grumbled, his mouth still half-full of food.

"No, it's actually a good idea," Vickie said. "And yeah, I appreciate your concern for my future. Not that it's really warranted since I can handle myself."

"I never said you couldn't handle yourself," he added quickly before he took a mouthful of his prime ribeye. "We're a team now, and that has certain implications. We might not need to be overly involved in each other's lives, but we can always help each other improve and grow. If that means you take a couple of days off work to listen to boring lectures, so be it. Besides, I'm fairly sure that your..." He watched her and the trace of a smile twitched at the corners of his mouth. "Older sister?"

"We don't even share the same name, man," she answered and laughed.

"I'll get it right eventually. Anyway, I'm sure Banks didn't only send you to me because she thought you needed to learn the lessons that come from working with your hands."

"Why did she bring me to you?" Vickie asked.

"I have no idea," he said honestly. "But I think we can work on finding out. I'm reasonably sure she wouldn't object to you getting an education either."

"Fair enough. I can't argue with that, even if I wanted to. But yeah, I'll think about it."

"That's all I ask."

# CHAPTER TWENTY-ONE

They didn't actually drink that much, although they did stay later than they had intended. At the end of the evening, each of them elected to take a cab to their respective homes.

Taylor and Vickie shared one since they were heading toward the same place. He told the others they could have a morning off and come in for the afternoon if they wanted to.

If he knew Bungees at all, the man would consider the morning off as a suggestion and merely come in a couple of hours late. He had no idea how Vickie would take it, but he was curious to find out. Either way, they'd had a long day and he had no intention of busting their balls over arriving a little late. Or a half-day late, in that case.

He wouldn't judge them too much if they decided to take his offer to heart and take the morning off. As the night had worn on, he'd realized that while the shooting probably hadn't affected him much, he was an odd person. He needed to remember that people who were more normal like Vickie or Bungees might not see it the same way he did.

After everything that had happened, they probably needed time to reconsider their life choices without being clouded by alcohol.

Even so, there was work to be done, and if the people involved weren't there to do it, he needed to. He was up at eight in the morning and still felt a little logy from the night before. There was stuff to do, however, but in this case, not entirely for the shop.

A quick cab ride took him to one of the nearby used car lots, where he spent time talking with one of the salespeople. He had a very distinct idea of what he wanted when he got there and thankfully, they were well-stocked with the kinds of trucks he would need.

The chances were that Banks would call him to head off and hunt something in the near future, and he would need something that could carry one or both of his suits. A truck was the only viable option, and it was easy to select a four-by-four that met his needs quite nicely.

The salesman was surprised when he offered to pay for the only slightly used vehicle immediately. Closing the sale took about as much time as was needed to transfer the money and drive away. She was smaller than Liz but he wouldn't hold that against her.

She had all the modern trappings except for an AI to manage the driving.

"I'll have to fix that about you," he said as he drove through the city. "Don't tell Liz I said this, but it's much easier to drive you in the mid-morning traffic than her. Which reminds me. We'll have to think of a name."

The dark purple four-by-four pickup had nothing to say to that. He started to wonder if he was merely shit at naming things in general but was saved from his train of thought stalling at the station when his phone rang. He still hadn't paired it to the Bluetooth in the new truck and had to pull over to answer it when he saw Banks was on the line.

"Good morning, Special Agent," he said with a smile. "What can I do you for?"

"You sound upbeat for someone who had an attempt on his life the day before." She sounded a little the worse for wear.

"People keep saying that like I haven't intentionally put myself in danger for years. It's like you expect me to handle it like a normal person."

"I guess that's fair," she acknowledged. "Look, I need to meet you. Have you had breakfast yet?"

Taylor was reminded by a low grumble from his stomach that he had not, in fact, had breakfast yet.

"Nope," he said simply.

"Good, can you meet me at Il Fornaio at the New York-New York Hotel on the Strip?" she asked.

"That's kind of rich for my blood," he pointed out.

"Your payment for the LA job is already in your account so don't give me any of that."

"Fine." He rolled his eyes. "I'll meet you there in…shall we say, twenty minutes?"

"See you then."

The traffic turned out to be a little heavier than he'd anticipated, and while the truck's GPS helped him to find the streets that were emptier and easier to navigate, he was running a few minutes late by the time he pulled into the entrance of the hotel and casino that had been built as a replica of the city it was named after.

As Banks had said, though, he wasn't doing too badly for himself, and not only because he had received a hundred-and-fifty-thousand-dollar-plus payday. He left the semi-new vehicle in the hands of one of the valets and headed inside.

Casinos were built to be a maze you never got out of and in which you wanted to spend your money at every turn, but this place was somewhat unique, he had to admit that. He'd never been to New York City before, but the way it was structured with the looks of the "buildings" inside made it feel like he was actually in the famed city. Well, not really, but tremendous effort had been put in to create the effect.

A few wrong turns made him even later before he finally found the Il Fornaio in question, and he was a little surprised. He had no real clue what he had expected, but the pristine restaurant was well yet warmly lit. Coupled with the modern but comfortable aesthetic to the marble floors and tabletops, it was not really anything like what he had imagined.

Taylor didn't really want to say that he had looked for one of the stereotypical establishments that were shown in Martin Scorsese movies—the kind that only served a variety of pasta to the mobsters who came and stayed while they plotted heinous crimes. Truthfully, though, it leaned slightly toward what he'd envisaged, especially with how the hotel and casino around them had been built.

He had to say it was a pleasant surprise. Since he had no

nostalgic ties to times past, modernity was definitely what appealed to him about it. The kitchen was visible, which gave the patrons a full view of how their food was prepared. It was a nice touch.

The breakfast crowd appeared to have already moved on to the rest of the hotel. A few still lingered or had arrived late so it wasn't completely empty, which meant there were enough patrons for him to not feel overly exposed in the area.

It wasn't difficult to locate Banks in one of the corner booths. She raised her hand and waved to him to call him over to join her.

"Our tax dollars at work, huh?" He gestured expansively and grinned. "Are you staying in the hotel too?"

"That's none of your business," she said. "But yes. It's actually a little surprising how low the daily rates are here."

"It's not really surprising since they want to draw you in and take the rest of your money at the casino."

"Which is why I stick to the room and the amenities. I'm not sure how much of this I will actually have to pay but all things considered, I think it's worth it, especially this place."

Taylor looked around a little warily. "Yeah, my first thought, when I came in here, was to wonder if they had a breakfast menu."

"Take a look." Banks passed one of the menus over to him. "I've come here almost every day. Their food is fucking amazing."

"It looks like you're not only enjoying the food." He raised an eyebrow at the champagne flute with yellow liquid inside. "Isn't it a little early to drink?"

"I'm taking a personal day. Sue me." She lifted her glass defiantly to her lips and took a sip. "Anyway, forget that. Do you want to order something to eat? Because I'm starving."

"Will you cover the bill?"

"In your dreams."

"Fair enough." He smirked. "I merely wanted to make sure this wasn't a date or anything."

"Again, in your dreams." She flashed him a mocking look over the rim of her glass as she took another sip.

A stout, middle-aged man with a grey goatee came over to the table and tugged a smile from her lips as she stood to greet him.

"Welcome back, Miss Banks," he said with a grin and shook her hand firmly. Taylor stood a little awkwardly and tried not to look at them. He didn't want to appear rude, but at the same time, he wasn't sure what the man was doing there.

"It's nice to see you again, Marcelo." Banks turned to Taylor. "This is Marcelo, manager of Il Fornaio and one of the most interesting people I've ever had the pleasure to meet. Marcelo, this is Taylor, a…business associate."

"And here I thought you would call me one of your friends," he said with a small grin.

"The way you two were bickering, I'd say that you two were friends," Marcelo pointed out with a slightly challenging look at each of them.

"See? I like this guy. He's very intuitive."

Banks rolled her eyes. "Business associate."

"Anyway," the manager said. "Niki has been one of my best customers. She always tips well and hasn't missed a single breakfast during her time here, so any business associate of hers is a friend of mine."

"Out of sheer curiosity, how long has she been coming here?" Taylor asked.

"Well, every day over the past week, but she has made regular visits over the past month and a half."

"Is that so?" He glanced slyly at the special agent.

Her eyes widened in panic at the man's words and she quickly and somewhat desperately changed the subject. "Okay, I think it's time we actually ordered, right Taylor?"

"I could have a bite," he said and patted Marcelo on the shoulder. "I was actually a little surprised you had a breakfast menu, but I'll opt for something a little more basic. I'll have the..." He looked hastily the menu. "Con Panche... sunny-side eggs with the applewood-smoked bacon."

"Con Pancetta Affumicata," the man said and pronounced the Italian words effortlessly. "Would you like anything else?"

"Yeah, and the...uh, Tosto Francese?" He wasn't sure if he said it right but what the hell. Food was food, whatever you called it.

"Nice pronunciation," Marcelo said with a chuckle.

"Thanks. I took Spanish in high school. Oh, and black coffee to go with it."

"Might I suggest a glass of orange juice? It fits well with the rest of the meal, in my opinion."

"Sure. Why not?"

"And the usual for me," Banks said.

"Of course, an Uova Salute with a Zampa d'Orso and a Latte Caldo?" the manager confirmed and he nodded before he headed back to the kitchen.

"I didn't see him take any of that down," Taylor said and narrowed his eyes.

"I don't think he needed to."

"What's a…Wova…" He consulted the menu briefly. "Huh, cholesterol-free eggs, fresh basil, potatoes, and fruits. It sounds healthy. What's that zampa thing, though? All it says is that it's a pastry."

"It literally translates to bear claw in Italian," she explained. "Well, bear's paw, technically, but it is simply a bear claw. They are very good here, though."

"So, why don't you tell me why you had me come all the way here," he said while he somewhat absently watched Marcelo give the kitchen their orders. "And don't say it was because you wanted company."

"I'll have to refer you back to your lonely, pathetic dreams."

"Did you find anything on the guys who shot my truck?"

"I'm still working on that," Banks replied.

"So you're checking on Vickie to make sure she's okay?" he pressed.

"Is everything okay with her? Is she shook up over the shooting?"

"She wasn't the one who was shot at, so yeah, she's as right as rain and thanks for asking." He laughed. "Maybe a little hungover. We took her out for a drink last night and she's smaller and her liver doesn't process the alcohol too quickly, so she's sleeping it off. I gave her and Bobby the morning off."

"Then no, I'm not checking in on her," the agent said. "I actually have a job for you."

"I'll have you know they shot my truck up, so I might be a little slower to get there."

"That won't be a problem, I don't think," Banks said. "This job is in Oregon, where a group of foresters claims up and down that they saw Bigfoot."

"And we care about those crazies making up crazy stories from what they saw when drinking why, exactly?" he asked, his tone deliberately sarcastic.

"Because they're not crazy."

"What do you mean?"

She sighed. "I honestly never thought I'd say this, but Bigfoot is dropping bodies."

His eyebrows raised and he stared at her. "Huh. No kidding?"

"I'm afraid not. Desk is working on the details for you right now, but I wanted to check in with you first to make sure you were up for the job."

"Why wouldn't I be?" A couple of waiters already approached with their plates. "Damn, they're fast."

"I really hope I don't need to remind you about what happened yesterday." She leaned back as the plates of freshly cooked breakfast were placed on the table in front of them, followed by their drinks.

"I wish people would stop," he protested. "It's not like you guys were the ones who were shot at."

"So, you're good to go?" Banks asked.

"Obviously."

"Awesome." She smiled. "Now…" She waved at his plate with her fork. "Enjoy your meal."

The smell alone was enough to make his mouth water, although that probably had something to do with the fact that he hadn't eaten anything since the night before. He took a sip of coffee first, then tried the food.

It was difficult to pinpoint what exactly it was that made it all different. It tasted amazing, of course, but there was something extra.

For some weird reason, it was like it tugged at the nostalgia in him and called him back to a time when all he really needed to think about was getting home in time for his favorite cartoons. Back then, his worries about food were minimal since his mom did the cooking, although he needed to help with the cleaning.

"Holy shit," he said, his mouth still full of pancake.

"I know, right?" his companion replied and attacked her food with a gusto that he'd not seen in her before.

Taylor swallowed and in that moment, decided to put all thoughts about shootings and hunting monsters aside for the moment and simply enjoy his meal.

Everything else could be dealt with later, anyway.

# CHAPTER TWENTY-TWO

"So," Taylor said into his phone. "Bigfoot. What are your thoughts? Does he exist or not?"

There was a moment of silence on the line and he could tell that Desk tried to decide if he was serious or not. He wasn't sure if he was serious or not either. It was a long drive to Portland, and while the new truck was a breeze to drive, it simply wasn't Liz.

For one thing, there was no option to turn the AI on and sit back to watch something or nap as the miles flew by. He needed to physically drive all the way for almost sixteen gosh-damned, long-assed, annoying and boring hours.

He could kill those fuckers for that alone.

Of course, he wouldn't complete the trip in one day. Banks had said that there was no time constraint like there had been on the last couple of jobs, so he would be able to find somewhere to spend the night before he started again the next day. He had already plotted most of the journey, having spent the morning after the fantastic breakfast packing what he needed and doing his research. Bobby, as always, was left in charge.

The afternoon had been spent driving the first leg, which gave him a head start for the following day. It was a good plan. He still felt like it had been a good idea but had failed to account for the mind-numbing dullness that came from not being able to focus on anything other than the road.

It was what everyone had done in the past and it wasn't like he hadn't ever done it before, but he had grown accustomed to certain luxuries that were now absent.

He added yet another reason to kill the fuckers in a very long and painful way.

His music had played to keep him company and helped to relieve some of the tedium of the trip until Desk called him. She was ready to provide the details of where he would go and what he was likely to deal with and he took the opportunity to stretch the conversation a little. Having someone to talk to really took the sting out of the miles.

"So tell me," he said, "do you believe the Bigfoot story?"

A fairly long silence followed during which he tapped his fingers on the steering wheel in time to the beat still in his head from the music and tried to imagine what she must look like deep in thought. It was a stupid exercise, but hey, it filled the gap.

"Honestly?" Desk asked finally, her tone cautious.

"Sure."

"I think you'll have to be a little more specific. The world is full of all kinds of crazy monsters, as I'm sure you're aware. So if the point of the question is to establish whether I am open to the existence of a Bigfoot creature, then yes, I am open to it. If the question was meant to ascertain whether or not I feel the Bigfoot creature does exist and has existed as stated in common American folklore, I have to say no. The evidence suggests that there is a possibility of similar creatures, but the creature as described is probably merely the result of people with impaired visibility who saw a bear or something of the kind."

"Huh. Well stated."

"I'm glad it meets with your approval," she said. "Where do you stand on the topic?"

"Basically the same as you," he replied. "I'm not sold on the whole culture around it, and yeah, I'm sure the people who supposedly saw Bigfoot probably didn't, but there is a possibility that it exists. I can't say for certain that it doesn't, but it doesn't really matter since whether a particular creature exists or not doesn't impact our lives."

"Well, in this case, I'd say it definitely impacts yours," she pointed out.

"Okay, I guess that's a fair point." A hunt for Bigfoot was obviously a high point in his work as a cryptid assassin, whatever the hell it turned out to be. He didn't actually think Bigfoot was out there, obviously, but if he had to go out there based on reports that the big guy attacked and killed people, there was no way he would keep this one quiet.

A long drive in the afternoon culminated in a break for the night at a small hotel a few miles off the highway. Before he resumed his drive early in the morning, he made a quick call to Bobby to make sure everything was still on track and set off on the second leg of his trip.

The truck had performed well and he felt confident about his purchase. Of course, he had done a check on the vehicle and so knew what he was getting into and even took it on a test drive before he completed the deal. But there wasn't much in the world that could test a vehicle more than a long trip and so far, this one had more than stood up to the challenge.

Taylor hadn't been entirely sure that he would keep her after the purchase but settled more and more into the idea of it. He still didn't have a clue what to name her but so far, she had proven herself. She carried the weight of two mech suits and cruised the road at the kind of high speeds he would get calls from Desk about, and she had shown no signs of problems.

Of course, that could change later but so far, he liked her.

He needed to slow as he came into the city of Portland, as Desk had directed him to head into the local FBI head-quarters where Banks had been able to fly in and set up shop. She had said he could fly and do the preparatory work alongside her, but he had declined.

For him, it was best to drive and he would be comped for all his expenses anyway. He wasn't a fan of being in a flying tube with a horde of strangers, and while he had full control of the phobia, it wasn't like he intended to constantly test it without any real cause.

An underground parking lot provided a safe place where he could leave the nameless lady and he headed into the offices Banks had been assigned for them.

It was odd to see her in an office situation, and while he knew he worked as a freelancer for the FBI, he still hadn't quite made the connection until there was a whole process of being searched and checked before he was allowed entry.

A couple of other agents studied him curiously but didn't say anything.

Banks came out to greet him with a small smile and gestured for him to follow her. "Don't mind the rest of them. They work here permanently and don't like it when outsiders come to interrupt their routine. We won't be here for long, so they won't have to worry about you too much."

"Fun times," he quipped, unruffled by the scrutiny. "Why do we need to be in a building again?"

"We don't need to be here," she replied. "We only need a location to look at the data that was collected to confirm that this is definitely a job for you, and I thought that having an office no one's using would be the best way to do it. Otherwise, I would have had to spend money and no one wants that."

"Not even you?" She shut the door to the office behind him. "Not even overspending your time in a hotel while lurking over me?"

"I'm keeping an eye on Vickie." She strode to the other side of the desk and dropped into the seat.

"Not for the past month and a half you haven't," he said with a grin.

"I needed to keep an eye on you too. And I don't know why we're talking about this. I don't have to explain myself to you."

"I merely wondered why you're such a regular in the city like Giuseppe said you were." His grin widened as she rolled back on her chair to open the window behind her.

"His name is Marcelo," Banks reminded him and opened the blinds to a limited and yet still good view of the city below them.

"Exactly," Taylor said, but his attention was drawn to the billboard hung directly above the window. It was an ad for a TV series that would hit the waves within the next couple of weeks and displayed a good-looking man with a square jaw and bristle on his chin. He held a gun and leaned against a doorframe while something approached from the darkness behind.

"What?" she asked when she realized he wasn't staring at her but rather at something behind her.

"What the hell is *The Savage?*"

"Oh yeah, there was an incident in which someone in a mech suit attacked a Russian safe house in Brussels," she explained. "I remember it being all over the news a little while ago. Anyway, footage went viral of the guy beating a couple of cops during his getaway, and people ran with it and called him The Savage. There were a couple of comic books about him and now, they're making a series about it, I guess. It's not really my thing, though."

"Huh." He grunted, half-amused and half-curious. "I might have to check that out."

"Sure, mindless action has you written all over it," she said with a small smirk.

"Of course it does. Anyway, I seem to recall you needed me here to do some job or another. I remember something about…Bigfoot?"

"Right." Banks took a deep breath. "Let's get to it. First

of all, we had a couple of reports from some of the locals that mention the sightings. We've dealt with those kinds of reports in the Pacific Northwest since forever, so no one really paid much attention to them until, again, a couple of hikers—or more accurately, self-proclaimed cryptozoologists—reported a couple of bodies in the area. Oh, and signs of Bigfoot too."

"So far, it seems legit. What did you guys find out there?"

"Well, the only people available to follow up were a couple of local police officers who found the bodies and put in reports of large animal sightings. As you can imagine, that drove the locals crazy. The result was that a whole horde of folks headed into the local forests to try to catch a glimpse of the big guy."

"How did that work out for them?" He grimaced when his mind joined the dots of for him. "You don't need to be a whatever-ologist to know that even bears could deliver a hefty body count if a large group of humans intruded on their territory."

"Well…many people didn't see anything." She pushed one of the files on the table across for him to take a look at. "Three of the groups weren't heard from again, though. Search parties were sent in after them, and…well… Take a look."

Taylor picked the file up and opened it to the pictures that had been collected by the search parties. It wasn't hard to tell them apart, of course, since it was clear which were from the original bodies seen and which were from the Bigfoot hunting parties. Most of them were of the bodies and the first few showed the five that had been found by the police. These were crisp and professional and displayed the corpses in a way that would be relevant to any investigations that might result.

He doubted that they would find anything to investigate, however. The remains appeared to have been in the mountains for a while, and while there seemed to have been considerable damage, especially to the torso and stomach, that could have easily been caused by wild animals that had found the bodies after their death.

The second set—which comprised a total of eleven corpses—was a little more telling. They were fresher, for one thing, and showed far more of what actually killed them, although he couldn't be sure if it would have been the damage to their stomachs and chests or the fact that they had been impaled on branches in the trees.

"Fuck me," Taylor said and scratched his jaw. "Have the families been shown these?"

"Not the pictures, no," Banks replied. "The bodies were returned, but…well, it's hard to explain that kind of shit."

"That's not a bear or a mountain lion," he said firmly. "I don't think there's much in the world that can pull that shit off. The only animal I know of that pegs its prey on trees and stuff are birds—shrikes, I think they're called."

"Yep. That was what I thought," she agreed.

"You thought it was a giant shrike?" He raised an eyebrow skeptically.

"Well, it's probably a little more complicated than that. But…yeah, unless you have any better ideas."

"I don't," he admitted. "But I know one thing for sure—this definitely sounds like our kind of job."

"Agreed. When can you head out there to investigate?"

"I don't know. I might need to put a little more time in to think this through." He shrugged and put the file on the table. "There are other possibilities to consider. What if this isn't goop-related? What if I'm actually dealing with a Bigfoot that likes to pin his victims on trees?"

"Well then, you shoot Bigfoot in his big head, come back to me to collect your reward, and for the love of God, don't get the media involved. If there's anything the FBI doesn't need right now it's the bad press that would inevitably come from us being implicated in the death of a beloved folklore character. And yes, even if he kills people by pinning them to trees."

"Well, I don't know… I kind of want to be remembered as the guy who killed the first Bigfoot."

"Well, if that happens, you don't get paid," Banks pointed out.

"I don't need to get paid. I'll have the book and film rights." His eyes lit up. "I'll be a fucking millionaire."

"It won't be that simple and you know that," she argued with a grin. "With that said, being the FBI agent who authorized a hit on Bigfoot does seem like it would be worth a pretty penny too. Do you think I could get someone really hot to play me, too?"

"I doubt it would be difficult," he assured her. "Besides, they'll choose someone who's really hot with large tits and no acting skills to play you all angsty anyway."

"I'll be sure to wipe my tears away with hundred-dollar bills." She tapped the desk. "Now, what say you we get this show on the road?"

"That sounds good to me."

## CHAPTER TWENTY-THREE

There was something to be said about the beauty of the forests in the Pacific Northwest. People always said it rained or snowed almost every day of the year, but in the days that had sunlight, it was a gorgeous place to be. Lush forests covered the landscape in a thick green blanket.

Today was not one of the good days. It rained incessantly, the kind of steady, driving rain that made it more difficult to climb through the damn forest than it really needed to be. Excessive rain was another thing he had never encountered in the Zoo. The self-created weather brought storms that usually cleared after a few hours and seemed to follow a pattern that only the jungle that created them understood. Occasionally, he'd encountered softer drizzle that lasted longer, but that didn't seem to be the norm, at least from his experience.

Even so, it didn't take him too long to begin his long climb through the hills. While the mud was difficult to navigate, he was certainly better equipped to handle it than most of the hikers who ventured out this way.

"You have the coordinates, right?" Desk asked and the comm line blinked active on his screen.

"Nope. I'm merely wandering around here blindly in hopes of finding whatever it is I can find." He pulled himself up a small incline and adjusted his heading toward the north.

"You're joking, I take it?"

"Yes, I'm joking. How the hell are you able to get any signal out here?"

"Well, the suit you're wearing was designed with the Zoo in mind," Desk said. "Of course, the jungle is able to interfere and even block signals, so comms usually only achieve a maximum of one to two kilometers. My point, though, is that your suit has a very distinctive signal that I'm able to track, follow, and even contact when needed. That should be no surprise to you."

"Well, no, but it sounds like you're talking to me over a phone line."

"I might be," she said. "But it's been uniquely programmed to make contact with your suit. There should be a signal powerful enough to allow me to contact you almost anywhere in the world."

"I assume the exception would be the Zoo," Taylor replied.

"Among other places," Desk admitted. "There aren't too many areas in the world with light satellite coverage these days, but there are a few. North Korea comes to mind."

"Huh, the more you know, I guess."

"Hey, Desk," Banks said and joined the link. "How is

Taylor doing? When will he reach the area where the bodies were found?"

"Should I say something?" he asked.

"Oh… I didn't realize this was a shared line," the agent said. "Oh, well, how are you doing, McFadden, and what time do you think you'll reach the area where the bodies were found?"

"What, no Taylor? And here I thought we were on a first-name basis all of a sudden."

"Well, we're not. "Now answer the question, McFadden."

"There's no need to get grumpy I'm merely making conversation." He chuckled. "As for how I'm doing… Well, the rain has slowed me somewhat and it is tough terrain, but I've made better time than the people did without a suit. With that said, I'm not really sure how much I'll be able to find out here. It's been days since the bodies were found, and with all the rain and other elements in this corner of the world, there's no telling how long useful evidence will last before it's washed away."

"Well, you never know what you'll find." The agent sounded dismissive. "Besides, you need somewhere to start, and there's no place better than where the monster was last seen."

"Should we get a bet going?" he suggested. "Whether or not it's actually Bigfoot?"

"Goddammit. Will you give it a rest?"

"Oh, would you rather we talk about how often you stay in Vegas to keep an eye on me instead? You know, I'm actually a little surprised you didn't volunteer to come into the forest with me this time. I seem to recall that you like to stick close to me. It would be all romantic and shit. Okay, sure, there's rain and mud, but that doesn't really matter when you're in a mech suit."

"I joined you that one time because I didn't trust you to get the job done," she reminded him caustically. "I've since learned the error of my ways and I know for a fact that there's no better way to hunt monsters than to send a monster after a monster. I trust you now, which is why I stayed behind."

"And yet you're still keeping an eye on me?"

"I'm keeping an eye on Vickie," Banks corrected him.

"Hey, Desk, settle something for me," Taylor said and addressed the third party in their link. "Does Banks keep such a close eye on the other freelancers? Is she this close to the rest of the operatives?"

"Don't answer that," the agent warned.

There was a moment of silence while Desk appeared to try to decide whether she would follow orders or not.

"She does not keep this close an eye on the rest of the task force operatives, no," the woman finally answered in a level tone.

"Dammit, Desk!" Banks snapped.

"Well, don't sound too disappointed," Taylor said. "I'm sure you're only keeping this close an eye on me instead of the others because you don't trust me, isn't that right, Desk?"

"I think it's less about trust and more about curiosity," Desk replied.

"If you say another fucking word, there's nothing in the world that'll save you from me," the agent all but snarled and sounded like she meant it too.

Desk had nothing to say to that, which told him that

she actually believed the special agent's threats. Still, he doubted he would need help from anything to keep him away from Banks' vengeful impulses.

"So, you pursued me, then?" he asked, unable to stop a small grin from spreading across his face. "And why would that be if it's not only about my qualifications? Do tell me the reason. Should I be blushing right now?"

"You should be doing your job right now." She instantly sounded like the consummate professional. "You appear to be approaching the location where the bodies were found. There should be all kinds of things for you to focus on other than the childish teasing you appear to be obsessed with."

"Well, like I told you, there won't be much for me to find. So, I might as well focus on the teasing. Talking mindlessly is like white noise for the brain. You simply let it run on automatic and eventually, it does what it's meant to do and things work."

"And what? You want me to hang around and let you ramble on at me until you find something you can track?"

"Well, unless you have a better plan to work with." He scrutinized his surroundings once more. The area did look vaguely familiar since he had studied the pictures on and off during the entire hike. It had taken him a few hours to get this high up and with little else to do than to try to determine what he had to find.

He should have considered a helicopter, but those fuckers were even smaller than flying tubes.

A couple of landmarks stood out and he realized that he had, in fact, located the first site. There had been five bodies in the trees around him and eleven more deeper into the forest and higher up into the mountains. There wasn't much else to see, exactly as he had predicted. The bodies were gone and all the blood had washed away, and all he was left with was the memories of what had happened.

"I...don't have a better plan, no," Banks admitted. "But you have to realize that it's a shitty plan to merely wait for something to happen while you run that mouth of yours."

"I'd hold off on judging it," he said quickly. The rain that had settled into weak but constant for the entirety of his climb had slowed further to barely a drizzle. That, fortunately, gave him a decent view of his surroundings. "I think I might have an idea."

"What makes you think that?" Banks sounded skeptical.

"I don't know." Taylor moved toward one of the trees closest to him and looked up. "It's not an idea—more of a thing, really."

"A thing?" The agent sounded confused.

"Don't question the thing. It's in progress. The bodies that were found in this location were the farthest from the mountains there to the east, and the other sites seem to lead up toward those same mountains. I can't say it's a path to follow but it's as close to it as possible— And then there's this asshole."

"What asshole?" Banks demanded.

"Can't you see the footage from my HUD?" he asked irritably as he studied the trees carefully.

"I have access to the live footage," Desk pointed out. "Banks doesn't. I don't want to overload the connection by having it stream to two locations at once."

"Well, whatever." He lowered into a crouch and peered

at the ground in front of him. "There are fresh tracks. It looks like a bear's tracks too."

"A bear?" the agent asked. "What kind of bear—a monster bear? Like that one near DC?"

"I don't think so." He examined what he'd found from every angle. "Only a regular fucking bear."

"Do you think it was a regular bear?" she pressed. "If it was, sure, kill it and come back."

"Regular bears do tear into their prey," he pointed out. "But they don't pin them to trees, mostly because that's a waste of energy. Bears in this part of the world need all the calories they can store because they don't eat much of anything during the winter. There are jungle cats that hide carcasses in trees to come back to them later, but they don't impale them on the branches. That's fairly unique to birds. Small birds, too, because the larger ones can carry their prey to their nests up in the mountains."

"Okay, I think I follow your train of thought. Wait…no, I'm lost again. It sounds like you're talking about a small bird that's still somehow big enough to pick a human up and impale it on a tree branch."

"Yeah, I won't lie, I'm a little confused too. So, I'd say you're following my train of thought just fine."

"Honestly? It sounds like you're lost," she snarked.

"Well, I am in the middle of the woods trying to find my trail of breadcrumbs. I'm not sure how I'm supposed to work this one out, but if I keep talking, I'm bound to stumble onto the answer eventually. You see? This is fun, chatting away like we're old friends."

"Trying to solve a mystery together," Banks said. "You make us sound like we're the Scooby-Doo gang."

"Do you think I'm Shaggy or Fred?" Taylor asked.

"You know that Shag is the British word for fucking, right?"

"You're right, Shaggy is a good fit for me. That makes you Daphne, and I guess Desk is Velma."

"I always liked Velma best," Desk said.

"See, it's all coming together. We only need a Fred for Banks to fall head over heels in love with. Daphne and Fred get together, right? Or is that only from the movies?"

"I think Daphne and Fred only had a mutual crush in the animated series," the agent said. "They never actually got together, as I recall. Also, don't we need a Scooby-Doo to be the Scooby-Doo gang?"

"Well, we have Liz, so she can be our Scooby." Taylor stopped abruptly, alerted by a faint shiver that traced up his spine. His path had brought him almost to the mountains now, close enough that he could already see an outcropping of rock that opened into a cave. Cautiously, he proceeded, his senses on high alert. The rain had almost stopped by the time he reached the opening. He wasn't sure what he would find inside, but he had the kind of feeling nagging at the pit of his stomach that told him he wouldn't like whatever it was.

"What did you find?" Banks asked.

"A cave. The bear tracks lead to a cave."

"It sounds like you found your monster."

"Maybe." He inched a little closer to the opening and the motion sensors and night vision kicked in to give him a better view of what was inside. "Maybe not."

It was hard to make out at first, but the bear was definitely in the cave. It didn't extend too deeply or if it did, the bear itself—a grizzly by the looks of it—remained near the lip.

A flicker of movement caught his attention. There wasn't only one bear, he realized, but a cub as well.

Grizzlies didn't like it when people came too close to their cubs and became aggressive, even if the humans didn't try to interact with the little one at all. The mother growled softly but remained beside her offspring. She could see Taylor at the entrance but didn't seem quite sure what to do about him yet.

No, he decided, she knew what she would do. She would stand her ground and protect her baby if he attacked, but she had no plans to do anything else judging by the way she nuzzled and calmed her cub.

"You're afraid," he said softly and took a careful step away from the cave. He had no intention to provoke any kind of reaction from the mother that obviously only wanted to be left alone.

"Who's afraid?" Banks asked.

"The bear. It's hiding inside the cave." Taylor looked around, more confused now than ever. "She's afraid. Now...what on earth would have a four-hundred-and-forty-pound beast so terrified that it will only defend and not attack when cornered?"

"I have a feeling you have an answer to that."

"I don't, unfortunately." His sensors pinged movement from the cliff above the cave. "But I have the distinct feeling that I'm about to."

CHAPTER TWENTY-FOUR

Rocks began to rumble down the cliff face as if something had dislodged them. He imagined that whatever it was had woken up and really didn't like him to stride around in his heavy metal suit.

Calmly and quietly, Taylor backed away from the rocks and rubble that rolled down the mountainside. Faint hints of movement caught his eye at first. It was hard to make out what the beast was and the only thing he could really see was the wings. The massive appendages spanned dozens of feet, almost as large as a small airplane, and fanned and waved like it tried to catch the wind before it took off.

"Oh, you are gorgeous," he said softly and smiled as he looked at the cliff, where the creature peered over the edge and down to where he stood.

"Do you see the monster?" Banks asked. "Repeat, do you have a visual?"

"Yeah," he said softly. "More importantly, I think it has a visual of me right now. Desk, would you mind telling and showing Banks that I'm about to try to kill what looks like a giant fucking pterodactyl?"

"A what?" the agent asked.

"A big, fucking, flying dinosaur!" he roared, spun quickly, and tried to get as far away from the cliff as he could. A thunderous screech issued toward him and the entire forest seemed to shake under the force unleashed when the monster took flight.

"What's with these Zoo monsters looking like dinosaurs, anyway?" he yelled as a rhetorical question to himself rather than for the benefit of anyone listening and hurdled a fallen log. "Well, at least we know what the fuck a grizzly bear is afraid of now, right? Something like that probably makes you feel like a rat trying to escape from a goddamn owl!"

"Are you talking to me?" Banks obviously hadn't grasped the full gravity of the situation.

"No, I'm talking to myself—shit!" He flung himself to the left as the beast swooped and the gargantuan wings flapped hard enough to cause a huge gust through the trees. "Another thing we seldom had to deal with in the Zoo was flying creatures—aside from the fucking locusts, of course, which seemed never-ending. There weren't many other winged mutants around the jungle and nothing this size that I recall personally."

It shrieked defiance at him, unable to dip beneath the tree cover. Instead, it perched on the treetops that groaned beneath its weight and tried to find an angle down. He continued to run and dodged constantly from left to right to make himself a more difficult target.

After a moment, he could almost hear the famed intelligence these creatures were known to have begin to tick in its head and had no doubt that it would find a way to reach him. It wasn't long before it flapped its wings, still grasping the top of one of the trees. The wood creaked and cracked under strain until, with a twist, the creature soared skyward with half the damn tree trapped in its claws.

"Oh shit. Oh shit!" Taylor drew his assault rifle from its place on his back and attempted to target the monster effectively as he pulled the trigger. He couldn't tell if he had even hit the damn mutant. If he had, the bullets didn't seem to do much damage as the monster continued to fly even higher until it simply released the huge section of the tree.

He pulled the launcher up on his shoulder, primed one of the rockets, and fired it. A comforting whoosh saw it on its way and a plume of white smoke trailed it to where it impacted hard with the falling tree. A blast flashed brightly and suddenly, it rained splinters and leaves around him.

A screech of annoyance was the immediate response from the creature and it banked sharply, circled once, and flapped its wings to thrust itself back to the cliff face. Monstrous claws curled around two boulders.

"Well, talk about a one-track mind," he muttered.

He wouldn't be able to reliably destroy the boulders in the air like he had the tree. While he could shoot at the beast itself, there was no tracking mechanism in the rockets themselves. He would have to fire and pray he would hit the target. When something moved that high up and that far away, he definitely wouldn't be able to fire accurately from this distance. And who wanted a random rocket to fall from the sky?

He needed a better solution and he needed it immediately. The boulders fell from the creature's hands, one at time. They spun almost lazily and with impossible accuracy to where he stood.

"Sonofabitch!" he roared and dove to the left as the boulders plummeted at frighteningly high speed now and bulldozed through the trees above him like they were made from paper. They thudded to a stop powerfully enough to shake the ground and buried themselves in the mud that had collected.

"No fucking way." Taylor growled and delivered a string of epithets as he pushed to his feet and looked up. The mutant swooped again with a series of screeches and roars. The force generated by its wings was almost powerful enough to knock him off of his feet without any kind of direct attack.

He raised his assault rifle and fired a couple of rounds at it. He knew they wouldn't actually do much good, but as long as he was able to do something, he could feel better about himself.

At least the two women made no effort to talk anymore. Chatting while he hiked through the forest was all well and good, but when he was engaged in a fight with what he'd come to the damn forest to kill, he didn't need distractions.

The flying beast collected two of the destroyed trees like they weighed nothing, elevated powerfully, and circled in an attempt to find a clean shot. He continued to duck and dart between the trees.

This mutant was a little too smart like it knew he was a threat already and it had to eliminate him. He somehow knew this wasn't a need to kill or eat him as it had the others. It merely wanted him dead and was willing to do almost anything to accomplish that goal.

*I need some fucking ideas here.*

A crazy, thoroughly stupid plan half-formed in his mind, but for it to work, he needed to be somewhere out in the open. Where had it pinned the bodies to the trees? There were clearings in the area that allowed it to reach down and snatch its victims, pull them up, and pin them to the damn branches.

"Oh, I'm so going to regret this," Taylor mumbled. He had to get it close enough for the rockets to be effective, and for that, he needed to draw it in. It had clearly become more and more frustrated with each failed attempt to crush him from afar. He could use the possibility that this would cloud its judgment to his advantage. All he had to do was draw it in so it would believe it had the opportunity to kill him.

His mind made up, he turned and pushed the mech as quickly as it would safely go as he returned downhill, which added to the speed. The beast overhead was more than capable of keeping up. It followed and tried to keep track of his movements, clearly looking for a way to reach him without being tangled in the trees where it already seemed to know it would be killed.

"Why do I always get the smart ones?" he muttered, more to himself than the two women he knew were listening. Zoo monsters were smart in general and maybe these needed to be even more so this far away from the jungle that would have sustained them if they hadn't spawned elsewhere.

He could see a break in the trees not too far ahead, and

so could the mutant. It began to move faster and higher and prepared to dive. Taylor primed one of the rockets in his shoulder for the strike.

All the warning he had was the frantic beeping from the sensors before the crackle of trees breaking him above told him he had made a couple of miscalculations.

"Oh shit!" he shouted as something grasped his midsection and twisted him. The rocket fired wildly and well wide of the monster that now had him clutched in its talons. It pressed down on his arms to hold them in place as it dropped to a heavy landing, its weight pinning him down.

He was much closer to it than he'd ever intended to be, yet the proximity brought encouragement rather than panic. Not many would see it as such, but the lack of a beak —replaced instead by a long line of razor-sharp teeth— meant it had no way to break through his armor.

No direct way, at least, and it appeared to know that and made no effort at all to try those teeth on the suit. All he could feel was the added pressure of the creature on top of him, mostly held off by the armor. Unfortunately, he couldn't move his arms and had no clear shot with the rocket launcher either, not without him being caught in the blast radius.

The wings flapped again. The suit was much heavier than the humans it had lofted before, but it would still make it. With incredible strength, the massive appendages drove the mutant skyward and Taylor's feet lifted off the ground.

It intended to do what eagles did when they couldn't

get through a turtle's shell. The monster would drop him from a great height so the armor cracked.

"Like...fucking...hell," he mumbled and struggled to pull his arms free. The right was pinned helplessly to his side, but the left was a little less constricted. If he could only move it a little more, he had a chance.

They climbed faster and the trees started to move away. Only the tallest were still in sight when his left arm suddenly came free. He gasped with relieved frustration as he reached for the sidearm still at his hip, yanked it clear of its holster, and pressed the muzzle to a foot that held him in an iron hold. Without hesitation, he pulled the trigger.

A surprised screech issued from his captor as the foot released him. He wasn't free, but he primed the rockets in his shoulder—two of them this time. He wouldn't take any goddamn chances.

The second claw released quickly when he pulled the trigger on his handgun again and a moment of vertigo filled him as he hung in the air and waited for gravity to kick in.

In the next moment, he began to fall. He gave himself one second before he launched the rockets. The white plumes clouded his vision for a moment and all he could hear was a loud screech of pain from the mutant before the twin explosions and the distinctive crackle and snap of tree branches breaking.

He met the ground hard enough to knock the breath out of him and immediately looked up. Two blackened holes had replaced the pterodactyl's chest cavity. It tumbled helplessly and its featherless wings caught and ripped on the trees as it finally plunged through to the earth below. The force of impact was so great that the ground shuddered, and he grasped a nearby tree trunk to steady himself, even though he was sprawled prone and wouldn't fall.

He needed a moment. The air was full of smoke, and he had trouble breathing. Maybe he had a cracked rib or his body simply needed time to recover.

"I need to stop taking these jobs." Taylor hadn't meant to say that out loud, but who the fuck cared? Finally, he managed to push into a seated position and stared at the still figure of the monster.

"Taylor?" Banks asked tentatively. "Are…are you alive?"

"I think so. The same can't be said for the big, winged bastard, though."

"Do you think there might be any more?"

"I very much doubt it. There was no nest up in the cliffs that I saw, but maybe Desk can check the footage to make sure—you know, zoom it or something for a closer look."

"I'm on it," Desk said quickly.

He groaned and used the tree to haul himself slowly and carefully to his feet. Honestly, he hoped like hell there weren't others because he sure as fuck did not want to have to face another one or climb the cliff.

"Desk?" the agent said, and he could hear the anxiety and impatience in her tone.

"One second," the other woman responded. "Okay… fortunately, you looked at the cliff long enough to get a good feed I could work with. I've enlarged and enhanced it, and I'm positive there's nothing up there."

"Yeah," he agreed as he peered up toward the cave and could faintly make out a large dark shape at the entrance.

"And momma bear is bringing her baby out. She wouldn't do that if there were another one of these fuckers to worry about."

"That's good enough for me," Banks replied. It sounds like we need a cleanup crew now. Come in for a debrief. Good work, McFadden."

"Yeah, yeah, don't start falling in love with me again," he grumbled.

"I think you are safe from that."

# CHAPTER TWENTY-FIVE

There was nothing more to do other than to move away from the forest location, peel his suit off, and head into the city. Despite his physical conditioning being on par with anything that could be found in the military, he could still feel the dull aches in muscles he never knew that he had. That aside, the pain in his ribs had eased and he assumed he'd escaped with bruising rather than anything actually cracked.

He would definitely be sore in the morning, but in the end, he had killed another monster, made the country a little safer, and walked away with one hell of a payday for his effort. There were worse ways to make a living and he had no desire to rethink his life choices.

Despite that, he would always complain, but that was merely to help his case when he presented the invoices and not because he had a genuine problem with how the jobs had gone down.

Banks' called him on the drive into the city.

"Do you miss me already, Special Agent?" Taylor asked

with a chuckle. "Oww," he finished and clutched his side. Even bruising could be a bitch.

"About as much as I miss having pimples as a teenager," she replied and punctuated it with a derisive snort. "Anyway, I'm processing your invoice now and it should be cleared by the bean counters in the agency soon."

"Really?" He had put in a couple of charges that he doubted he would get, which included the price for a few repairs his suit would need.

"Unless there's something you'd like to add or subtract on your invoice?"

"Nope, I have nothing to change. I'm curious, though, since I expected you guys to contest every charge like an insurance company. You are the government, after all. While you love taking money, you hate giving it up."

"That's a fair comment, but you should know there are plenty of folks in the government who would rather pay their freelancers well and let them get away with a little something here and there rather than play the penny pincher and lose them to corporate interests." She paused for a moment. "You're not trying to get something past me, right?"

"I would never," he said and feigned a southern accent. "The very nerve. How dare you? My honor, ma'am. My honor is insulted, I say!"

"Well, you can go ahead and challenge me to a duel to restore it," she replied with a laugh. "But I'll have you know I'm one hell of a quick draw, so you'll probably end up dead."

"What if I choose swords? Do you know anything about using those?"

"According to the ancient laws of…uh, dueling or whatever, the person who is challenged gets to choose the weapons," she replied smartly. "With that said, do you know anything about using swords?"

"No, but I assume that since I'm bigger and stronger than you, I'd be able to use that to my advantage since you don't know either. But yeah, you'd get to pick the weapons. Question—can I wear one of my suits during the duel?"

"Well, we can establish that kind of shit when you get to a bar and we have a drink to celebrate a job well done. I'll text you the address."

"I'll be there but I need to find a hotel and take a shower first. I don't know if you know anything about hanging out for extended periods in a mech suit but let me tell you that the smell does indeed get funky. I'll maybe get there in twenty minutes—or thirty, depending on how easy it is to find a hotel in the area."

"I'll see you then." She hung up and he continued into the city of Portland. The bar where she had chosen to meet him was a local dive and not entirely interesting but not terrible either. It seemed the perfect place that enjoyed a stream of regulars who would come in every night for a drink or a binge and stagger to their nearby homes.

At least, that was what it looked like from the online reviews, and who was he to question those?

"Still, a drink is a drink," he said to himself as he pulled into the underground parking garage of the hotel he'd chosen.

He had no intention to stay in the city for longer than a night since he needed to return to the shop to help Bobby and Vickie get their orders out in time. Check-in was a simple process and he took the keycard, headed to the room for a quick shower, and left. The bar was within walking distance from the hotel, which had been a primary motivation when he'd chosen it. He wouldn't have to spend extra on a cab.

The establishment looked almost like it had been described. An older gentleman shared bar duty with a younger trainee and both poured drinks that seemed to be exclusively either neat whiskey or beer from a bottle or a tap. Those who asked for complex cocktails would get a sour look from them, which perhaps explained the two predominant choices.

The waitress seemed a little nicer and smiled and waved at the regulars she recognized. She probably lived mostly on the tips she received, while the other two had a living wage. From what he saw, no one could claim it had a huge turnover, and they probably made only enough to keep the doors open and everyone paid.

Still, it did have a kind of comfortable, lived-in atmosphere that made him feel at home. He eased his jacket off, careful to move slowly to protect his bruised ribs, and hung it over his arm as he joined Banks among the small group of patrons. The heat of the shower had eased some of the pain so he assumed it wasn't all that serious, but it was still tender.

"It's nice that you could make it," she said as he took his seat across from her. "I thought you would have wanted to have an early night and get an early start tomorrow."

"The night's still young, so I can still do that. But I might as well have a drink and take in the local scene of the Pacific Northwest. And—don't take this the wrong way—but you're actually not that bad as a drinking buddy."

"How am I supposed to take that the wrong way?" she asked and took a sip of her drink.

"You could have assumed I was hitting on you, said something along the lines of 'ew, no' and walked away," he replied smoothly as his own beer arrived. "You have to admit it is a fairly likely scenario."

"Sure, it's not that unlikely," she replied with a shrug. "With that said, though, you shouldn't take it the wrong way when I say you're a fun drinking buddy too. And I'd say that the way for you to take it the wrong way would be to say I was hitting on you and make some kind of lewd remark that would make me say 'ew, no' and walk away. Maybe after splashing this beer in your face."

"Fair enough." He chuckled. "Can I ask you something?"

"Only if I have the option to not answer," she countered smoothly.

"Why is it that you pay so much more attention to me than to the other members of this task force? It's not because you think I need the help. You've seen my credentials and if you didn't believe them, you've seen what I can do with your own two eyes. You have no reason to doubt me. So why hover?"

The agent shrugged and seemed to try to decide what to say. "I'm not really sure. You have to understand that this task force is kind of my baby. I wasn't the one who came up with it, but when the offer came my way, I took it because I believed I could pull this shit off. As yet, the people I've hired as freelancers have been the epitome of low risk and low reward, and while people have watched every move I've made, I've managed to keep them at bay. When you were brought in, I needed to pull too many strings and owe an astronomical number of favors to get you on my team. You were a considerable risk on my part so I'm only…making sure that my investment is sound."

"Okay, I can live with that," he said with a firm nod. "But let me explain again. You don't need to keep your eyes on me all the time. I know what I'm doing, so if you'd rather keep an eye on the other folks you're working with, that might be time better spent."

"I'm not wholly convinced." She shook her head. "But keep up the work you've been doing, and I will be."

"Fine. I'll leave it at that then," he agreed, raised his glass, and clinked it with hers.

He noted that her gaze shifted to the door as he took a sip and something akin to panic crossed her face before she quickly regained control of herself. She looked at her drink, not to take a sip but to think about what to do next.

What could have her this unsettled?

Taylor turned when a small group arrived and three young women and a man stepped through the entrance of the bar. They didn't appear to be regulars, but the waitress was quick to greet them, all smiles, and told them to take a booth and that their orders would come along shortly.

Banks' gaze was focused on one woman who stood ahead of the others and scanned the room like she was looking for someone—his companion, he assumed.

The special agent was quick to gain her feet when the woman caught sight of her and damn near jogged over to the door and gestured for her to come closer. He turned and leaned in a little to hear what they were saying.

"What are you doing here, Jennie?" she asked, her voice heated, and she sounded a little annoyed.

"Hey, sis, it's nice to see you again. It's been a while," Jennie answered with a smile. "That's how you're supposed to greet a sister you haven't seen lately in case you need some pointers."

"Hey, sis, it's nice to see you again. It's been a while," Banks repeated woodenly. "Now, what the hell are you doing here?"

"Well, I heard you were in town and more importantly, I heard he was in town, so I thought I might come over and see how you two are getting along. Oh, and I brought some friends, so don't feel like you need to hang out around us all the time."

"I...dammit." Banks growled in frustration. "I told you to stay away. Find someone you like and spend time with him or her. Preferably someone with a job who's boring and makes a ton of money like maybe a banker or something. Stop chasing after tail that'll only get you in trouble."

"I appreciate you looking out for me," the other woman responded. "But you have to realize I'm my own person and you don't get to tell me what to do."

"I know." She raised a hand to her forehead. "I only wish you would take what I have to say seriously."

"I do. But I don't need to follow your every instruction. I'll hang out with my friends now, but it would be nice if you came over to share a drink with us. I think you know them."

"Yeah, I do. I don't think I remember their names, though."

"I'll text them to you." Jennie waved. "Later, sis."

Taylor was quick to realize that the conversation was wrapping up and turned in his seat before Banks returned and took her seat across the table.

"Who was that?" he asked. The conversation revealed that the woman in question was her sister, whom she had mentioned was a scientist who had spent some time in the Zoo. He was curious about whether the special agent would share that information with him.

"Oh, yeah, an acquaintance of mine," she said blandly. "Beeswax.

"First name Nunya."

"What is that—Italian?" he asked with a small grin and turned to face toward the seats he couldn't see. "Otherwise, her parents must have hated her."

# CHAPTER TWENTY-SIX

B obby sighed.

It was easy enough to open the shop without Taylor there and he honestly didn't mind doing it. The alarm system had been transferred to him like it usually was when his boss made one of his out of town trips. He would receive the alerts when he arrived and nothing would happen until he was already inside and able to shut the system down for the day.

The basics of it were no problem at all. What was annoying, however, was that his phone buzzed with virtually step he took. It was as if Taylor had wanted to know every move that any intruder might make and had set the system so he would be alerted every inch along the way.

It was like a damned Police song—the rock group, not the law officers.

While it made sense in a situation where their security was breached, it was still beyond frustrating. He especially hated that he had to deal with it when he arrived at the shop for the start of what promised to be a long day's work.

Maybe that was why Taylor always had the grid shut down before he arrived. Right now, he knew he'd arrived to trigger everything so simply ignored the warnings.

He unlocked the door, pulled it up, and stepped inside. Vickie was already hard at work on the pieces he had assigned to her. These only needed the simple electronics repaired, something she already knew a thing or two about, but they still had to be fixed before they could put the third suit together and ship it out.

"Morning, Bobby," she said, entirely focused on her work. "I hope you don't mind but I was up early and decided to get some of this done before you got in."

"Why would I mind?" he asked and placed his customary delivery of coffee and donuts on the table to be consumed at their leisure.

"I don't know…I assumed you and Sir Tay-Tay would prefer to keep an eye on my work to make sure I don't burn anything out." She delivered this in a slightly teasing tone but still didn't look up from what she was busy with.

"Hell, I ain't no helicopter parent," he said with a deep chuckle and took a bite from one of the donuts. "With me, it's sink or swim. If you get it wrong and burn something out, that piece will come out of your paycheck."

"Fair enough," she conceded. "But don't think I'll make a shit-load of mistakes simply to save you guys money."

"It's not likely to happen," Bobby grumbled. "Taylor probably wouldn't charge you the five hundred bucks it would take to replace a data relay."

"That's sweet, I suppose. But I guess I could still afford it. He is letting me live here rent-free, after all."

"And how's that working out for you?" The man was genuinely curious.

"Like he said, it's better than living on the street, and the Wi-Fi is actually downright decent. Aside from that, though, it's definitely more of a temporary situation, and I'm already looking into getting a place of my own. I have the feeling he likes his privacy too, so he'll be happy to see me gone."

That was a fairly sound assumption.

Taylor did like his privacy, and while he was unlikely to voice any kind of complaint, Bungees knew the man well enough to realize that he would be anxious to have the place to himself once more. It was why he had elected to live in the strip mall instead of finding a place actually suited to…normal humans.

It wasn't like he couldn't afford a place of his own.

The sound of tires over concrete brought his eyes up from his coffee and toward the garage door he'd neglected to close. It wasn't like they expected any visitors, but Taylor had insisted that they keep the place locked down given the possible dangers they might face.

When the SUV pulled up in front of the garage door and two men exited, both toting firearms, he realized that his boss might not have been paranoid.

Or maybe he was, but that didn't mean that there weren't people out to get him. He turned toward his shotgun.

"Now, now—no need to get fussy," one of the men said and aimed his weapon at Bobby's head with calm precision. He seemed comfortable with the weapon but still far from a consummate professional, which made Bobby a little nervous. Top-notch pros were less likely to react in stupid ways. "We're not here for either of you, strictly speaking. Although, having said that, we won't think twice about giving your brains a new access to oxygen if you try anything funny. So, why don't you move away from those tables, nice and slow, and no one will get hurt, understood?"

The second man aimed his weapon at Vickie, whose hands were already up. They moved away from the furniture, which allowed the second man to approach them and run a quick frisk for weapons.

"Hey, hands off the goods," Vickie protested with no response from the gunman.

"They're unarmed," the man said finally and stepped away to join his friend. A bandage peeped out from inside his shirt.

"You're the dumbasses who tried to pick a gunfight," Bobby noted, more for Vickie's benefit than for that of the two men.

"No shit, Sherlock," the first man said. "Which means we're here for your boss, not you, so if you'll go ahead and stay fucking still, no one will be hurt. Well, except for him. Now move outside, keep your hands on your heads, and face the SUV while my partner here picks your boss up for a little one-on-one time. How does that sound to you?"

"Are you really asking or merely playing the nice guy to reduce the possibility of one of us resisting?" Bungees asked to draw the attention toward himself and away from Vickie.

"Well, I tried to be a nice guy so the reasons are moot." The captives moved to the SUV and faced it with their hands above their heads as the second one moved through the strip mall.

The building was large, but given that it was mostly abandoned, it didn't take long for him to return.

"He's not here," he said.

"And you looked everywhere?" his partner asked.

"No, I peeked into every room and asked him politely to step forward." His tone had a sharp and sarcastic edge.

"You—Jet Li-looking asshole," the first man called. "Where's your boss?"

"How the fuck should I know?" he asked and shrugged. It wasn't a lie, technically. Taylor had said he was on his way back, which meant he could be anywhere between Portland and Vegas by this point.

"Shit. Well, plan B it is, then. You two"—he waved his gun—"get in the car. We'll go for a little ride."

"Do you expect us to simply go along with this?" Bobby asked and gasped when something hard and metal struck him in the kidney. He doubled over and fumbled to rub the place on his back where he had been struck when he suddenly found it difficult to breathe.

"Your compliance really isn't a concern," the second man said. "Now get in the fucking car."

"Fuck you, asshole!" Vickie snapped, her cheeks pink with indignation.

"You don't want any of what I am right now," the assailant retorted and pressed the barrel of his pistol to her head. "Now, unless you want to explain to flight attendants why you walk with crutches for the rest of your life…" He shoved her head with the point of his gun. "Get in the fucking car—now!"

An early start had obviously been a good idea, of course, but as the miles dragged on, Taylor wondered if he didn't simply want to change his mind about this no-flying business, even though it would mean confronting his phobia on a regular basis. It was worth consideration, at least until Liz was fixed or until Bobby could install a compatible AI into the new truck.

Maybe they could take the one in Liz out, put it in the new one, and replace it when she was fixed.

Admittedly, they would then have to reprogram the device to a new vehicle twice, but it had to be better than having to actually drive everywhere Banks needed him to be. He really did miss the freedom and relaxation the AI brought to the process.

The music helped, but in the end, listening to the random shit people played on the radio lost appeal almost as quickly as listening to the pre-selected songs from his own playlist on repeat.

But, when the early start stretched toward a later finish, he knew he would reach the shop before nightfall. There was no way he would subject himself to a night in another crummy motel. While his own abode wasn't much better than the average motel, it was still his and the Wi-Fi was at least functional.

Provided that Vickie didn't decide to download something and hog all the bandwidth.

The sun was only starting to set when he managed to reach Vegas in record time. Or better time than his trip up to Portland anyway, and the traffic into the city was much lighter than he'd experienced when heading out. It wasn't long before he turned into the strip mall. Usually, this would have transferred the security programs from Bobby's phone to his, and as he could see none of it, he assumed his friend was working late.

Or maybe Vickie needed access to the building's security.

It wasn't something he would have done, but she was the one who was living in the building and if she wanted to have people in while was away, that was her call.

His eyes narrowed as he turned into the back and saw the garage door still open and most of the lights on with no one in the shop. It wasn't unrealistic for them to perhaps leave things as they were for a quick trip to the bathroom, but he would still give them a piece of his mind for it.

Anyone could have waltzed in and taken hundreds of thousands of dollars' worth of merchandise that simply sat out in the open.

Taylor slid out of the vehicle, pulled his phone out of his pocket, and pressed the quick-dial for Vickie's phone. She would definitely hear his complaint about this. Bobby as well.

He looked around, a little startled when the girl's ringtone played softly in the background. She wasn't the kind to leave her phone anywhere, paranoid type that she was, and yet there it was on the floor under one of their worktables.

"Oh...that is not good," he muttered and ducked under

the table to retrieve the device. It turned on automatically and immediately opened to a web link that evidently led to a location on a map.

"Huh. I would have thought she would at least password-protect this," he said softly as he opened the link and followed it to the map, on which a bright red dot pinged just outside of Vegas.

The caption on the bright red dot read, *I'm here, moron.*

"Yeah. This is really not good," Taylor grumbled and turned his attention to the room. There was no sign of where Bobby might be, so his second step was to call the man to make sure he was safe.

"Of course—straight to voice mail. I assume they destroyed your phone." He shook his head as he finally accepted the suspicion of foul play as fact. The message left by Vickie told him where she was, but he didn't know how she managed to transmit her position if she didn't have her phone.

Still, she only called him a moron when she was serious, and this seemed to be about as serious as she could ever get. Somehow, she'd found a way to make sure he knew where she was.

He wouldn't be able to do this alone, he realized. Much as he hated to admit it, he needed help. Worse, he needed the help of someone who was the absolutely last person he wanted to fill in on this particular situation.

"Special Agent?" he said when the line was picked up. "I'm afraid I'll need your help."

"Do you miss me already, Taylor?" Banks asked and laughed.

He would have appreciated the irony of the situation

any other time, but he shook his head. "I really didn't want to make this call, but I assumed you'd want to know that it looks like Bobby and Vickie are missing. And unless they eloped for some reason—I wouldn't judge, Bobby is an absolute catch—they've gone missing. Vickie left her phone in the shop with a link that opened to display her location."

A moment of silence passed and he gave her time to think things through. "I'll catch a plane and will be there in a couple of hours."

"There's no need to involve the FBI, except maybe Desk," he said. "I merely need to make sure they're in trouble before I head in as the cavalry."

"I'm coming to Vegas," she insisted.

"That's really not—"

"Vickie is my cousin, Taylor," she said firmly.

"Oh." He grunted and ended his protest. "Well then, welcome to the team, Special Agent Banks."

# CHAPTER TWENTY-SEVEN

The woman hadn't been kidding when she'd said she would be there in a couple of hours. Taylor had to assume she had wangled a flight with some of her FBI connections since he thought it took far longer than that to get through security at the airport.

But no, only two and a half hours passed before Banks arrived. She pulled up in one of her SUVs, spilled out of the vehicle, and looked like she was about to kick up a storm.

"First of all, I have no idea how this happened," he said in anticipation of her line of questioning. "I was in Portland with you, and Bobby was supposed to keep an eye on her. I'm still trying to work out what happened."

She nodded. "Don't worry. I've put off yelling at you until Vickie is safe. What do you know?"

"I checked the security tapes, and it looks like the guys who took a shot at me came back." He pulled his laptop up and showed her the footage. "They might have come looking for me, but I can't be sure. Maybe they were actually there for Vickie from the beginning. She said people might come after her because of what she did. Which…is what exactly?"

"Which is not relevant. These aren't the ones who would target her," the agent said quickly. "I'm reasonably sure they were hired to deal with you, though, and decided to take some leverage when they couldn't find you."

"Right." He couldn't fault her logic, and she knew the girl's situation way better than he did, obviously. "Vickie left her phone behind. It wasn't locked when I picked it up and it opened to a link."

He showed that to her as well and she tilted her head and stared at the caption under the red blinking light.

"My guess is that I'm the moron in question." He shrugged and managed a half-hearted grin.

"Well, that sounds about right. Have they contacted you yet or—"

Her voice cut off when his phone rang. They both looked at it and he scowled at the unregistered number.

"Don't worry. I already told Desk to run traces on all the calls to or from your phone," Banks assured him. "Pick up."

Taylor did as he was told and pressed the button to put it on speakerphone.

"May I assume that I'm speaking to Taylor McFadden?" a man said over the line.

"Sure, go ahead. I have no idea who you are, though."

"You might have a clue since you put a bullet in me not that long ago. That was nice shooting, by the way. It seems like you've had the relevant training."

"You know us Americans and our shooting ranges," he agreed blandly, although anger coiled within him.

"Listen up," the man snapped. "I assuming you want to see your friends again, so you know the drill. I'll give you a list of demands and you'll comply without involving the cops or the feds. If you do, everyone goes home happy. Fortunately for you, the list will be short and sweet. It starts with you getting ready to meet us in person tomorrow morning."

"How am I supposed to get ready?"

"Stay near your phone for one, and in a car for two. You'll do a little driving. I'll send you the coordinates tomorrow morning at an unspecified time, and you'll have an hour to meet us. I've already texted you a proof of life picture, so all you need to do is stay on your toes and you'll hear from us soon."

He checked his phone and, sure enough, a picture with both Bobby and Vickie holding a newspaper from that morning waited in his inbox.

"This isn't your first kidnapping, is it?" he asked. Or maybe they watched too many action series. It almost seemed cliché enough to appeal to the two men, who hadn't yet shown any indication that they might be remotely top-league.

"Wait by your phone, Mr. McFadden, and be ready to move alone when we give the instruction." The man hung up.

"Did you pick anything up?" Banks asked.

"Nothing that we didn't already know," he said. "At least we have it confirmed that they have Bobby and Vickie and they're being kept alive. It's a start, anyway. Another step would be if Desk was able to trace the call."

"Why?" she asked and gestured at the girl's phone.

"Because if she managed to establish a location, we can confirm that the beacon on that phone is actually Vickie." His phone rang again from another unknown number.

This time, he already knew who it was, accepted the call, and set it on speaker. "Desk, you have me and Banks on the line."

"Hello again, Agent Banks," the woman said in a surprisingly calm voice. "How are you feeling?"

"I'm still a little frayed," Banks replied honestly. "Do you have anything for us?"

"I have a location, which I've sent to you right now."

"Can you coordinate it with a location that's already on Vickie's phone?" he asked. "I'll send you the link now."

There was a pause while she followed the link he texted to her. "Yep, it's the same place. And the link is actually to a track my 'insert name here' in Vickie's name. She must have some kind of a tracking device on her body or clothes, one her captors haven't found."

"Well, now we do have something." He took a slow, deep breath. "We know they'll keep them alive at least until tomorrow morning and that they don't know we have a way to track them."

"And that knowledge will definitely help us." The agent looked a little less stressed now that she had actual information to focus on. "Now to decide what to do next."

"Well, among other things, this lets us know where they want to make an exchange, which means we can get there earlier than the hour they have planned. What makes the most sense might be to arrange a little trap of our own."

"Oh…I like that." Her smile was evil.

"Yes, I thought you might."

The morning in the desert was inevitably chilly. Some people tended to forget about that, and as the sun started to come up, Jon began to regret not having brought a warmer jacket as they waited outside the city for McFadden to drive out to meet them.

"Did you send the text?" he asked as Mike came around their SUV.

"Yep. He should be on his way right now." His partner looked at their hostages. "We might have wanted to give him less time, though. I'm freezing my nuts off out here."

"I know the feeling, but no, it had to be an hour. We calculated that carefully to give him enough time to reach us while making sure he doesn't have time to plan any nasty surprises along the way."

"What will you do when he gets here?" the all but bald girl asked and looked like she shivered as much as they did.

"Nothing too bad," Mike said. "None of this is personal. We're merely trying to persuade your boss to pay what he owes. We're not the mob, after all."

His partner shrugged. "Well, the guy paying us is the mob and McFadden needs to know that. He's kicking against the family here, and they don't take shit from anyone. That's why they hired outsiders like us who know the job, but that doesn't mean we need to let things devolve into brutality. That's just savagery."

"Yeah, because kidnapping is the epitome of civilized," the man retorted and flexed his arms against the plastic bindings that held him secure.

"Hey, it was either this or torch the building with you

guys in there," Jon snapped. "The boss wanted us to send a message and that is exactly what we will do, end of story. McFadden will walk out of here with only a couple of holes in his kneecaps or maybe a few broken fingers if he's nice and shows a new appreciation for the hard work extortionists do in his area. He will be a little wiser and yet still walk."

"Well, technically, with crutches and a fair amount of pain," Mike clarified.

"He was the one who decided to be an ass and ignore the reality of the situation, so I guess he should have expected it."

The large man with his hands secured behind his back merely rolled his eyes and leaned against the wheel of the SUV. Mike had wanted to leave them in the car where it was warm, but his partner didn't want to risk the possibility that they might somehow manage to free themselves and throw a wrench into the works. They didn't need that right now, so the two hostages were seated outside in the cold with their captors.

Not for long, though, if all went well.

"So, have we officially decided to shoot him in the knees?" Mike was curious.

"Only if he's troublesome," Jon replied. "There's no need to waste bullets if we don't have to, right? If we give him something to remember us by, we're all good."

"I don't know," Vickie said. "Kidnapping us and messing with his business is bound to make Taylor incredibly pissed off."

"In that case, he'll get a couple more bullets to the knees, a huge hospital bill, and a permanent limp." Mike gestured with the pistol in his hand. "All of this could have been avoided if he had come to work yesterday. We could have done the business there, extracted his promise to pay our boss his price, and that would have been that. But no, he needed to take a personal day and drag this whole job out."

"Not that I'm too bothered. We'll bill the client for all the extra trouble," his partner stated irritably.

The two hostages didn't have much to say beyond that, which gave the kidnappers nothing else to do while the minutes ticked by. The extended silence made the wait seem like forever.

Jon glanced continually at his watch, half-afraid that they might be running late. He didn't want to have to make a point—although he knew it was sometimes necessary to show that they were serious—but he would prefer to keep things clean and tidy. The kidnapping had been yet another spontaneous decision and while it wasn't necessarily a bad one, it honestly wasn't something either he or his partner had much experience with.

Still, it was something to consider for the future. If they wanted to make it in this industry, they would need to up their game to include a wider repertoire. Kidnapping wasn't exactly a rare occurrence, although he'd never personally been asked to do it. So yes, while this was something of an irritating and unexpected development, it had potential as a learning curve. If he looked at it in that light, he wasn't above putting a few bullets in the large man to let McFadden know they meant business.

Killing the girl would only piss him off more and would therefore be detrimental to their cause. There really was no need for bloodshed aside from what McFadden himself owed—which wasn't actually that much, given the degree of trouble he'd caused the local mafia.

"We have incoming," Mike said and gestured with his gun to a cloud of dust raised by what seemed to be someone driving across the desert toward them.

Jon checked his watch. "He's ten minutes early. The idiot must have run a few red lights to get here. He's in something of a hurry, isn't he?"

"I'd be too if I was trying to save my friends," his partner said with a shrug. "Let's not overthink this. Keep it simple, get everything done, and we'll be home before dinner. Maybe we can do Benihana's next month?"

He nodded, a little distracted by the four-by-four that stopped some twenty yards from where they were parked. McFadden didn't want to give them any cause to be anxious, which was good. He clearly worked with a level head and had no intention to make trouble.

The driver's door opened and their quarry stepped out. He kept his hands raised and his movements smooth and deliberate.

"Who should I aim my gun at?" Mike asked in a whisper.

"At the girl, dumbass," Jon replied. "That way, there's a better chance that he won't want to cause any trouble."

His partner nodded and complied as McFadden walked slowly to where they stood, stopped about halfway between his car and theirs, and kept his hands raised. He had expected the cold from the looks of it and appeared to have dressed in layers with a biker jacket outermost

It was a nice jacket too. It would be a shame to get blood on it.

"It's nice to see you're taking us seriously, Mr. McFadden." Jon spoke loudly enough but almost conversationally. "We do appreciate you coming alone. You have to understand that it's in everyone's best interest to finish this quickly and with minimal fuss. I do have to say that you probably won't make that biker gang meeting you're dressed for."

"You're a funny guy," McFadden replied, his voice laced with sarcasm. "How will we do this, then? You never did say what you wanted to meet me out here for or the reason why you kidnapped my friends and left the property wide open. That was rude and dangerous, especially in that neighborhood. How am I supposed to pay anyone if all my shit gets stolen?"

"Well, we were a little too busy to care about how you run your business," he answered. "Of course, if you really cared about that, you would have simply paid the bill for insurance like a regular person and everyone would have been happy."

"What can I say? I don't do well with extortionists. It's simply not in me."

"I was afraid you'd say that," Jon said. "Since it is me who will have to give you an attitude adjustment."

He really didn't want to do this—it was one thing running drive-bys, "liberating" a stranger's possessions, or conducting various other operations that did not require too much close-up and personal beyond a little thuggery. But from the look McFadden gave him, a simple breaking of the fingers wouldn't do it. Well, he'd wanted to expand his repertoire and there was no time like the present to plunge into the deep end.

With what he thought was admirable calm, he raised his pistol, aimed it at the man's knees, and pulled the trigger twice.

He stared in shock when not only did the man not even move, it seemed as though the bullets had ricocheted into the ground beside him.

# CHAPTER TWENTY-EIGHT

He couldn't help flinching a little when the gun went off. It was loud and the emptiness of the desert made the crack seem only that much louder. He also felt the impact around his knee area, which confirmed that the man was a fairly decent shot.

Taylor already knew that, having squared off against him before. However, his intention was not to enter into a gunfight with the man. No, what he had in mind was much closer and one hell of a lot more intimate.

A moment of confusion crossed the kidnapper's face as he tried to make out what had happened. It was the kind of second he needed to take advantage of.

"Surprise, motherfucker!" he roared, not only for his benefit as he pushed toward the man who now inspected his gun as if he thought it might have misfired.

They had been able to track the kidnappers thanks to Vickie's tricks, which allowed them to prepare for the situation before they had even received the text. Banks had set up in the distance, having armed herself with a sniper rifle she was cleared and trained to use. It wasn't something she had brought up with him before, but it was the perfect solution.

Not that she needed to tell him everything. He wasn't her keeper, after all.

She would wait for her shot behind him, and he had yelled the chosen codeword for when shit would go down.

That moment was now, and while he disabled the guy who liked the sound of his own voice, she needed to make sure his partner didn't get too excited and take any shots.

Thankfully, the man swung his gun away from where it aimed at Bobby and Vickie, who were seated on the ground, their hands behind their backs, and pressed against the wheel of the kidnappers' vehicle. A couple of rounds pinged off Taylor's chest and deflected away from his exposed head and into the sand behind him.

Not coming with a helmet had been a risk but was one he'd needed to take. There was no way they would let him approach wearing the helmet that came with Bobby's hybridized mech suit.

Taylor moved to close the distance between himself and his adversaries far more rapidly than they thought he could. The shock was apparent in their eyes when he reached the mouthy one before his target fully registered his approach. He darted his hand forward to grasp the hand that held the pistol, squeezed hard, and twisted the weapon free before he tossed it aside.

"Fuck!" the man shouted and stretched to reach down to his ankle, possibly for a knife or sidearm in a holster. All he found was a knee to the face, which drove him back a couple of steps as his attacker followed and held him firmly to keep him between him and his comrade's line of fire.

"Any fucking time now!" Taylor shouted to Banks, who took her time in choosing her shots. He would have to move and risk taking a couple more rounds to center mass in an effort to tackle the uninjured man against his own SUV.

A small puff of dust lifted from the second man's clothes and he uttered a groan that sounded like he'd had the wind punched out of him. The kidnapper staggered a couple of steps before he jerked against SUV and fell with a grunt.

A quarter of a second later, the crack of the rifle was heard.

Taylor nodded in satisfaction and let the first man drop, clutching his nose and groaning in pain. With both kidnappers disabled, he picked up the weapon he'd tossed aside and snagged the revolver strapped around the man's ankle before he moved over to inspect the condition of the second man.

Another groan and the lack of any blood spray told him that Banks' target wore body armor and was still alive. Fortunately, he wouldn't get up for a dance session anytime soon.

"How did you know he wore body armor?" Taylor asked and kicked the gun the kidnapper had dropped out of reach.

"I didn't." The agent sounded annoyed. "I'll be right over, assuming you have the situation handled?"

"Yeah, I'll make sure there aren't any more surprises waiting for us." He studied the two men, unsure of which one had it worse. Even with a smaller caliber bullet, a hit in the chest while wearing body armor still felt like getting hit by a car. He knew that much from personal experience.

The other man dealt with what looked like a broken nose and possibly a concussion too. Both deserved what they'd received, to his mind. Once he was sure they weren't packing more weapons, he moved over to where his friends waited.

"You took your damn time," Vickie said with a small smirk as Taylor pulled a knife out and cut the plastic around their wrists and ankles.

"Sorry. I couldn't decide what to wear," he replied honestly.

"Sure," Bobby grumbled, pushed up from the ground, and stretched before he rubbed the feeling back into where the bindings had dug into him. "How did you find us quickly enough to set up a sniper nest?"

"That's on this one here." Taylor helped Vickie stand. "We were able to track her thanks to her dropping her phone, which let us keep up with you guys on the road. It was delicate work but wouldn't have been possible without quick thinking, squirt."

"I only did my job, boss," she said.

"Where did you hide the tracking device anyway?" he asked. "I have to imagine they would search you for shit like that."

"You'd be right. But most people tend to ignore my piercings. My nose stud has a small transmitter implanted. Like I said, I have people who want me dead or gone and I don't want to make it too easy for them to accomplish that."

"Well, it was good thinking. Although…yeah, I don't think Banks will ever forgive me for letting you out of my sight."

"She's the one who called you away," she pointed out and scowled at her captor, who still nursed a very, very painful chest.

"That's true, but I'm sure she won't see it that way." He looked up as Banks jogged over. She had reached them surprisingly quickly, given that she'd set up about two hundred and fifty yards away from where they now stood and carried her rifle.

"How are you?" the agent asked, a little out of breath. "Are you hurt? Fucking hell, I knew I shouldn't have let you out of my sight."

"I'm fine too, by the way," Bobby interjected.

"I don't really care about you," the woman said bluntly and he laughed.

"It's nice to see you again too, Special Agent," he said.

"I'm fine," Vickie said. "And if you take me out of the shop, I swear I'll run away and stick it out with them anyway."

"We'll talk about that later," Banks said. She turned her attention to the two men they'd overpowered.

Taylor moved over to where the first man sprawled a short distance away, grasped him by the collar, and hauled him roughly to shove him beside his partner.

"What will we do about these two?" he asked.

Banks shrugged, her expression hard. "They can choose between having their skulls crushed or heading out on the next flight to the Zoo. I'm feeling reasonable."

"How about you go fuck yourself instead?" the first man asked from behind his broken nose.

Taylor scowled at him and raised his hand to give him a smack across the face but stopped after a couple of inept whirs of motion from his suit. Without an HUD, he'd needed to calibrate the damn thing by touch and there were some issues to deal with still.

The man laughed, which prompted him to pick up the pistol the kidnapper had dropped and shoot him in the knee.

His scream of pain carried into the dry air of the desert, not that there was anyone within ten miles to hear him.

"Now that'll cost you your life in the Zoo," he told the man with a chuckle. "That's assuming you don't have seriously mad hopping skills."

"Well, I think we need to get clear of the area," Banks said. "I don't know if anyone might have heard the gunfire or not. Taylor, do you want to take these two in your four-by-four and I'll drive their SUV with Vickie and Bobby?"

"Fuck no," he said vehemently. "That's a new car and if they bleed on the leather, you might have to deal with them being shot. You take Vickie in my car and I'll take Tweedledee and Tweedledum-ass in their SUV. Let me know where you need them to be dropped off. Bungees, do you mind helping me?"

"No problem," his friend said with a small grin and cracked his knuckles.

"I'll text you the details," Banks said. "Come on, Vickie."

# CHAPTER TWENTY-NINE

"So, you'll keep working with us?" Taylor asked as they exited Jackson's.

It wasn't that late but still the kind of hour that prompted Taylor to contemplate a late day tomorrow or maybe even simply giving the two the morning off.

They had earned it, having finished off the five mech suits they had to repair with a day to spare before their next shipment came in. They could have the morning off and perhaps some of the afternoon too.

"I eventually got Niki to agree that your property was basically the safest place in the city for me," Vickie said. She seemed to stagger a little, and he placed a hand on her shoulder to steady her. "You built a damn fortress in there, so even though there were mistakes made, I'll stick it out with you two losers. She will keep a much closer eye on what we're doing, but other than that, things should be about the same."

"So, what—will she move into the strip mall with us?"

"What's that supposed to mean?"

"You do know she's practically lived in Vegas since you started working with us, right?"

"No, but that doesn't surprise me," the woman said with a shrug. "Even though we're only cousins, she's always been more like the big sister I never had and kind of wanted, but not really."

"Well, she cares about you a ton, and that's something, I guess," Taylor said. "Not like there are too many people in the world who care for folks enough to help them like Banks did you."

"I guess you're right." She pulled the door open and stepped out into the parking lot. "Still, having her looking over my shoulder can be a pain, honestly."

"I know how you feel. I'm fairly sure she wants to keep an eye on me too. She said something about me being an investment when it came to her task force and wanting to make sure it paid off or something."

"Sure, that's what she says. But it sounds more like she wants to keep an eye on you for other possibly nefarious reasons."

"And I'm sure you're not using nefarious right," Taylor said with a shrug. "I don't really care, though. She's a good enough agent, partner, and even sometimes drinking partner, but there's nothing else going on there."

"What are you talking about?" Bobby asked.

"There is no chemistry at all," he explained. "Only some light chit-chat here and there but there's nothing more to make of that."

"Sure, keep saying that," Vickie said. "You might actually believe it one day."

"Yeah, so what kind of trouble did you get into that might have had you shipped out to the Zoo?" he asked.

"None of your business, that's what," she replied quickly.

"Oh, well, I've heard that one thrown at me fairly often before." He chuckled. "But there's no reason for you to be fussy about it. I'm only saying that since she pulled you out of a tight situation, you might be wholly biased in your views."

"What the hell is that supposed to mean?"

"Nothing. Ignore me. I'm a little wasted."

They were interrupted when another group exited the bar behind them, laughing loudly and generally making a racket while Marcus the bouncer eyed them closely. Taylor wondered how close the man had been to throwing them out before they decided to leave of their own accord.

"Hey, big guy, I wouldn't bother with that one," one of the men shouted and strolled over to where Taylor, Bobby, and Vickie stood. "With that kind of haircut, you have to know you're dealing with a Dina van Dyke situation here."

Vickie scowled at him and tried to take a step away as he approached.

"I told you," Taylor said and shook his head. "Humans are animals, only a little more intelligent but not sharp enough to know when their own lizard brains are playing them. Do you know how to fight?"

"You mean like biting and scratching and then running away?" she asked. "Because I have a black belt in those."

"You might want to work on a more effective form of fighting," he said lightly. "It might give you a leg up if you are ever caught doing your hacking and are sent to the

Zoo. You'll have something to help you stay alive for a little while."

"Gee, thanks for your confidence in my abilities," she said and rolled her eyes.

"Hey, man, didn't you hear what I said?" the drunk oaf asked and patted Taylor on the shoulder. "You're digging in infertile soil there, pal, and you don't look like the kind of guy who can turn a no into a yes—although I'm sure if you tried hard enough, you might be able to change that."

Vickie looked at Taylor. "With that said, do you still think I should learn to fight?"

He shrugged. "I don't know. You might benefit from a little demonstration. What do you think? It'd have to be a little quicker than I'd like but hey, you never know when you'll learn something."

"Stop ignoring me," the drunk man shouted. "Stop messing around with your girl and pay attention."

Calmly, he turned to face the man in question. The heckler was big, powerfully built, and had the look of someone who liked to get into fistfights. Still, he offered nothing he hadn't faced before.

"She's not my girl, pal," he said and his deep voice rumbled. "And she's not my sister either since I can see that's where your brain will go next. She's my employee, and if you think I'll let an inbred pissant talk to her like that, I'll have to teach you a few manners."

The man took a step back instinctively but shook his head as if to convince himself that he was still in the driver's seat of this engagement. "You have to be crazier than I thought if you think she'll put—"

That was about as much as Taylor intended to hear

from him. He caught him quickly by his collar and yanked him closer, leaned forward, and drove his forehead into the man's nose. A soft crunch and a gargled scream of pain followed as he sagged, clutching his face.

His friends rushed forward to help but stopped when he stepped closer and stood over their grounded comrade.

Marcus moved tentatively, possibly to intervene, and he shook his head to tell the bouncer he had it under control.

"Now, do you guys want to try me?" he asked and tilted his head to regard them with open amusement tinged with a warning. "Or do you want to go ahead and call an ambulance for your one-pump chump of a friend here?"

The other three already doubted their chances, but a glance at the bouncer who stood poised to join the altercation quelled whatever fight they still had in them and they pulled back. One called an ambulance and Marcus stepped casually into his usual position in the doorway of Jackson's.

"And that's how you deescalate a situation by rapidly escalating it," Taylor said and turned to Vickie. "Now, do you want to share a cab? I kind of want to make it an early night. There's this place Banks introduced me to that serves the best breakfast in the city. Seriously, the food there tastes like what my grandmother used to make."

"It sounds like there's a good dose of nostalgia there," she said.

"Yeah, I'll take you to try it sometime. You'll see what I mean."

CHAPTER THIRTY

"I'm right here, standing in the hills outside of Los Angeles," Carey said into his phone. "There were reports of Zoo monsters sighted in the area but we were unable to enter while the fires raged. Our brave firefighters have now extinguished the blazes with their valiant efforts and have begun to pull out of the area. We've monitored the situation closely and are reasonably sure that only the fire teams have been allowed entry. We've taken this small window of opportunity to sneak in while odd patches still smolder around us. Since there was no sighting of the monsters reported from the population centers around us, we have to assume the beasts were caught in the fires."

"And if they were here," Zach interjected on the live ZooTube broadcast, "we'll be able to get verifiable proof that the government has been hiding the fact that there are Zoo monsters on US Soil. Bodies have been found everywhere from New York to Seattle, and no one's done a damn thing. They're blaming Bigfoot, for God's sake."

Corey nodded. It had been five months since he'd

agreed to team up with the other Zootuber to boost both their viewer counts, but he could tell that his supposed partner tried to steal the viewers to his own channel by his attempt to present as many conspiracy theories as possible. He didn't even bother to research what he was trying to say. Merely saying everything loudly and calling everything a conspiracy was still popular with the Zootuber audience.

He'd thought it would be a passing fancy, but some of the original films and series on the streaming service emphasized the conspiracy theories, so they had become more and more popular.

"Anyway, we've walked through this area and we can't help but notice how devastating the fires were," Corey continued. "There are many people still working to continue to keep the fires in check, but this is the area where reporters and even a couple of firemen reported seeing animals that definitely weren't the kind you'd see in this part of the country. Not only that, no local zoo has reported any animals missing, so they won't be able to pull the same shit they tried in Florida."

They continued to move through the ravaged aftermath of the fire's destruction. It had been a huge pain in the ass —and a costly exercise—to get clearance from the fire department via someone who needed hot cash in a hurry. He wasn't even sure the expense was necessary as they didn't really expect to find anything. All things considered, they wanted to drum up their new series based on a game that would be released in a couple of months.

Still, you never knew. They might be the first channel of their type to actually find something.

He pressed pause on the recording when they reached a charred log and he took a deep breath. "Goddammit, I can't remember the last time I breathed regular fresh air."

"Stop complaining, man." Zach looked a little out of breath. "And get back on the stream. We have over thirty thousand viewers on this, and if we play it up more, they'll spread the word for us. Won't need to get that marketing gig."

"Fine, but if I wanted to do this much walking, I would have stuck to my job as a bartender." He restarted the live stream. "Sorry about that, guys. We needed a second to get our bearings. Right now, we're headed roughly north-northwest to where the fire was the most intense and—what's that?"

His partner turned quickly and squinted at a burnt shape on the ground. "It looks like a bobcat. They have those around here, right?"

"I don't think so," Corey said as he moved closer, picked up a nearby stick that was mostly intact, and poked the corpse gently. Not many other channels would go that far.

"Nope, not a bobcat," the other man said. "They have short tails, don't they?"

"And no…uh, spike at the end," he responded softly. "What is it—oh, God. I think I'm going to puke!"

After the third jab, the brittle skin broke and a dark-blue sludgy liquid began to ooze from the break to spread over the ashes.

"That's no bobcat," Zach said excitedly. "That's…that's a monster. Something that bleeds blue and has a stinger on its tail? That's totally a Zoo monster."

He was right, Corey realized. He leaned in and let the

camera on his phone get a better shot of the creature. "Holy shit… You saw it here first folks. Tell your friends that Corey and Zach have found proof that there are alien monsters on US soil."

The chances were that people would simply say it was a fake, but he didn't care. They'd found it and no one would be able to take that away from them.

The story continues with Sacrificial Weapon, available now at Amazon.com and through Kindle Unlimited.

# AUTHOR NOTES

## JANUARY 18, 2019

Thank you for reading this story and joining me in the back for a little weekly update. I hope you enjoyed Taylor, Bungees, Niki and Vickie. I have finished reviewing book 03 and will be getting into book 04 super soon!

I don't want to get too Behind the Scenes (check out our podcast here!), but Taylor's story is a reaction to something I've been feeling for a while, promulgated by the media.

**WEEKLY UPDATE**

Last year, I had put a goal for our company to accomplish publishing four hundred (400!) books.

We didn't make it

(We were somewhere between three and four hundred books released) but more than that, the goal I set wasn't the end goal. (*Editor's note: We published on the high side of 350*)

The end goal was to "**Test Ourselves**."

Meaning, I wanted to push our company so hard, we knew what we could accomplish and to grow our backlist, providing us a large group of stories for our fans to read. It was a "BAHG," which is short for Big Hairy Audacious Goal.

Otherwise known in the company as **"Are you f##king kidding me?"**

In 2018, where the theme was "Let's prepare for 2019 where we do 400 books," we built an infrastructure towards the goal of making that happen. We put on our thinking hats and sharpened our pencils to figure out how to get to 400. What stories were we going to do? Who (exactly) were going to be doing it? How would we get 400 covers done? How many words of editing would we need to be able to accomplish?

*(The answer is a metric sh##load.)*

We went running through 2019 like a bunch of teenagers trying to catch free cash raining from the heavens. It was a lot of fun, but man oh man, was it dangerous!

*Lynne: I edited between 800k and 1.2m words per month last year, as did my co-editor. Holy schnikes! No wonder we're tired! But we did learn a lot, mostly that we could not sustain that pace, so for me, see the theme below and substitute "the editing team" for "ourselves."*

We broke (more) than a few things, but in the end, we survived. We are stronger, more capable, and more than that, we are wise beyond our years. (*Editor's Note. I'd say wiser. "Wise" just challenges us to come up with better, more creative errors, which we also found out last year we were capable of.*)

How can I say that? Because wisdom comes with doing, and the more you do, the more wisdom you earn.

On average (a very odd word, but the best one I can

use), a publishing company will put out up to twenty-four books a year.

Some, like Baen Books, do about seventy-two a year.

We published four to five times Baen Books' total and twelve times that of an average publishing company.

So, we acquired a LOT of wisdom, pushing the company and our creativity. Some of the wounds we suffered I'm sure will heal in 2020. Some won't.

So as we come into 2020, we have a new theme, and it is…

**The Year of Unf##king ourselves.**

How's THAT for a theme?

;-)


Ad Aeternitatem,


*Michael Anderle*

CONNECT WITH THE AUTHORS

**Michael Anderle Social**
**Website:**
**http://lmbpn.com**

**Email List:**
**http://lmbpn.com/email/**

**Facebook Here:**
https://www.facebook.com/OriceranUniverse/

https://www.facebook.com/TheKurtherianGambitBooks/

https://www.facebook.com/groups/320172985053521/
(Protected by the Damned Facebook Group)

OTHER ZOO BOOKS

**BIRTH OF HEAVY METAL**

He Was Not Prepared (1)

She Is His Witness (2)

Backstabbing Little Assets (3)

Blood Of My Enemies (4)

Get Out Of Our Way (5)

**APOCALYPSE PAUSED**

Fight for Life and Death (1)

Get Rich or Die Trying (2)

Big Assed Global Kegger (3)

Ambassadors and Scorpions (4)

Nightmares From Hell (5)

Calm Before The Storm (6)

One Crazy Pilot (7)

One Crazy Rescue (8)

One Crazy Machine (9)

One Crazy Life (10)

One Crazy Set Of Friends (11)

One Crazy Set Of Stories (12)

**SOLDIERS OF FAME AND FORTUNE**

Nobody's Fool (1)

Nobody Lives Forever (2)

Nobody Drinks That Much (3)

Nobody Remembers But Us (4)

Ghost Walking (5)

Ghost Talking (6)

Ghost Brawling (7)

Ghost Stalking (8)

Ghost Resurrection (9)

Ghost Adaptation (10)

Ghost Redemption (11)

Ghost Revolution (12)

**THE BOHICA CHRONICLES**

Reprobates (1)

Degenerates (2)

Redeemables (3)

Thor (4)

Printed in Poland
by Amazon Fulfillment
Poland Sp. z o.o., Wrocław

58457519R00186